Sara glared in affectionate exasperation at her brother. "Spanish doubloons. Diamonds. Rubies. The whole thing is a Peter Pan treasure hunt."

"It's a calculated risk with the possibility of substantial financial reward," a man's voice said from directly behind her.

Sara whirled in her seat, her eyes narrowed against the glare of the setting sun. No one had to introduce her. She knew without a doubt she was facing the infamous J. C. Hawk.

"Fool's gold. The whole scheme is ridiculous."

"How do you do, Mrs. Riley," Hawk said politely, ignoring her tirade. "Welcome to Tyiskita."

Tyiskita. Sara repeated the name silently. It was a strange and wonderful place. But it wasn't Never-Never Land. And she wasn't Wendy Darling. And the man in front of her certainly wasn't Peter Pan. He was real. Very real. A contradictory thought crossed her mind—he could very definitely be Captain Hook!

Dear Reader,

Get ready for a double dare from Superromance!

The popularity of our Women Who Dare titles has convinced us that Superromance readers enjoy the thrill of living on the edge. So be prepared for an entire *month of living dangerously!*

Leading off is this month's Women Who Dare title, *Windstorm*, in which author Connie Bennett pits woman against nature as Teddi O'Brien sets her sights on a tornado chaser! But our other three September heroines also battle both the elements and the enemy in a variety of exotic settings. *Wildfire*, by Lynn Erickson, is a real trial by fire, as Piper Hilyard learns to tell the good guys from the bad. In Marisa Carroll's *Hawk's Lair*, Sara Riley tracks subterranean treasure—and a pirate—in the Costa Rican rain forest. And we're delighted to welcome back to Superromance veteran romance author Sara Orwig. Her heroine, Jennifer Ruark, outruns a flood in the San Saba Valley in *The Mad, the Bad & the Dangerous*.

For October's Women Who Dare title, Lynn Leslie has created another trademark emotional drama in *Courage, My Love*. Diane Maxwell is fighting the fight of her life. To Brad Kingsley, she is a tremendously courageous woman of the nineties, and as his love for her grows, so does his commitment to her victory.

Evelyn A. Crowe's legion of fans will be delighted to learn that she has penned our Women Who Dare title for November. In *Reunited*, gutsy investigative reporter Sydney Tanner learns way more than she bargained for about rising young congressman J.D. Fowler. Generational family feuds, a long-ago murder and a touch of blackmail are only a few of the surprises in store for Sydney—and for you—as the significance of the heroine's discoveries begins to shape this riveting tale.

Popular Superromance author Sharon Brondos has contributed our final Woman Who Dare title for 1993. In *Doc Wyoming*, taciturn sheriff Hal Blane wants nothing to do with a citified female doctor, and the feeling is mutual. But Dixie Sheldon becomes involved with Blane's infamous family in spite of herself, and her "sentence" in Wyoming is commuted to a romance of the American West.

Please enjoy **A Month of Living Dangerously**, as well as our upcoming Women Who Dare titles and all the other fine Superromance novels we've lined up for your fall reading pleasure!

Marsha Zinberg,
Senior Editor

Marisa Carroll

Hawk's Lair

Harlequin Books

TORONTO • NEW YORK • LONDON
AMSTERDAM • PARIS • SYDNEY • HAMBURG
STOCKHOLM • ATHENS • TOKYO • MILAN
MADRID • WARSAW • BUDAPEST • AUCKLAND

Published September 1993

ISBN 0-373-70565-4

HAWK'S LAIR

Printed in U.S.A.

ABOUT THE AUTHOR

Hawk's Lair is the eighth Superromance novel from the writing team of Carol Wagner and Marian Scharf, the sisters who write under the name Marisa Carroll. The story was inspired by a recent trip to Costa Rica by Ms. Wagner and her husband. The sisters, who live in Deshler, Ohio, have been writing together for about ten years. "It's just real fun to keep bouncing (ideas) off each other," Ms. Sharf said in a recent interview. "We just keep bouncing them back and forth till it sounds like Marisa Carroll."

Books by Marisa Carroll

HARLEQUIN SUPERROMANCE
268—REMEMBERED MAGIC
318—GATHERING PLACE
418—RESCUE FROM YESTERDAY
426—REFUGE FROM TODAY
437—RETURN TO TOMORROW
515—ONE TO ONE
529—KEEPING CHRISTMAS

PROLOGUE

"I DON'T KNOW WHAT you expect to accomplish, dragging two kids along with you to some godforsaken banana republic, some jungle outpost," Wade Riley said, scowling across the table at his ex-wife.

"It's not some godforsaken jungle outpost," Sara replied patiently. "It's my brother's home. And Costa Rica isn't a banana republic. They have a stable democratic government. They don't even have an army. It will be a great experience for the kids."

Wade merely grunted in reply and went back to punching numbers into his calculator. "I still think your brother ought to be committed. He's got to be crazy, squandering Zack's education fund like this." He bent his head to scowl harder at the figures that came up on the screen. "A certifiably mad scientist."

"That's not true at all." Sara's reply was vehement, but also defensive. Her brother, Dr. Elliot Carson, was a botanist, and a very good one. But he did tend to get too tied up in his work, studying the plants of the southern Costa Rican rain forest. Since the death of his wife five years earlier, it was all he seemed to care about. At least until this business with J. C. Hawk had surfaced. The last time Sara had seen her brother was three years ago when he returned to Fort Wayne, Indiana, for his son Zack's sixth birthday. He'd stayed exactly seventy-two hours. Zack, who barely remembered his father, hadn't even cried when he left.

"Then he's a patsy and this guy he's working with is a crook. How the hell did they get hooked up together, anyway?"

"They met while Elliot was doing research in the Spanish archives in Seville. He gave Elliot permission to do plant research on his property."

"This guy sounds like a real humanitarian," Wade said sarcastically. "I'll bet you don't even know what he does for a living."

"I intend to find out."

Wade looked skeptical. "You?"

"Yes."

He shook his head. "What a family."

"Wade," she said, holding on to her temper out of habit, as she'd done so often over the years. "I thought you came over to talk about plans for Megan's graduation party, not to browbeat me about Elliot's behavior."

"But fifty thousand dollars." Wade had never been easily sidetracked. For years Sara had just floated along in his wake. When he'd moved out of the house two years ago, she'd suddenly found herself adrift on the current. She still wasn't swimming free, more like dog-paddling along. But she was getting stronger every day. She had to, with three kids to raise. Not that Wade didn't do what he considered "his share." He did. And he'd never once missed a support payment. But he just wasn't "there" for them anymore. He had a new young wife, a new life, and Sara and their children didn't figure prominently in it.

Sara ran her fingers through her naturally curly, shoulder-length brown hair, trying to tame its flyaway tendencies. Wade looked up at her and frowned. Sara put her hands on the table and tried to stop fidgeting.

Her ex-husband never looked at her without Sara feeling he was comparing her unfavorably to his new love. It made her uncomfortable. It made her angry.

Wade's new wife was a study in cool sophistication. Her hair was sleek and blond. Her body was just as sleek and her skin tanned and golden, even in the middle of a long Indiana winter. She was a successful accountant and businesswoman. And nine years younger than Sara.

And Wade had changed, too, since the divorce. He was tanned and sleek as well. And he'd had a series of hair transplants to thicken his thinning black hair. He was forty-two. He looked ten years younger.

Sara was thirty-seven years old and, at five feet seven inches tall, weighed twelve pounds more than the insurance tables said she should. She'd noticed a few laugh lines around her green eyes when she looked in the mirror these last couple of months, and a few gray hairs. But she was the mother of two teenagers and the guardian of a lively nine-year-old nephew, and she figured she was entitled to both those combat badges.

Wade was the one who had always been obsessed with growing old. Maybe that's why he'd quit loving her when she was no longer quite so young. Or maybe it was because she was just plain Sara—Lewis and Clark Junior High School art teacher, housewife and mother—and probably always would be. Before the divorce her pride hadn't let her ask him what had gone wrong. Now, most of the time, she no longer cared.

"Dad! When did you get here?" their seventeen-year-old daughter, Megan, asked, coming into the room with the remains of a carry-out pizza in a box. She wasn't quite as tall as Sara, but was slim and leggy, with curly strawberry blond hair and dark-lashed brown eyes.

"Half an hour ago," Wade replied.

"Want a piece of pizza?" she asked, offering the box to her father.

He shook his head and patted his newly flat stomach. "No thanks, sweetheart."

"Dad, wait till you see the absolutely incredible bathing suit I got for the band trip to Florida. It's just adorable."

"I'll bet it is," Wade said dubiously. "Is it a bikini?"

"Of course." She gave him the dimpled smile that from the time she was five weeks old had never failed to win her what she wanted from her father. "But not a 'bikini' bikini. Just a bikini. You'll approve."

Wade grunted. "Now, tell me again. When do you leave?"

"The day before Mom and the brats," she said, rolling her eyes. "It'll be heaven being away from them for two weeks. You haven't forgotten I'm coming to stay with you and Felicity, have you?" Megan's high school band had been invited to perform at Disney World during spring break and she'd been adamant about refusing to accompany Sara and the boys to Costa Rica if it meant she would miss the trip. Sara had been adamant that she not stay home alone. Fortunately, before the issue got serious, Wade had invited her to stay with him and her stepmother, something he hadn't done before.

"Don't forget, the band returns from Florida five days before the boys and I fly back from Costa Rica," Sara reminded them before Megan began wheedling for permission to drive Wade's new sports car.

Father and daughter looked at her with identical brown eyes and identical expressions of pained tolerance.

"I'll be fine in Florida, Mom," Megan said, as though reassuring a rather dense child. "The school is practically sending more chaperones than kids." She wrinkled her nose. "Bummer."

"Cut her some slack, Sara," Wade said, coming down on his daughter's side as the cool, laid-back buddy he'd always wanted to be, instead of co-disciplinarian and father figure. "She's a smart kid. She's not going to do anything to make her old man unhappy."

"I know who's going to be paying my tuition at Purdue next fall," Megan said, wrapping her arms around his neck and giving him a big hug. "I'll be good as gold."

"There," Wade said, looking as pleased with himself as Megan was. "I've done my part. The rest is up to you."

"It always has been," Sara said, but the remark was drowned out by the arrival of fourteen-year-old Benjamin and nine-year-old Zackary. Her nephew was being dragged along at the end of a leash by a mutt whose fondness for splashing through mud puddles and playing in the rain had given him his name. The dog was very large, long-haired, exuberantly friendly—a real ladies' man and a guilt offering from Wade to the boys after he'd moved out of the house.

"Dad, did you come to pick up Puddles? We'll be leaving for the jungle in three days. He's supposed to stay at your place while we're gone, you know," Benjamin reminded him, pushing his glasses up on his nose.

Sara swallowed a smile. She'd bet the new Mrs. Riley wasn't thrilled to be baby-sitting a dog. She just hoped Wade didn't leave Puddles tied out in the yard the whole time they were gone. Late March weather in Fort Wayne was changeable and a long way from springlike and balmy.

"I'll stop by and pick him up on my way home from the office the day you leave," Wade hedged. "He'll be all right out in his doghouse until then."

"Don't leave him out at night," Zack warned, leaning against Wade's shoulder. "He'll bark at every sound he hears."

Her ex-husband put his arm around the younger boy and pulled him onto his lap, but only smiled at his son. "I'll take good care of him."

"I'm going to miss the first Little League planning meeting," Zack announced, with a scowl that was a carbon copy of Wade's. Physically, Sara's nephew resembled his dead mother, with dark hair and fair skin, but his mannerisms were carefully copied from Wade and were pure Riley. The divorce had been harder on Zack than on the others. As sometimes happened, Zack, a very athletic little boy, had a much better rapport with his uncle than Wade's own son did.

"I'll call the coach and let him know why you're not there," Wade promised, and this time Sara didn't doubt he would do as he said. "Don't worry, they'll save a place for the star pitcher on the city league championship team."

"Yeah." Zack brightened immediately. "Megan says they have cannibals and terrorists and all kinds of poison snakes in Costa Rica. She says we're all going to be murdered in our beds."

"No such luck as far as she's concerned," Ben grumbled, showing a fourteen-year-old boy's typical disdain of an older sister. "Unless she gets run over by Goofy in a golf cart at Disney World."

"Ben," Sara said warningly.

"Come on, Zack. Let's go check out what to take along on the plane. I've got two really great new computer mags I don't want to forget to pack."

"I'm taking my Super Squirter water gun," Zack said, jumping across the family-room floor like a large, red-T-shirted frog. "I'll take care of any old poison snakes and giant man-eating lizards that come around."

"And I'll save *you* from airport security," Ben said, following his cousin out of the room in a slightly more sedate manner.

"My hero," Sara said, laughing.

Ben looked back over his shoulder and rolled his eyes. "Bye, Dad," he said, going through the doorway into the hall.

"See you in a couple of weeks," Wade called back.

Sara's smile faded away. She rested her elbows on the table and folded her hands beneath her chin. She hoped the boys enjoyed the trip to Costa Rica. She wanted Ben to start having fun again. He'd taken life far too seriously since he'd become "the man of the house." And Zack. She wanted more than anything for him to get to know his father. And for her brother to admit he needed to be with his son. The problem was she didn't know where to begin for certain. Zack's personality was almost exactly the opposite of his father's, as Ben's was from Wade's. She knew from her own experience that such differences made it difficult for them to find common ground. Elliot had even more problems dealing with Zack, because the little boy reminded him too much of what he had lost, instead of what he still had. Somehow, while they were in Costa Rica, she had to help them both come to the conclusion that they needed to be a family again. Just the two of them.

The only trouble with that dream was she didn't know how to accomplish it without being separated from Zack—and as desirable as the outcome was, the thought of giving up custody of her nephew was almost enough to break her heart.

"Now." Wade's voice broke into her thoughts. "Quit giving me the runaround, Sara. I want to know just exactly what your screwball of a brother intends to do with nearly half of Zack's inheritance."

Sara had known this was coming from the moment she'd informed Wade she was taking the children with her to Costa Rica over spring break. By adroit verbal maneuvering, and some outright evasions, she'd managed to put off today's meeting until it was too late for Wade to stop her from going.

"He's investing it," she said, choosing her words very carefully.

"In what? Some company called Hawkslair? What is that—a commuter airline? A coffee plantation? What?"

"It's none of those things." Sara straightened in her seat. "It's an investment company."

"What kind of investment company? Sara, you know there are a lot of fly-by-night outfits in Central America. They lure gringos down there, show them a pineapple plantation, or a coffee *finca,* or something that won't make a cent after the first year, and try to get people to invest. I'd have thought Elliot had been there long enough not to fall for some scheme like that. But then, he never did have a practical bone in his body."

"It's not any of those things." Sara interrupted before he could get launched on the subject of what he considered her brother's main faults in life. Dear Lord, how was she going to say this? She didn't believe it herself.

"Well, who owns it? It's an American company. The money's being transferred to Costa Rica through an American bank."

"J. C. Hawk owns it. He's Elliot's landlord at Tyiskita."

"Ti-is-kee-ta." Wade repeated the four syllables as if he'd never heard them before. Tyiskita was the tiny village on the Pacific coast of Costa Rica, just north of Panama, where Elliot had been living for the past three years. Wade knew that as well as she did.

"Yes."

"What the hell does he have to invest in there? Monkeys? Parrots?" Wade put both hands on the table, scowling at her now instead of the calculator.

Sara scowled right back. She might as well get it over with. "Buried treasure," she said, pleased to hear her voice come out steady and clear.

"Good God," Wade exploded. "That idiot brother of yours has lost his mind."

"I'm sure he wouldn't risk Zack's inheritance on some fly-by-night scheme."

"What do you mean? He already has. It's a done deal, as far as I can tell." Wade folded his arms across his chest and leaned back in his chair as he eyed the papers on the table before him. "As his accountant I ought to stop payment on this check."

"No." He'd gone too far. It was true Wade was Elliot's accountant. It was true he cared very deeply for Elliot's son. But he was no longer a member of the family. Elliot's behavior wasn't his concern. It was hers.

"But digging for buried treasure? Are you sure?"

"Yes." Sara had enough doubts of her own about her brother's conduct—and about her trip to Costa Rica.

But she wasn't going to admit them to her ex-husband. "He's helping to finance this guy's search for hidden Spanish gold on his property."

Wade shook his head. "This is ridiculous. Buried pirate treasure? How the hell am I supposed to explain that to the IRS? I was right—your brother is nuts. He's certifiable. He's spent too much time staring at bits and pieces of trees and bushes under his microscope. The heat and humidity down there must have addled his brain."

"Wade, you're exaggerating."

"Who does this guy Hawk think he is, the reincarnation of Bluebeard or Jean Laffitte? The man is obviously a charlatan—or worse yet, an out-and-out crook."

Sara hated to admit it, but she felt the same way. J. C. Hawk *was* a twentieth-century pirate. "I know." She sat up a little straighter in her chair. "Someone's got to talk some sense into Elliot and it might as well be me."

"Sara, you're going to go charging down there and get yourself in over your head," he warned, narrowing his eyes. "A man like that will chew you up and spit you out in little pieces." He was trying his best to intimidate her. Well, it wasn't going to work. She'd gotten over being intimidated by the likes of Wade Riley a long time ago.

"No, he won't." She gave him back look for look. "When I get to Tyiskita, I intend to confront both my brother and this J. C. Hawk face-to-face and find out just what the hell is going on down there."

CHAPTER ONE

"BELOW US is Golfito," the pilot of the small, single-engine plane informed Sara in his excellent but heavily accented English. "It was a banana port before. Now it is a free port for Ticos." Elliot had already told her that *Tico* was the word Costa Ricans used to refer to themselves. "Got a Japanese microwave oven there for my sister last week. Good deal."

Sara merely nodded. She was too busy concentrating on keeping the small plane in the sky to make polite conversation. With three passengers and all their luggage, the aircraft seemed dangerously overloaded. The pilot, however, had no such apparent qualms.

"Tyiskita is one half hour south," he said, circling the airport before heading out over the ocean. "About three hours overland."

"I bet there's no McDonald's down there," Ben said wistfully, craning his neck for a better look at the town strung out on a spit of land between the jungle-covered cliff and the Golfo Dulce.

"This place is a real dump," Zack said loudly.

"Zack, be quiet." Sara raised her voice over the engine noise. "Your father says it's a nice town."

"Yeah, sure."

"Civilization as we know it has ended," Ben muttered loudly enough for her to hear.

"It's an adventure, guys," Sara said, hoping her own anxiety couldn't be heard in her voice. "Loosen up. Enjoy yourselves."

"I hope I know what to say to my dad," Zack confided loudly to his cousin.

"It'll be okay," Ben yelled back. "I wish we'd had time to stop for burgers and fries in San José. My stomach's growling." The boys had seen advertisements for all their favorite fast-food places on the trip across Costa Rica's capital from the international airport to the private airfield where their young Tico pilot was waiting to ferry them to Tyiskita.

"We'll get something to eat as soon as we get settled," Sara promised.

"We'd better, or I'll be starved to death before we get the suitcases out of the plane."

"Me, too," Zack echoed, a frown pulling down the corners of his mouth.

The pilot pointed to the ground. "Here begins the land belonging to Allied Fruit," he said. "They are bankrupt now. Many of the trees died of disease. Prices dropped all over the world and here the government taxes bananas heavily. The *nortes* left and the *campesinos* have taken over some of the land."

Below them smoke from several small fires eddied up to meet the clouds. Behind them in the Talamanca Mountains, the smoke from much larger fires was visible. The hills were barren all the way to the sea and cows grazed over the sparse pasture land. Firsthand, Sara was witnessing the destruction of the rain forest, which she'd heard so much about. It was a sobering sight.

"What are *campesinos?*" she asked.

"Squatters. Farmers who have no title to the land."

"What can they grow here?"

"Very little." The pilot leaned close to make himself heard. "Some grain, a few cattle. Then the land will be worn out and they will move on and it will be nothing but scrub. Still, the *campesinos* have nothing else they can do and their families must eat. Families are very important to us. You have fine, strong children yourself."

"Thank you," Sara said.

They left the derelict banana plantation behind and flew over the lush green forest, which began as abruptly as if a line had been drawn in the earth.

"Tyiskita," the pilot said. "The land has been in Señor Hawk's family for many years. He has only lived here about a year himself."

"What did he do before that?" Sara asked. No one seemed to know any details about Hawk's life.

The pilot shrugged, a very Latin gesture that said a great deal. "Who knows? We'll fly over the compound so that they know we are here. The big house on top of the cliff is Señor Hawk's. The *cabañas* are for the *touristas* who are beginning to come." He pointed off in the distance. "The landing strip is at the village. It is only a few minutes' walk along the beach. Longer in the Jeep."

"Is that it?" Ben hollered over the roar of the engine and the rush of wind through the open windows. "It looks like Tarzan lives there."

Sara was thinking the same thing. Several thatch-roofed buildings were visible against the cliff face. Someone came out of the largest of them and waved up at the plane, then headed for a beat-up old Jeep parked on a narrow roadway that ran down to the village through a cut in the trees.

"It's Elliot." Sara waved, not even caring if her brother couldn't see her so far above him.

"*Bueno.*" The pilot dipped the wings of the plane. "They have seen us. The village is just over the ridge." As he spoke, it came into view, a scattering of thatched huts and wooden buildings with rusty metal roofs. A large stream ran alongside it, dropping down out of the heavily forested hills that brooded over the village, tumbling over rocks until it reached the sea. The beach was wide and smooth and the tawny sand glowed golden in the strong afternoon sunlight. On the beach were farmlike buildings behind a barrier of coconut palms. Two big work oxen were penned in a corral near a barn. Dogs and small brown children tumbled about in the yard.

"How pretty," Sara said. And as different from Fort Wayne, Indiana, as night from day. A big white boat floated lazily at anchor beyond a headland. "What's that boat out there? A yacht?"

The pilot shook his head. "A salvage ship, *señora.* A bunch of loco *nortes* are searching for a lost treasure ship."

"Like *Treasure Island,*" Zack echoed. Sara had been reading the Robert Louis Stevenson classic to him at night the past few weeks.

"Yes, or Peter Pan," the young man replied with a grin. "Loco."

Sara was surprised by the information, but she tried not to show it. So Hawk had rival treasure hunters to deal with. No wonder he was in such a hurry to find the gold.

"Fasten your seat belts. We're going to land."

The plane set down in a long narrow pasture between the scattered houses of the village and the sea, and moments later Sara was standing safely on the ground. Several villagers, their features reflecting a mixture of Spanish and Indian heritage, came out of their houses and gardens to greet the pilot. He handed one of them the mailbag, and most of the others followed the man back to what appeared to be the largest and most important of the buildings that lined the single narrow street. The men didn't speak to Sara, but smiled and tipped their woven straw hats to her as they walked away.

Half a dozen laughing, brown-skinned children continued to observe the gringo strangers from a distance, but at a shouted word from a woman standing on the front porch of one of the houses, they ran off down the beach. Several moments later, a short, slightly overweight young woman, with sky-blue eyes and red-gold hair pulled back into a ponytail, emerged from the main building and walked toward the plane. She was wearing cutoff jeans and a faded green T-shirt, and looked far more Irish than Tico.

"Hi," she said, offering her hand to Sara as the pilot and Ben began to unload their luggage. "The mayor, Señor Escobar, told me you'd arrived. My name's Emily Wycheski. I'm with World Bible Missions. I run the clinic. Welcome to Tyiskita village."

"Thank you," Sara said. "I'm Sara Riley and this is my son, Benjamin, and my nephew, Zackary Carson."

"Hi," Emily said, smiling at both boys, but her eyes were fixed on Zackary.

"Is my brother coming to meet us?" Sara wished she were standing in the shade. The late-afternoon sun was as strong and bright as summer midday in Indiana. It made her a little dizzy. It had been a very long day. She was hot and tired and more than a little bit nervous about what lay ahead.

"He'll be here in a few minutes. I heard the Jeep coming down the hill." A very tall, very athletic-looking young man with the same red-gold hair and friendly smile as Emily joined the group. "Hi, I'm Luke Wycheski, Emily's cousin. I'm here for a while to help her out." He held out his hand to Sara and grinned at the boys. "Welcome to Costa Rica."

"Where are you from?" Zack asked with devastating frankness. "You talk a little funny."

"Canada," Luke answered. "We were born and raised in Windsor. That's across the border from Detroit."

"Luke's a good kid," Emily said, smiling fondly at her cousin as the young man swung a heavy duffel bag to his shoulder and carried it over to the shade of a coconut palm. "He took off a semester from college to come down here and help me out. He's been a godsend. Your boys will be fine with him."

"I'm glad there's someone here who speaks English. Neither of the boys has any Spanish."

"Send them down to the school in the mornings if you can get them to come. They'll pick it up quickly enough, and it will be a treat for the children to have visitors their own age. We don't get many outsiders here as yet."

"Hey, Mom! It's Uncle El!" Ben hollered, pointing to the rough-running Jeep that had just come into sight along the dusty street.

Zack held on to his sports bag containing his treasures and stood as close to Sara as he possibly could without looking like a baby.

"How long has it been since they've seen each other?" Emily asked.

"Three years," Sara replied. "It's been that long for all of us."

"Then you don't need me and Luke to complicate the family reunion."

"Maybe that would be best," Sara agreed. The truth was Elliot really didn't want her and the boys to be there. He'd gone so far as to make the three-hour trip into Golfito himself to telephone and ask them to postpone their trip. But it was too late; she had already bought the plane tickets. She was determined to find out exactly what J. C. Hawk was up to with Elliot's money, and no one was going to talk her out of it.

"Come down to the village and visit anytime," Emily said, turning away with a wave of her hand. "My door's always open."

"Thanks. I'd like that," Sara said, and meant it.

Luke said goodbye as well, and followed his cousin back to the village. They both waved to Elliot as he passed in the Jeep, but he didn't stop to speak.

He pulled up under the shade of the coconut palms just as Sara got there. "Hi, sis."

"Hi, El." Her brother hadn't changed much in three years. He was still lean and rangy. His brown hair might be a little thinner; and there might be a few more lines at the corners of his eyes, but that was all.

"Hello, son."

"Hi," Zack said, still standing close to Sara.

"You've grown," Elliot said, as though not quite believing what he saw.

"I'm starting pitcher on my Little League team," Zack announced proudly.

"Good. That's real good."

Elliot didn't get out of the Jeep, and Sara's heart sank. She hadn't expected Elliot to come flying out of the Jeep to gather his son in his arms; he wasn't that demonstrative and never had been. But she'd expected more than this cool assessment of the boy.

"How are you doing in school?"

"Okay," Zack replied, not offering any details. Zack, like many children, was a good student in subjects that interested him and not so good at those that did not.

"Hi, Uncle El," Ben said, bounding up to the Jeep.

"Benjamin," Elliot said, smiling for the first time. He gave Ben a playful punch on the arm. "You've grown a foot."

"Dad," Zack said, drawing Elliot's attention away from Ben, "do you have a baseball bat here?"

"What?" Elliot looked as if he hadn't heard correctly.

"A baseball bat? Do they play baseball here?"

"I—I don't know," Elliot said, getting out of the Jeep at last, but not to embrace his son, only to start loading their belongings into the back. "I've never asked."

"Baseball is very popular in Central America, I understand," Sara said hopefully.

"I need a bat to practice so I'll be ready for tryouts when we get back home." Zack looked as if he wanted to cry, except that it was such a sissy thing to do. "I need a bat and Aunt Sara said I couldn't bring one."

"We had way too much luggage as it was," Sara explained for what seemed to her like the hundredth time.

"Maybe some of the kids in the village have one," Ben suggested helpfully. "If they're not too poor."

"They might." Elliot sounded dubious. "You could ask Emily or Luke. Emily's the village nurse, but she's been filling in at the school since the government teacher left last month. Or ask Hawk. He might even have one up at his place.''

"Not him. He's a crook," Zack blurted out before Sara could stop him. "A crook and a con man."

Elliot swung around. "Who told you that?"

"Well, that's what Uncle Wade said."

Sara considered letting her ex-husband take all the blame, but her conscience wouldn't let her. "Zack's only repeating what he heard us say."

"Zackary, I don't want to hear you talk that way about my friend again, do you hear?"

"Yes," Zack said, scuffing the toes of his sneaker in the sand. "I hear."

"And you ought to know better, sis."

"I'm sorry, El. I should have been more careful. Little pitchers have big ears."

Elliot looked at her with narrowed hazel eyes. "I suppose Wade thinks I've lost my mind loaning Hawk that money."

"He thinks . . ." Sara began, then decided she might as well speak her mind. "To hell with Wade. *I* think you're making a mistake, El."

"Are you going to start arguing about this already? You haven't been here fifteen minutes."

"Yes," Sara said, "I guess I am. But I don't want to," she added hurriedly. She'd hoped they could have a few pleasant minutes together, before the painful subject of J. C. Hawk had to be raised. Obviously she'd been as naively overoptimistic about that as she had been about Elliot and Zackary's reunion.

"Okay, then, we won't. Truce?" Elliot asked, holding up his hand Indian style, as they used to do as kids.

"Truce," Sara said, laughing self-consciously as she did the same.

"Hey, guys," Elliot called out. "This Jeep's loaded way over the legal limit. How about taking the beach path back up to the lodge? Just follow the stream down to the stepping stones. Turn right along the beach until you hit the steps at the bottom of the cliff."

"Is it safe for them to go alone?" Sara asked before she could stop herself. She hated sounding like a mother hen all the time, but she'd always been a worrier, and it hadn't become any easier when she was suddenly faced with raising three kids on her own.

"They'll be fine, sis. It's a whole new world for them here."

"For me, too," Sara reminded him. "I think I ought to pinch myself. I can't really believe we're finally here."

"The squirrel monkeys will be coming to feed any time," he told the boys as they raced up to the Jeep. "If you hurry, you can get a ringside seat on the dining porch. And if you get there ahead of us, tell Olivia— she's the cook—to break out the soft drinks. My treat."

"Do you have ice?" Ben asked.

"Sure," Elliot said. "All the comforts of home."

"But you don't have electricity. That's one of the reasons Megan wouldn't come. She can't live without her curling iron and her blow dryer."

"We have a generator for running the computers and the radio, and electric lights in the evening."

"And the refrigerator?"

"It's gas. I'll show you how it works sometime."

"Great. C'mon, Zack. Let's get going."

"Your mom and I will meet you at the dining porch."

"What if we miss the path?" Zack asked.

"Then you'll have to walk all the way back to Golfito and catch the next plane. You can't miss it. Get going," Elliot said gruffly.

"Okay, Dad."

Sara hoped she was the only one who noticed the slight hesitation before the word *dad*.

The boys started off. Luke Wycheski came out of one of the hutlike houses nearest the stream. With a wave to Elliot and Sara, he fell into step beside the youngsters.

"Good. Luke's going along," Sara said approvingly, as she climbed into the passenger seat of the Jeep.

"Emily probably sent him out to lead the way. She's a great gal and Luke's a good kid. And so is Zack. You've done a fine job with him, sis. Thanks. Your taking him after Mindy died saved my sanity."

Sara laid her hand on his arm. "I love him," she said simply. "I want him to be happy." They were both silent a moment as the Jeep lurched over the sandy, narrow street that cut the tiny village in half. She wanted to get this over with before they reached Hawk's stronghold. "We've got to discuss this matter of Zackary's money."

"I thought we called a truce. Aren't you even going to give me a chance to ask how Mom and Dad are doing? And Megan and Wade? I can't believe you let her go to Florida alone." Elliot shifted gears as the venerable Jeep started up the steep, rutted trail where the street ended and the jungle began.

"Megan's with a hundred other kids from the band and more than twenty chaperons. She's almost eighteen and she's got a mind and a life of her own, or so she keeps telling me. Wade..." she paused "...is Wade. He's madly in love with his new wife and he's had hair transplants. Mom and Dad are fine, and if we return safe and sound with no visible injuries or exotic diseases, they're thinking of coming to visit you next winter, so be ready for them.''

"Great," Elliot moaned. "That's all I need. You and Mom both here trying to organize my life in the space of eight months.''

"I didn't come here to organize your life. I came here to find out just what you're doing with Zack's money.''

"Lecturing me on my fiscal irresponsibility is a hell of a reason for coming to one of the most beautiful places on earth.''

"And one of the hottest," Sara said, fanning herself with one hand while she plucked at the thin cotton of her blouse where it stuck to her skin just above the lace edge of her bra.

"Yes, but look at the view.'' Elliot pulled into the clearing where the main building of the compound, the one she'd seen from the air, was located. An opening in the dense underbrush at the cliff's edge gave a glimpse of the achingly blue Pacific and the misty gray-green jungle headland that separated Hawk's land from the village.

"It is beautiful," Sara agreed. "It's like something out of a fairy tale.'' She laughed, leaning her head back to eye the canopy of green leaves high above them. "Thirteen hours ago I was driving to Indianapolis in a snowstorm.''

"Hard to believe, isn't it? There's a toucan," he said, pointing to the big black bird with the familiar gaudy-colored bill in a tree to their left. "Did I mention you can bird-watch from your cabin?''

"No, you didn't, and it *is*," Sara said, shielding her eyes from the sun with her hand as the toucan flew away with a raucous cry. "A real live toucan. And not in a zoo." Elliot had said "toucan" the way she'd have said "robin" or "sparrow" back home. "This is great. This is unbelievable. I feel like I'm on *Wild Kingdom* or something." She sat up straight and fixed her eyes on her brother's face. "But we still have to talk."

"You can talk till you're blue in the face, sis. But it won't change anything." Elliot's jaw was set, his expression mulish. Sara felt a little of her confidence slip away. She knew that look, that stubborn tone. Elliot had made up his mind and he wasn't going to budge.

"You can't possibly believe there's buried treasure here." Sara looked around her in disbelief. She tried hard to sound completely sure of herself. In truth, it was a whole lot easier to believe in buried treasure here, on the edge of the vast Pacific, with toucans and monkeys and palm trees swaying in the breeze, than it was back in the snow and cold of Fort Wayne, Indiana.

"It's a documented fact. There is treasure here."

"Who documented it? Hawk?"

"And myself." Elliot tightened his grip on the steering wheel. It was obvious he was trying to control his temper just as she was. "That's where I met Hawk. In Spain. In the archives. You ought to go there someday, sis. It's a fascinating place. We were both looking for the same thing. Although I didn't find that out until later."

"What were you looking for?"

"The whereabouts of the wreck of the *Mary Deere,* an English merchantman that went to the bottom of the Pacific with all the gold of the Lima treasury in her hold."

"Hawk was there, in Spain, researching the wreck as well?"

"Yes. For different reasons, coming at it from different directions, but yes, we were looking for the same thing."

"How do you explain that?"

Elliot shrugged. "I guess you could call it fate."

"I just can't see you searching for sunken treasure galleons."

"I wasn't, exactly. But even botanists have their legends of lost treasure. They're just a little bit different from everyone else's."

"And your particular lost treasure led you to this place and a business association with J. C. Hawk?"

"Yes."

"How?"

"One of my old professors was also a student of Spanish history. A real Indiana Jones type," Elliot began. "There are lots of stories of Spanish missionaries who cataloged the plants and flowers of Central and South America. They brought back tales of almost-miraculous cures from injuries and diseases. Even today we've barely begun to understand the pharmacological potential of the rain forest."

"Birth-control pills, antibiotics, painkillers. Maybe even a cure for cancer. I know that much," Sara said, hoping to forestall a botany lecture. "Is that what happened? Did you find one of those priests' journals?"

"I found reference to one. His name was Father Benedicto Juarez."

"And?" Sara prompted, trying not to be distracted by a trio of small brown monkeys scrambling across the grass toward a tree stump piled high with bananas.

"He came to Tyiskita one hundred and seventy-five years ago on the *Mary Deere*," Elliot explained. "He

died here. His journal is still here
much for sure."

"At the bottom of the ocean in a
ship?" Sara hoped her dismay wasn't a

"No, the journal's hidden in a sea cave
the beach."

"How did it get there?" Sara asked, con...

"I'll try to explain. It's a long story, but here are the high points. One day the viceroy of Peru woke up to find Simon Bolívar and his revolutionaries camped on the doorstep of Lima. The viceroy and the Church fathers loaded as much of the treasury and as many precious Church artifacts onto the *Mary Deere* as she could hold."

"You said the *Mary Deere* was an English ship. I thought England and Spain were at war in those days."

"They were, but the captain of the *Mary Deere* was a Scotsman, not an Englishman. The viceroy had done business with him before. He thought he could trust him. He was wrong."

"How does your Father Benedicto and his journal come into this?"

"They sent along a handful of priests to guard the treasure. One of them was Father Benedicto. He had become something of an embarrassment to the Church, because he'd started preaching on the wonders of nature and the jungle, and the superiority of the Indians' way of life—what few of the poor bastards there were left after nearly three hundred years of Spanish rule. The bishop probably figured he was killing two birds with one stone—saving the loot and getting rid of a radical. In the end, Father Benedicto was the only one to survive the pirate takeover and the subsequent sinking of the *Mary Deere*."

y, I'll buy your story so far," Sara said reluc-
ly. "He buried the journal in the cave before he
died, I suppose. Do you know where the entrance to this
cave is?"

"Not really," Elliot admitted. "No one knows for
sure anymore. It's been almost two hundred years.
There have been hurricanes and earthquakes—even a
tidal wave or two."

"I understand why you feel the journal could be of
value to you in your work," Sara said, choosing her
words carefully. She didn't want to start a fight with her
brother. Their time together was too short to spend it
arguing. "But even if you salvage it, you might not be
able to read it. After all, it's been exposed to the elements for almost two centuries. Are you sure it's worth
risking your son's future to possess it?"

"You're right about one thing," Elliot replied. "The
information inside the journal will be invaluable. I'll be
set for life and so will Zack. They'll be knocking my
door down to get at it. Major universities, Japanese in-
vestors, even big pharmaceutical companies like Wainright—"

"Wainright Pharmaceuticals is the company that
backs your research, isn't it?"

"Yeah." Elliot's eyebrows pulled together in a frown.
"They've got a stake in a salvage ship down there in the
bay. Along with a lot of other people."

"I saw it," Sara told him. "The pilot pointed it out
when we flew over the village."

"They're looking for the treasure of the *Mary Deere*
the same as we are. And they more than likely got the
idea from my research." He dropped his chin onto his
knuckles for a moment and looked off into the distance. "I wasn't thinking too clearly that year after

Mindy died. Searching for clues to the whereabouts of Father Benedicto's journal and the shipwreck was like a quest, a challenge that kept me going. Obviously, it interested others as well.''

"What's Hawk getting out of this?" Sara didn't dare let her pain for her brother's loss soften her stand. "More to the point, what's he contributing financially to this wild-goose chase?"

"I told you, sis. There really is a treasure. Not all of the gold and jewels were lost with the ship. The journal's only part of it. Emeralds and gold. Spanish doubloons. You saw the size of that recovery ship. Next time we're in the village, I'll take you out to see their equipment. It's state of the art. If they don't find what they want down there pretty soon, it'll only be a matter of time until they pick up on the legend of the treasure in the cave. It isn't a secret in the village. The story's been passed down for generations. They don't talk to outsiders much, but word's bound to get around, sooner rather than later. Money talks, even here. Hawk's been working on this for years. I owe it to him.''

"You don't owe him anything," Sara said in exasperation. "This whole thing is pie in the sky. A Peter Pan treasure hunt."

"It's a calculated risk with the possibility of substantial financial reward," a man's voice said from directly behind her.

Sara whirled in her seat, her eyes narrowed against the glare of the setting sun. No one had to introduce her. She knew without a doubt she was facing her adversary, the infamous J. C. Hawk. She was at a disadvantage, still sitting in the Jeep, while he stood beside it tall and slim and insufferably sure of himself.

"Fool's gold. Buried treasure, my foot! The whole scheme is ridiculous. Spanish doubloons. Diamonds. Rubies. Who ever heard of such a thing?"

"How do you do, Mrs. Riley," he said politely, ignoring her tirade. "Welcome to Tyiskita." He leaned forward, one booted foot on the floorboard of the Jeep, a hand on his knee and the other braced on the windscreen. His muscled leg was very close to her hand. She could feel the heat of his skin against her arm. He was watching her closely from eyes as dark and hard as obsidian. His hair was dark as well, as black as a moonless jungle night, without a speck of gray, but too short to be worn tied back in a club with a bit of satin ribbon. He wasn't wearing a white shirt with long full sleeves, or tight black pants with a pistol stuck in his belt, either. He had on an ordinary khaki shirt, open at the throat to reveal a triangle of bronze skin and crisp dark hair. His shorts were khaki, too. The fabric, soft and faded from much washing, stretched taut over broad shoulders and muscled thighs. "For your information, the treasure most likely consists of emeralds and gold coins," he said in a low, rough voice that raised the hairs on the back of Sara's neck. He gave no indication whatsoever that he'd been discomfited by her scrutiny. "Although there might be one or two rubies scattered among the doubloons."

"Ill-gotten gains," Sara said, sounding like a schoolteacher and hating it.

"Exactly," Hawk replied equitably. "Stolen from the Incas and the Aztecs by the army of the King of Spain and by the Catholic Church, and then in turn stolen from those noble gentlemen by the crew of the *Mary Deere.* We're looking for a tiny fraction of that precious cargo, I admit, a portion so small that no one has

ever missed it, but one that's worth a fortune at today's prices. And all of it buried beneath this cliff for
almost two hundred years. It isn't a ridiculous quest, or
a scam, Mrs. Riley,'' he said harshly, as though reading her mind. "I don't deal in fantasy. Only cold, hard
facts.'' His smile was no more than a faint, upward twist
of his lips. "And I'm not a crook. Or a charlatan.'' He
straightened suddenly, stepping back from the Jeep in
one quick, fluid movement that took what was left of
Sara's breath away. "That one little bit of the *Mary
Deere*'s treasure is here. On my land. It's real, not a
fairy tale. And it's there for the taking. What is it they
say?'' he asked rhetorically, one dark-winged eyebrow
lifting slightly. "To the victor belongs the spoils?''

Ill-gotten gains. Pirate curses. Pieces of eight. Dueling pistols and cutlasses, red with blood. Deserted jungle islands covered by... Sara looked around her at the
quarreling monkeys in the trees, at the orchids hanging
in pale pink-and-mauve clusters from the lower
branches, at the ocean waves on the beach far below.
This wasn't an island, but as near as made no difference.

Privateers.

Errol Flynn.

Captain Blood.

She was suddenly dizzy from a mixture of heat and
fatigue—and J. C. Hawk. It was a potent combination, far too heady for her to handle with aplomb.

With a whoop and holler, the boys and Luke Wycheski appeared at the cliff edge through a break in the
undergrowth, huge flowering bushes that might or
might not be azalea. They looked hot and thirsty, and
came running toward the Jeep as though they had been

trekking through the jungle for days or weeks instead of less than half an hour.

Sara almost sighed aloud in relief. Her children. Her reality. Tyiskita was a very strange and beautiful place, but it wasn't make believe. It wasn't never-never land. She wasn't Wendy Darling.

And the man in front of her certainly wasn't Peter Pan. He was real, very real. But he was still a pirate.

CHAPTER TWO

A FLOCK OF SMALL green-and-red parrotlike birds were feeding in the trees just below the dining porch. Sara picked up the field glasses that Elliot had loaned her and studied them for a long moment. "I wonder what they're called," she said aloud.

"They're crimson-fronted parakeets," Hawk answered, coming up beside her so quietly, she hadn't noticed he was anywhere around.

"Oh." She gave him an angry glance before the antics of the feeding parakeets drew her attention back to them. "You startled me."

"Sorry," he said, not sounding sorry at all.

"Thank you for telling me their name," she added, trying to sound more gracious than she felt.

"You're welcome," he said with equal coolness. "They eat fruit. A lot of fruit. My fruit." He watched the small flock dip and wheel as they headed off toward the orchards farther up the hill, as though on cue. "See what I mean?"

"That your guests are able to study and enjoy them must make it worth the cost," Sara said, more civilly this time.

"I have had very few guests so far. But you're right. It's a fair trade-off."

"Mangoes and star fruits in exchange for parakeets and toucans." Sara smiled. She had every intention of tackling him about the treasure-hunting scheme, but she had more than a sneaking suspicion that if she wasn't careful how she went about it, he would just fade away into the jungle as quickly and as silently as one of the big hunting cats he so resembled. "We don't have anything like them in Indiana."

"I know." He changed the subject. "Did you enjoy your lunch?" The words were stiff and formal, as though he didn't often engage in polite small talk. No wonder he got along well with Elliot. She could imagine days on end going by in this place without the two of them exchanging half-a-dozen words.

"Yes. Olivia is an excellent cook."

He nodded agreement as he walked to the bookcase along the back wall. His footsteps made no sound. Each movement of his body was carried out with an economy of movement, an unconscious grace that made Sara's heart catch in her throat. "There's an excellent reference guide to the birds of Costa Rica here," he said, laying the book on the table. "It's in English."

"Yes. I saw it." She didn't say more, because she was afraid he would turn around again and notice how closely she'd been watching him. She focused her attention on something else. There was a surprising number of books on the wooden shelves. Most were in English, but quite a number were in Spanish, several in French and even one or two in German.

She wondered if all those books belonged to Hawk. If he read them, or if they were only for the pleasure of the few tourists who were beginning to find their way to this remote corner of the world.

"Are your accommodations satisfactory?"

"Yes. Very nice, actually." Her cabin was perched high on the edge of the cliff. It consisted of a sparsely furnished sleeping room, and a stone-flagged veranda with two rope hammocks, a table and two chairs. A resident iguana lived in the rafters, ate mosquitoes and startled Sara half out of her wits every time he crawled down to sun himself on the stone ledge facing the ocean.

"Good. I trust you slept well?"

"Like a baby."

"Some people find the sound of the surf distracting."

"I was out like a light the minute my head hit the pillow." That wasn't quite true. She'd rehearsed what she was going to say to him more than once before she'd finally fallen asleep.

"I'm glad to hear that."

"Mr. Hawk." She'd had enough small talk. It was time to get down to business. She didn't know when she'd get another chance to talk to him alone, to insist that he release Elliot from their agreement, give him back the money that had been intended for Zack's education.

"Just Hawk will do."

"Okay." She looked down at the binoculars, searching for just the right words, just the right tone of voice. "I—"

"You want to know what in hell kind of fly-by-night scheme I'm throwing your nephew's inheritance away on," he interrupted. "You want proof of my good intentions and you want results. Now. Today."

"Yes," Sara said, her temper rising, her good intentions blown away like so much smoke on the wind. "There's no use beating around the bush about it. That's exactly what I want."

"I'd like to oblige you," he said, clearly not wishing any such thing. "But we're about to be interrupted.

Here come the kids." He turned his attention to the boys as they came racing onto the porch from the direction of the path that led to Tyiskita's water supply farther up the cliff. Elliot was a few steps behind them. "How's it going, guys?" Hawk asked, once more the courteous host.

"Fine," Ben answered politely.

"We were looking for snakes," Zack responded bluntly. "We didn't find any."

"You walked too fast. And you made too much noise," Ben said accusingly.

"This is supposed to be the jungle, isn't it?" Zack asked, ignoring his cousin.

"Yes," Hawk replied gravely, standing with legs slightly apart, towering over the boys. "It is."

"I want to see something besides monkeys," Zack insisted. "A tiger, or a big snake, or something like that."

"They don't have tigers in Central America," Ben pointed out.

"The natives call the jaguar 'tiger,'" Hawk said. "But they've been hunted almost to extinction here. They are very rare and they hunt at night. I doubt if you'll be lucky enough to see one."

Zack nodded, accepting that. "But what about snakes?" he persisted.

"There are snakes."

"Big ones?"

"Yes."

"Poison ones?"

"Some of them."

"Why haven't we seen any?"

"I told you why," Ben snorted.

"Because the snake doctor keeps them away," Hawk said, rendering both boys speechless with the statement. Then he turned and walked away, with nothing more than a slight nod in Sara's direction.

"Wait. I'm not finished . . ." Sara found herself talking to thin air.

Zack and Ben watched him go in fascinated silence, then rushed to the table, where Elliot and Sara had taken seats. "Did you hear that?" Zack asked, his voice rising. "Poison snakes and snake doctors. What's a snake doctor, Dad?"

"A man that the natives believe has the power to charm snakes and heal snakebites."

"I want to see a snake," Zack insisted. "The poison frogs are neat." He glanced in the direction of the glass aquarium at the far end of the porch, which housed several of the tiny, brightly colored and dangerous amphibians. "I mean, I'd love to see one kill a mouse or something, but those guys just sit there and hop around a little bit. And you won't let us try and put some of their poison on the end of a spear to go out and kill something ourselves to see how it works." He sounded aggrieved. "But a snake doctor. A real live snake doctor. This I've got to see."

"Me, too," Ben said and added, "please."

"All right," Elliot said, giving in so readily Sara suspected he wanted to visit the snake doctor nearly as much as the two youngsters. "Let's go see if he's home. Want to come along, sis?"

"Of course," she said, smiling. "I wouldn't miss this for the world."

"I don't pretend to understand how he does it, but the natives, both the Ticos and the Indians, swear by him," Elliot explained as they neared the long, low, tin-roofed building that housed the school, the post office, Emily Wycheski's clinic and the cantina, and that formed the center of village life in Tyiskita. "His name is Ian Carter-Stone. Wait till you meet him."

The snake doctor, Sara soon learned, was a small, round-faced black man, a Belizian who'd met and married his wife, a village girl, while she was working in a hotel in San José. He was wearing a T-shirt, blue jeans and tennis shoes and a Yankees baseball cap. Sara wasn't impressed by his physical appearance until she looked into his eyes. His expression told her the truth: like Hawk, he was a very powerful man in this place and knew it.

"So," he said in lilting, Caribbean-accented English. "You come lookin' for de snake doctor to charm away ol' *terciopelo,* hey?"

"What is *terciopelo?*"

"De velvet one, lady. De fer-de-lance," Ian Carter-Stone replied with a grin. "Very bad snake, mon. Very bad. And dey don't like to be disturbed. No, mon, don't like it at all." He nodded portentously toward the other men gathered on the porch of the building. One of them repeated his words in Spanish for the benefit of the others. "Don't go lookin' for trouble, pokin' around disturbin' dey's rest, I say. Leave de gold where it be. If you want to make money for dis place, den let de hotels come. Dey get us all plenty colones."

"*Sí,*" chorused several of the other men, although Sara suspected they didn't understand most of what Ian Carter-Stone was saying. "*Muchos* colones."

"Hawk, him tink he know best for everybody here. He don't. Him say just a few *nortes* at a time. Bring dem in for a little while. Make dem work. That's good for de trees and de monkeys, mon. But it ain't no good for us."

"What can you do if one of us is bitten by a snake?" Sara asked. At the moment, she didn't care about big beachfront hotels versus small numbers of ecotourists, or village feuds, or even buried treasure. All she could imagine was one of the boys being bitten by a poisonous snake, here, as close as she ever wanted to be to the ends of the earth.

"You bring dem me. I fix," the snake doctor said mysteriously. "I call de snake from de woods. You kill him and everyt'ing be all right."

"Why won't you kill it for me?"

"No." He shook his head. "If I kill him, his spirit be mad at me. Don't worry. If him bite you or dem little ones, I give you somet'ing to take away de poison. You be all better real quick."

"What will you give me?" Sara persisted.

The snake doctor smiled hugely. "Why, magic, of course."

"Magic. I—I don't believe in magic."

Ian Carter-Stone shrugged. "Too bad for you. But if you want to see what I say is true, I'll call de snakes." He lifted his hand. The crowd grew hushed. There was no sound but the rustling of the sea breeze in the treetops and the murmur of the surf. At that time, in that place, she could believe in a kind of magic, the magic of Ian Carter-Stone's power over his fellow villagers and his belief in himself.

"No," she said. "I believe you."

"Good." He nodded again, leaning forward so that only Sara could hear. "Now remember. If snake gets you or yours, don't go wit' Hawk. You don't go to yo' brother, either. Dey call plane. Send you to hospital in

San José. You be dead 'fore you get dere for sure, mon." He pointed to a fat black finger at each of the boys. "You hear me? Come to me you get bit by ol' *terciopelo,* or a big bushmaster drop down out of a tree on top o' you. I save you."

"Okay," Zack said, clearly awestruck.

"Thank you." Ben was a bit more skeptical.

"Since Aunt Sara won't let you call any snakes out of the woods, can you show us some at your house?" Zack asked.

"I have de skins. I show you, so you know what good snake and what bad snake." He made a regal, courtly bow in Sara's direction. *"Con su permiso, señora."*

"Aunt Sara, please, can we go see the snakeskins, please?"

"I'd like that, Mom," Ben added.

"Of course." She might not believe in Ian Carter-Stone's magic, but that was no reason to deprive the boys of their grisly treat. "Hurry back."

The youngsters followed the snake doctor to his home. The other men drifted off, leaving Elliot and Sara standing alone.

"You might like to know I keep a supply of antivenom here at the clinic. And Hawk has some up at the lodge as well," Emily Wycheski said from her clinic doorway.

Sara hadn't noticed her standing there before. She looked over at the missionary nurse with a smile. "I'm glad to hear that. I'm afraid I can't be as openminded about folk remedies as I should."

"I don't pretend to know how Ian works," Emily admitted, walking out onto the covered porch that ran the length of the building. Her hair was pulled up into a damp knot on top of her head. She looked as fresh and clean as if she'd just gotten out of the shower. She smiled at Elliot and bade him good-afternoon. "The people here—all over Central America and the Caribbean, as a matter of fact—have great faith in their snake doctors. That alone demands my professional respect. However, Dr. Carter-Stone doesn't return the courtesy." She smiled ruefully. "He will barely give me the time of day."

"Don't antagonize the man," Elliot warned. "I've been trying to get him to tell me how he works for the past eighteen months. Too bad this business about the hotel has set him at odds with Hawk. He's become as closemouthed as a clam."

"He's feuding with Hawk?" Maybe she had more in common with the snake doctor than she'd first supposed, Sara thought.

"It's over the hotels locating down on the beach," Emily explained. "Ian and several men in the village think it's a good idea. Hawk and most of the other residents don't."

"But Elliot told me Hawk *is* interested in bringing tourists to stay at his place."

"Only a few at a time," Elliot explained. "You've heard of ecotourism, haven't you, sis? Where small groups of students and teachers, tourists, *nortes* come and pay good money to study and work at restoring the rain forests."

"Limited numbers in controlled situations," Emily added. "No poorly regulated commercial developments like the big beachfront hotels up north."

"Exactly." Elliot beamed at her approvingly. "No big spenders, no casinos. Just aging hippies, students and starving scientists like myself."

"Hawk's on one side of the fence and Ian Carter-Stone is on the other," Sara said, beginning to understand.

"Yes." Emily's mouth turned down in a worried frown. "The issue has caused a lot of tension here these last six months. And I'm afraid before it's settled, it's going to cause a lot more."

CHAPTER THREE

HAWK HEARD HER coming from a long way off. It wasn't that she was making a great deal of noise, but rather that her presence had disturbed a number of the more skittish residents of the rain forest. He'd learned long ago to pay attention to the habits of the denizens of whatever jungle he was in. If you didn't, you could wind up dead.

"Good morning, Mrs. Riley," he said, not looking up from the repair work he was doing on the water-wheel that supplied most of the power to the generator. He couldn't afford to lose the small but necessary part he was replacing by being polite. If he did, there would be no electricity for two weeks, until he could get another one. She'd like that even less than his lack of good manners.

"I need to talk to you, Mr. Hawk," she said, her forceful tone spoiled by her being out of breath. "About my brother's investment in your treasure hunt."

"I didn't expect you to be up this early in the morning."

"With three kids to get up and off to school every morning, not to mention getting there on time myself, I've never had much choice. You're up and around pretty early yourself."

"This is the tropics. It's best to get the heavy work done in the cool of the day."

"That makes sense. I'm sure you've guessed I didn't follow you up here to make small talk."

"I figured as much. Just out of curiosity, how did you track me down?"

"I—I saw you from the shower." The bathroom in Sara's cabin was located outside the building, on the veranda. It was surrounded by a shoulder-high stone wall and a low, overhanging thatched roof that screened the facilities from the path leading up to the waterfall that provided Tyiskita's water and electricity.

"You were watching me from the shower?"

"I was watching your macaw," she corrected him sharply. "She'd landed in a tree just a little way up the cliff and she was making a terrible racket."

"He," Hawk corrected her. "The bird is a male."

"Oh."

"Have a seat," he said, motioning to a rock at the side of the stream.

"No, thank you." She remained standing. Her hair was damp, pulled up in a knot on the top of her head. She hadn't been birding from the shower, he realized. She'd been taking a shower when she spotted him, and she hadn't wanted him to see her naked or she probably would have come outside and collared him then and there. "Mr. Hawk, about the money."

"Like I told you before, my name is Hawk. Don't bother with the mister." He looked up from his work. She was watching a column of ants carrying their booty back to the nest.

"Are they soldier ants?" she asked, edging closer to the fallen tree trunk along which the insects were traveling. "Where are they going?"

"No, they're not soldier ants. They won't swarm all over you and cut the flesh from your bones like the ones in the old Tarzan movies. They're leaf-cutter ants. They eat leaves, and they're taking those back to their nest. You can probably find it if you follow them."

For a moment she looked tempted to do just that. "I've never seen anything quite like it. Except on television, of course. Do you think the nest is very far away?" Hawk felt a tug of amusement at her almost childlike enthusiasm, but he didn't let it show. He'd heard enough about Sara Riley from her brother in the past weeks and months to know that it would be a mistake to underestimate either her intelligence or her determination to get back the money Elliot had invested with him.

"Remember to watch out for snakes when you get off the main path."

That brought her up short. "Maybe I'll look later. Now we need to talk." The reference to the snakes was an unfortunate one. She obviously considered him a snake in the grass, a member in good standing of the reptile family. It recalled to mind her primary reason for being where she was. She gave the column of marching ants one last, almost wistful look, but when she turned her green eyes on him, they were narrowed with animosity and distrust. "I want you to give my brother his money back."

"I can't do that, Mrs. Riley," he said, wiping his hands on a piece of oily cloth.

"Call me Sara," she said abruptly. "I'm not Mrs. Riley anymore."

"All right." He stood up. The top of her head was at eye level. She tipped her head slightly to maintain eye contact. He wasn't above intimidating a woman if it served his purpose, but something told him that wouldn't work with Sara Riley.

"Why not? Why can't you give him back his money? If you were an honest man, as you claim to be, you'd do it."

"I'm no crook."

Surprisingly, she nodded. "I'm sorry," she said politely. "I shouldn't have said that."

"Apology accepted." He smiled. The old saying about catching more flies with honey than with vinegar might work with a suspicious and skeptical schoolteacher as well. The smile caught her off balance, as he knew it would. She hesitated, but only for a moment. She didn't smile back.

"Okay, maybe you aren't trying to cheat my brother out of his money, but it doesn't change the facts. This whole treasure-hunting scheme is ill-advised—ridiculous, in fact. I'm here to ask you to call it off for my nephew's sake. The money—"

"You think an awful lot about money, don't you?"

"I like money as well as the next person," she answered without hesitation.

"You must. You certainly spend enough time talking about it."

"I'm a single parent with three children to raise. I have to think about money and their futures."

"Zack isn't your child."

He'd scored with that one, but she didn't let it stop her. "He's my nephew and I love him dearly. You may find it hard to believe, but the money isn't the only reason I'm here. I want Zack to be with his father." For a moment he was certain he saw a flash of pain darken her eyes, but it must have been a trick of light and shadow, because with her next breath she returned to the attack. "But Zackary's future with his father isn't the subject we're discussing at the moment. Zackary's inheritance is."

"His father is investing the money for him," Hawk said in a low growl.

"Investment!" She gave an unladylike snort. "Flimflam, more like."

"I don't take advantage of my friends," he said. He took a step closer, wondering just how far he could push her before she turned and ran. "And I don't like being called a flimflam artist."

Sara stood her ground. "I don't scare easily," she said, "and I don't change my mind. A bad risk is a bad risk, no matter what you call it."

Hawk backed off. He'd been called worse names than crook and con man by far more dangerous individuals than Sara Riley. He couldn't and wouldn't risk Elliot's friendship for the momentary satisfaction of putting his schoolteacher sister in her place. "There's some risk involved, I'll admit. But that's the way of most worthwhile achievements in life."

"This isn't the same as playing the stock market."

"I never pretended it was. Come here." He reached out and wrapped his hand around her wrist—a small wrist. But her resistance was strong.

"Where are you taking me?" she demanded, digging in her heels.

"Up there." Hawk pointed with his free hand. "I want to show you something."

"I can't climb up a waterfall."

"Yes, you can. The water's only a few inches deep this time of year." The rainy season was due to begin in a couple of weeks. "C'mon."

He let go of her arm. He knew she would follow him. They started climbing. It wasn't a particularly difficult or steep climb, but he was aware it had to be hard on Sara, unaccustomed as she was to the tropical heat and humidity. He'd been born and raised in central Illinois himself, only a couple of hundred miles from Fort Wayne. Although he hadn't been back there in twenty years, he remembered what it was like—as different from Tyiskita as Fort Wayne was from Oz.

"Wait," she called breathlessly, halfway up the last and steepest drop of waterfall. "I have to catch my breath." Hawk looked back. She was kneeling by the edge of the streambed, scooping water over her wrists and arms. Her face was flushed. Her pink T-shirt was damp and clinging. She wasn't wearing a bra, he noticed. No sane woman did in this heat. Her breasts were nice—not too big, not too small. She had nice legs, too. Her hair was brown, fine wisps escaping from the knot on top of her head to curl around her cheeks and the back of her neck. Her eyes were green, and so clear you could look straight into her soul. He wondered if she realized he could read her every thought in those eyes— and use it to his advantage. She was five or six years younger than he was, he guessed. Not a beauty, but not bad-looking. Pity she was such a pain in the ass.

"It's cooler at the top," Hawk called down in that low raspy tone that set the edges of Sara's nerves on fire.

She stood up, wishing looks could kill. He was so damned at ease, standing there on a big boulder, legs slightly spread. He was wearing khaki shorts again and a white shirt, open halfway down his chest, with the sleeves rolled back to expose bronzed and muscled forearms. A modern-day pirate for sure. He even looked the part, with that sharp blade of a nose, high forehead and heavy dark eyebrows. He was in his early forties, Sara guessed. A hard man, accustomed to getting his own way, and dangerous as a cornered lion when he did not.

"Come on, Mrs. Riley."

"I told you. It's Sara, not Mrs. Riley." But he'd started climbing again and probably hadn't even heard what she'd said. She followed him, although she wanted nothing more than to stay where she was, take off her shoes and dangle her feet in the surprisingly cool water.

"There's a bench up here on the path where you can catch your breath," he said, reaching down to help her over the last lip of stone. His hands were scarred, as though by fire, and work-roughened.

"Path?" She was hot and winded, and knew that her face was as red as a beet. He pulled her onto the path as though she weighed no more than a feather. "There's a path? Why didn't you tell me before?"

"Because it would take three times as long to get here that way. I'm a busy man, Sara Riley. I don't have all day to spend arguing with you."

"I keep telling you, you don't have to argue with me. Just give my brother back his money and I'll be on the first plane out of here."

"You sure as hell have a one-track mind."

"My nephew's fu—"

"I know. Your nephew's future is at stake." He looked at her, his eyes dark as midnight, his face impassive. "Why aren't you down there giving the third degree to your brother instead of me?"

Sara was caught off guard by the query. He'd backed her into a corner again, making her explain her actions, when he was the one who should be explaining to her. She was going to have to be very, very careful what she said to this man.

"Believe me, I would be if I thought it would do any good. But it's like talking to the wall," she said, because he already knew it was the truth. "He thinks you're on to something big."

"I am."

"It's too big a gamble." She was beginning to sound like a broken record even to herself.

"Your brother wants Father Benedicto's journal as badly as I want the rest of the treasure."

"How do you know it's even still here? What if Father Benedicto didn't die here? What if he walked out of the jungle and took it with him?"

"He didn't."

"Can you be sure?"

"Elliot obviously didn't tell you everything about Father Benedicto." He pointed to an opening in the undergrowth, a rocky outcropping that looked out over the ocean. Tyiskita, both Hawk's land and the village, lay spread out below them. There was a rustic bench a little way back from the cliff's edge and a narrow path dropping away down the slope. A short distance below them, Sara could see the thatched roof of a building she hadn't noticed from below.

"My house," Hawk said, answering her unspoken question. "Sit down." He indicated the bench.

Sara sat.

"What else is there to tell?" she asked, as Hawk braced his shoulder against the trunk of a tree, looking out over the blue-green water.

"Do you see that boat out there?"

"Yes," she nodded. "The treasure hunters. Elliot told me about them." Even from this distance, she could see small figures with scuba gear walking around on the deck. "They're looking for the wreck of the *Mary Deere*."

"They have a basketful of high-powered, big-money backers—Arab sheikhs, Japanese real-estate tycoons, even a couple of pharmaceutical companies that have heard the legends about the treasure—and Father Benedicto's journal. If they don't find what they're looking for down there, they'll come looking here."

"Can they do that? I thought you owned this land."

"I do. It's been in my family for generations. But I'm just one man. And this is Central America. If you have enough colones to grease the right palms, you can do just about anything you want, short of murder. Sometimes you can even get away with that."

"Your family's owned this land for generations, you say. Is that how you came to learn about the legends? From the natives in the village?"

"I heard the story from my grandfather years ago. My ancestor was a member of the crew of the *Mary Deere*."

The captain himself, Sara decided. She would just about bet on it. The man was the descendant of a pirate. "If you knew all along where the treasure was, why were you searching the archives?"

"Legends aren't facts."

"Somehow I'm not surprised to hear your great-great...great?—" she wasn't certain how many generations they were talking about here "—grandfather was a pirate."

"Not a pirate, exactly," he said, shifting position so that he faced her as she sat on the bench. For a moment she thought he might be going to smile again. "My great-great-great grand*mother* was the captain's mistress. Her name was Mary Hawk. She was an Englishwoman, something of an adventuress. Did Elliot tell you her part of the story?''

Sara shook her head. ''He didn't mention her. I think for my brother, Father Benedicto's journal is the only thing that's truly important.''

''You're right about Elliot. That's the kind of man he is. But the gold and emeralds are real, too. Our kind of treasure, Sara Riley—yours and mine.''

She pretended not to hear him.

''It was Mary Hawk's share of the booty,'' he went on. ''The other crewmen insisted she be able to keep it when her lover marooned her here along with Father Benedicto.''

''Did the pirates maroon him...them...because of the journal?'' Sara asked. Elliot hadn't told her this part of the story.

''Possibly,'' he said with a shrug. ''Evidently he was the only one of the viceroy's guardian priests who wasn't put to the sword when the crew turned pirate. Mary Hawk saved his life. She made her lover promise to put him ashore wherever they made landfall. For whatever reason, he agreed to her request. But later it seems the captain couldn't quite bring himself to believe her interest in the priest was purely... humanitarian. He was young, and not bad-looking, or so the family legends say. The captain ended up putting Mary ashore as well.''

''Was she in love with him?''

One of his dark-winged eyebrows raised slightly. ''I have no idea. All we know is that she was pregnant when she left here six months later on an English warship. Father Benedicto stayed behind to minister to the Indians—and perhaps to expiate his sins? Who knows.

But before she left, he helped Mary Hawk bury her share of the treasure in a cave. She couldn't take it with her. It would have made her a marked woman when she returned to London. She could have been transported or hanged."

"Is that what happened to her?" Sara asked. "Was she eventually hanged as a pirate?"

"No. Nothing so drastic. Actually, she managed to make a good marriage a few years later. To a minor nobleman, a younger son. They came to America. She had four more children, only one of whom lived to adulthood. We've lost track of that branch of the family. My great-great-grandfather was her bastard son, Joseph Hawk."

"And you're named for him?"

Hawk nodded.

"Did she ever come back?" Sara heard herself ask. Had Mary Hawk loved the young, handsome priest so deeply she'd tried to return to him? Or had she forgotten him, grown old and stout and set in her ways, a proper Victorian matron, her colorful and adventurous past obscured by a veneer of gentility and respectability?

This time Hawk did smile, a quick twist of his lips, nothing more. "Don't tell me you're getting interested in my family legend, my wild-goose chase!"

"I'm interested in hearing all the facts," Sara said, not smiling back. It would never do to let him know how interesting she found his tale.

"All right. I'll tell you the rest." He covered the distance between them in two quick steps. He leaned over the back of the bench, close, but not touching. She could feel the heat of his skin, smell his soap and the faint musky odor of his sweat. "She did want to come

back, although she never got the chance. Maybe she
loved her husband enough not to hurt him. Maybe she
just couldn't find her way back. I don't know. But I do
know that years later, after her husband died, she told
the story to my great-grandfather, her grandson, when
he was a very young man and she was a very old
woman. He was cut from the same bolt of cloth, a real
adventurer, in an age when it was still possible to make
or lose a fortune on the turn of a card.''

"He came to Tyiskita to find Father Benedicto for
her?"

"Benedicto was long dead," Hawk said bluntly. "He
came here to find the treasure she'd left behind."

"I don't believe that. Love is the most important
thing. She sent him to find the man, not the gold."

"Believe what you want," Hawk said with a shrug.
Sara couldn't be sure, but she thought she detected just
the faintest hint of amusement in his whiskey-rough
voice. "It doesn't matter to me. What does matter is
that by the time my great-grandfather got here, the ter-
rain was altered beyond recognition by earthquakes and
hurricanes. The entrance to the sea cave where Mary
Hawk had hidden her treasure was gone. All he could
do was buy the land above it. He did it for her, but when
he got back to the States, she was dead. Off and on
through the years, my family's come looking, but until
now we haven't had the time or the resources to make
an all-out effort. It's still down there somewhere—the
emeralds and the gold, millions of dollars' worth. But
it will take money and the proper equipment to find the
entrance after all these years."

"That's where my brother and his son's money comes
in." Time to get visions of lost lovers and pirate adven-

tures out of her head. Time to get back to the issue at hand.

"Elliot wants Father Benedicto's journal as badly as I want the gold," Hawk said bluntly. He straightened in one single, fluid movement, bringing Sara to her feet as well. "And I intend to see that he gets it." He took her by the arm, not hurting her, but giving her no chance to pull away. "Look out there. You may not recognize it, but that's the best surfing beach between California and South America. Three big hotel chains are vying for permits to develop the coast between here and Golfito. I don't want that."

"You can't stop progress." She couldn't come out and tell him that after only two days in Costa Rica, she didn't want to see that, either. It was ridiculous. She didn't know anything about the economics of this place. Maybe a big hotel nearby would be the best thing that ever happened to Tyiskita village—if not to the rain forest.

"I can damn well try."

"That's why the treasure hunters down there in the bay are a threat to you as well, isn't it?" she asked, turning so that he had to look at her. "If they're successful in locating the wreck of the Mary Deere, they'll bring even more notoriety to your little Eden. And if they aren't successful, they're liable to come after your treasure just like you said."

He was looking at her with dark, shuttered eyes, his face hard and set. He was very strong, she realized, as she felt his fingers tighten almost imperceptibly on her arm. Strong and utterly ruthless. Yet she wasn't frightened of him, not really. Deep inside she felt a slight, unfamiliar flutter of excitement. "You intend to get to it first, even if it takes every dollar you have."

"Yes." The word was a low, deep rumble in his chest.

"And my brother's as well."

"Yes."

"What are you investing?"

"Everything I've got."

"More ill-gotten gains?" Sara asked.

"I spent twenty years in the Marine Corps," Hawk said harshly. "And five more years doing...government work, shall we say? I earned every penny the hard way."

Somehow Sara hadn't expected him to say anything else. "You really believe the treasure is here, under the cliff, waiting to be found?" The flutter of excitement was back, stronger than before.

"Yes." Again his fingers tightened fractionally on her arm. There was still no pain, but Sara wondered if she would have a bruise by morning.

"The risk," she said, almost to herself. What if they did find the treasure first? What if Mary Hawk's treasure was theirs to share?

"Life is a risk," he growled. "Let go. Take the chance."

"Even if you find the treasure, there will be other claims." She had to keep her head, not to be carried away by this sudden rush of adrenaline through her veins. Treasure hunting. She'd never imagined herself doing any such thing. "The Costa Rican government. The government of Spain, or Peru. Even the Catholic Church." What *would* it be like to just let go, ride the whirlwind, as he'd told her to do?

"I'll cross that bridge when I come to it. I'll tell you one more time. What I set out to do I usually accomplish," he said without a trace of modesty. "Remember that." His next words were a threat, plain and simple, but still, absurdly, Sara felt no fear. "What I find I keep and no one, including you, Sara Riley, stands in my way."

"All right," she said, looking pointedly at her arm. She tried very hard not to let her growing excitement show. She still didn't approve of what he was doing, but she just couldn't stop herself from wanting all of a sudden to be part of the search. He released her abruptly and stepped back, giving her space.

"We'll make a deal," she offered. "I'll give you ten days. If you can prove to me in that time that you can somehow recover the treasure, I'll leave this place, go back to Indiana and you'll never hear another word from me."

"No more sabotaging my character with your brother?" he asked. His face didn't change expression, but Sara thought perhaps the look in his eyes wasn't quite as deathly cold.

"That's correct."

"Will you help in the search?"

"What?"

"Come treasure hunting with us, Sara Riley. It will save money." This time he did smile and Sara felt like smacking him.

"Okay," she said, ignoring another traitorous flutter of excitement. She couldn't let herself get too carried away. Hawk was only including her in the hunt to keep an eye on her, of that she had no doubt. He didn't fool her for a moment. But two could play that game, and his invitation meshed with her own plans for keeping him under surveillance. That was all. "I'll come treasure hunting with you. To keep you honest, if nothing else."

"Deal."

Sara caught herself wishing he would smile again.

"Deal." She held out her hand. "But only for ten days," she reminded him, as he folded his big rough hand around hers. "If you don't have something concrete to show me by then, all deals are off. And then watch out, Joseph C. Hawk. Watch out."

CHAPTER FOUR

TWO DAYS LATER they found the cave.

Or rather, Zack found the cave.

He was hunting for poisonous frogs, hopping on and off the steep pathway up the cliff, poking a long stick into every nook and cranny, when he simply disappeared.

Or at least that's what Ben told Sara when he came running along the pathway to find her.

"Mom! Come quick. Zack fell in a hole."

"Oh, Lord. Is he hurt?"

"I don't think so. Me and Uncle El and Zack were looking for the entrance to the cave over there." Ben pointed beyond a stand of ferns that blocked her view. "Uncle El said it looked like a good place—"

"What happened?" Sara interrupted, pushing Ben ahead of her, back the way he'd come.

"Zack hollered he'd found something. And then he just disappeared." Ben sounded more excited than frightened. "I mean, one second he was there, waving and hollering to beat the band, and the next, *pffft.*" He made a sweeping motion with his hands. "He was gone. Vanished. Just like that. It was awesome. Then we heard him yellin' and cryin' and found the hole he fell down. Uncle El stayed beside the opening. He told me to get you and Hawk."

"Hawk—" Sara stopped short. "Yes. That's a good idea. Go get Hawk. Tell him what happened. He'll know what to do." She might not like the man, but she wasn't stupid enough to ignore his expertise in a situation like this.

"I'll run all the way."

"Hurry," Sara urged. "But first tell me exactly where to find them."

"They're right over there," Ben said, pointing beyond a small rise. "Just keep walking. Can you find them by yourself?"

"I'll be fine," Sara assured him. "Now hurry. Can you find your way back here okay?"

"If I can't, Hawk can."

Sara hurried forward, calling her brother's name as she ran, refusing even to think about running into one of Ian Carter-Stone's deadly minions on the narrow, overgrown path. The canopy trees towered above her. Parakeets and monkeys jabbered in irritation as she passed beneath them, disturbing their siesta. She kept her eye on the path, moving quickly but carefully. She couldn't afford to be careless now and trip and fall over one of the many vines and tree roots that crossed the path every few steps. She called Elliot's name again. He answered from somewhere just ahead of her. Breathless, she topped the rise and there he was, kneeling beside a small dark hole in the ground surrounded by ferns and trailing vines and capped by a huge overhanging boulder.

"Elliot, is he all right?" She slid to a halt beside Zack's father.

"Aunt Sara? Come and get me," Zack cried. "It's dark and smelly down here."

"Zack, honey, are you all right?"

"I want *out!*" Zack yelled, so loudly Sara was almost certain he wasn't hurt.

"Damn, sis. I swear I didn't turn my back more than thirty seconds and he was gone," Elliot said. He was hunkered down in front of the hole, staring into the darkness. His eyes looked stricken, his complexion pasty.

"It's not your fault, El. He's just about the most inquisitive child I've ever seen." Sara moved up to pat her brother on the shoulder. Then she, too, peered into the hole. "Zack, are you okay?"

"Yes. I want *out!*"

"As quick as we can manage, honey."

"You come down, okay? I don't want to be here in the dark. You won't get hurt. It's like a slide. Kind of," he amended. "You can make it. Come and get me."

"Honey, don't you think it would be better if your dad came down? He's a lot stronger than I am."

"No! I want you." He began to cry.

"Sit tight, son," Elliot called out. "Don't move around unless you can see where you're going."

"I can't see a thing," Zack wailed. "It's too dark."

"What should we do?" Sara asked.

"There's no telling what it's like down there. If Zack gets too scared, he's liable to start moving around. We don't know if he's in a passageway, a room, or God help us, a chimney that goes all the way through the hillside to the beach. But if I go down now, you and Hawk will have a hell of a time pulling me back up."

"We'll manage."

"Aunt Sara!"

"Hold on, son. I'm coming."

"No! I want Aunt Sara."

"I'll go," she said, making up her mind.

"No, Sara. He's my son. I'll go," Elliot insisted.

Their voices must have carried clearly down into the cave.

"Aunt Sara, you come. Not my dad."

Elliot looked stricken.

Sara laid her hand on his arm. "I'm all he's had for a long time, El. After only two days, you can't expect him to turn to you when he's scared and alone. I'll go. I can make it through the opening. And I don't weigh that much," she added with a nervous little laugh. "Between you and macho-man Hawk, you should be able to haul me back up. I'll stay with him until you can figure out a way to get us both out of there."

"The prudent thing to do is wait for Hawk," Elliot said, sounding frustrated and hurt by Zack's rejection.

"I know that," she agreed, swinging down into the hole, "but we can't leave Zack alone in the dark. Give me your hand." Elliot steadied her as she squirmed into the opening feet first. She held on to his hands as long as she was able, then took a deep breath and let go.

It was a longer drop than she expected, but not dangerously so. For several moments after she landed, she sat in the wet, muddy gloom and tried to still the pounding of blood in her ears. She took a quick inventory and decided that, beyond a few scratches and bruises, she'd survived the descent intact.

"Aunt Sara!" Zack launched himself into her arms. "Help me climb out of here."

"I can't, sweetie," she said, giving him a fierce, hard hug. "You're right. It's kind of like a slide—a real slippery one. We'll need a rope. We're going to have to wait for Hawk and Ben to bring one."

"Did you tell Ben to bring back a flashlight?" Zack asked, clinging to her like a limpet.

"No," she said, laughing a little, with a mixture of equal parts relief and unease. "But I'm sure Hawk won't forget a flashlight."

"It's pretty spooky down here."

"I've already figured that out." Sara studied their surroundings now that her eyes had adjusted to the darkness. She could see a few feet in both directions. She shivered and drew Zack closer. Elliot had been right. They appeared to be in a small room or passageway of a much larger cave. Below them, and very far away, she thought she could hear the rush of waves against stone. Was it possible? Had Zack, a child, searching at a child's-eye level, found Hawk's lost treasure cave so soon?

"Sara? Are you two all right?" Elliot called from above.

"I'm fine." She hugged Zack again. "We're both fine."

"Hell and damnation. What's *she* doing down there?"

It was Hawk. There was no mistaking that gravelly voice. Or the exasperated tone.

"I came down to be with Zack," Sara called back, scrambling to her feet. She remembered just in time to stand up slowly. She had no idea how low the ceiling was. Tentatively she stretched her hand over her head. The hairy filaments of a root or spiderweb brushed her fingers. She snatched them back, rubbing her dirty hands down the sides of her shorts. "If you don't like it, you can sue me for trespassing. But first get us out of here."

DAMN, that woman was a handful, Hawk thought, as he tied a net bag containing a heavy flashlight to the end of the rope he intended to use to rescue Zack, and lowered it down the hole.

"What's she doing down there?" he repeated. He could hear her singing—humming really, some nursery ditty he'd long ago forgotten the words to.

"Zack wanted her," Elliot said. "He wouldn't have anything to do with me going down after him."

"The kid's scared," Hawk said. "He wants what's familiar. Don't make too much of it."

"He's kind of afraid of the dark sometimes," Ben offered. "And so is Mom. They always sing little songs and stuff when the lights go out, to keep the monsters away. That's what she's doing now. Hear her?"

"Great. That's all I need. A woman who's afraid of the dark at the bottom of a twenty-foot hole in the ground."

"Maybe she's afraid of the dark," Ben said, coming to his mother's defense, "but she went down there anyway. I think that's pretty brave."

"Yeah, kid," Hawk said, grudgingly. "You're right. Sara, move away from the opening," he called out. "I'm going to drop the rope. There's a flashlight tied to the end." There was no response from below. Hawk frowned. What the hell could have happened to her in thirty-seconds' time? "Sara!" This time her name was a command. "Answer me!"

"Yes." Her voice trembled, all the righteous indignation of just moments before washed away.

"Are you all right?" She didn't sound right at all. Was she going to go to pieces on him down there in the dark? "Stand back. I'm coming down."

"No." She sounded more herself this time. "Don't be ridiculous. You can't come down here. We'll all be trapped."

Hawk snorted. If neither of them was injured, and an earthquake didn't cause the walls of the cave to collapse at that exact moment, getting the two of them out of there would be a piece of cake. "I trust your brother to pull us back out," he hollered. "Don't you?"

"Yes. I'd trust him with my life," came the unhesitating reply.

"So would I. Now, quit arguing and stand back." He was learning very quickly how to deal with Sara Riley. Attack. Keep her off guard and then talk sense to her. He had to give her that—she listened. She didn't always take advice with good grace, but she listened. And she learned fast. Two qualities that were essential to staying alive in the shadowy world he'd left behind.

Hawk gave Elliot a few last-minute instructions for pulling his son out of the hole and then lowered himself into the gloom. The cave smelled of wet earth, mold and decay, and very faintly, beneath the other heavy, damp smells, there was the tang of the sea. Elliot had been right about one thing—the boy had fallen into a chimney, or some kind of extension of a sea cave. With any luck at all, it was Mary Hawk's cave. His cave. As soon as he got Sara and the kid safely out of there, he was going to go exploring on his own.

"Watch your head," Sara warned as he dropped onto the wet, muddy rock floor. "The ceiling is very low." She was holding the flashlight with both hands. The beam pointed at his chest. At least she'd had the sense not to shine it directly in his eyes.

Hawk surveyed the small room. Sara didn't oblige him any further by swinging the beam of light away from his body. As far as he could tell, the room narrowed quickly into a pitch-black passageway that more than likely dropped straight down to the sea. If they were lucky, very lucky, it might descend at an angle that wouldn't require climbing equipment to negotiate.

"Let's get out of here," Zack whispered loudly. "Aunt Sara found something nasty in the corner of the cave."

"What?" Hawk demanded, his gaze swinging to the spot where Zack was pointing.

"Nothing," Sara said quickly. Too quickly, it seemed to him. "It was nothing. This place just gives me the creeps, that's all."

"Let's take a look."

"No." He already recognized that stubborn tone of voice.

"Okay." Obviously, whatever she'd seen, she wasn't going to show it to him in front of the kid. If that's the way she wanted it, then that's the way it would be. "Let's get Zack out of here. I'm going to tie this rope under your arms and then your dad's going to pull you up."

"Wow!" Zack croaked. "Just like in the movies. Is Ben up there to see this?"

"He's there."

"Awesome. I wish he had the camera. Do you know if he brought the camera? He could take pictures and I could show the kids back home."

"We didn't have time to pick up the camera," Hawk informed him as he secured the rope around Zack's chest. He'd spent very little of his adult life around children. It was amazing how resilient they were. He'd expected the boy to be sniffling and tearful. He was scared, all right. But excited as well. Still, when he stopped to think about it, he probably shouldn't have expected anything else, with Sara Riley raising the kid.

"Ready?" Hawk asked. When Zack nodded, he began his instructions, "Put your foot in my hands." He laced his fingers together. "I'll boost you up. Then just holler up to your dad that you're ready, and he'll pull on the rope while you climb up the side."

"Awesome. This is just like one of those TV shows. You know, where they call in the 911 guys and save people from all kinds of things? We could be on TV when we get back home."

"Yeah. Sure. Now be quiet, kid. Save your breath for the climb. Ready?"

"Ready."

"Okay. One, two, three. Go." With a grunt and a small avalanche of mud and stones, Zack was gone. Hawk was alone in the near darkness with Sara. "You're next," he said. "Time to head back up into the sunlight. But first, show me what you found down here that scared you half out of your wits."

"I'm not scared half out of my wits," she snapped.

"Okay then," he said, lifting a hand in surrender. "What did you find down here that scared you almost speechless? Was it a snake? Or a big scorpion?" Now that he'd formulated his plan of action as far as Sara Riley was concerned, he didn't see any reason to vary his approach, even though they were temporarily entombed twenty feet below ground. Besides, he had the suspicion that if he went soft on her right now, she'd dissolve in tears of fright and reaction.

"It wasn't alive," Sara said, still clutching the big flashlight as if her life depended on it. Elliot had lowered the rope again. It slithered to a halt inches from her shoulder. She took an involuntary step backward, then sidestepped quickly with a little, hastily stifled squeak of alarm.

"You sure as hell sound spooked to me."

"Well, you're wrong. It just threw me, is all. And I didn't want Zack to see. He's scared enough already."

"He sure seems to have gotten over it all right. I wouldn't put it past the little hellion to sell the story to some TV producer, just like he said."

"He is resourceful," Sara said proudly. "But this..."

"This what?"

"That." She pointed into the corner. "Over there."

"Give me the flashlight," Hawk demanded. She was definitely spooked. For some reason he refused to recognize, that bothered him more than it should have. "What's down here with us?"

"I don't need the flashlight to see what it is," Sara said in a voice that was shaky but calm. Hawk relaxed a little. He should have known by now she wouldn't go to pieces on him without a damn good reason. "I already know." She stepped away and pointed to a shallow overhang on the far wall. "It's there. I stumbled over it a few minutes ago." She wiped her hand down her shorts as though trying to scour away a bad memory. "It's a skeleton. A human skeleton. Do you think it could be Father Benedicto himself?"

CHAPTER FIVE

"No," Hawk said. "It's not Father Benedicto." He dropped to the balls of his feet beside the remains, playing up the flashlight over the scattered and discolored bones.

Sara tried not to look at the sightless, staring skull, tried not to think of what it might be like to be disturbed by the light after years and years of darkness. She knelt beside Hawk. "How can you be sure it's not him?"

He was sifting purposefully among the bits and pieces of bones with the tip of the deadly looking knife he carried in a sheath on his belt. He didn't even turn his head when he answered. "This skeleton is old, but not that old."

"Oh," Sara said, before she realized how disappointed she sounded. "Then it's not one of the pirate crew, either?"

"No." He stood, sweeping the beam of the flashlight along the cave wall. "It's probably some poor bastard of an Indian. Or one of the villagers. A couple of the old-timers might even remember someone walking off to fish or hunt one day and never returning." He reached down with his free hand and pulled Sara to her feet.

"What's going on down there?" Elliot shouted. "Is something wrong? Are you both okay?"

Sara gave a guilty little jump. Poor Elliot. Here she was in a real pirate cave, discovering skeletons, and he was waiting up at the top with two overexcited boys and a handful of rope.

"We're fine," Hawk called back. "Sara's ready to come up. I'm going to do a little exploring first."

"Oh no, you don't," she said, repressing her guilt at leaving her brother on the surface to baby-sit. She was hot and filthy and tired, but she wasn't about to crawl back out of this hole until she saw everything there was to see. "I'm coming with you."

"No, you're not."

"Oh yes I am. You asked me to help find the treasure yourself, remember? Consider me Elliot's representative."

"Officially?" he asked, one dark eyebrow lifted slightly.

"Maybe not officially," she said, flushing. "But the fact remains, I'm down here and Elliot's up there. If this is your pirate cave, I'm going to be right beside you when you find Mary Hawk's treasure."

"Don't you trust me?"

"No," she said bluntly. "I don't know you well enough to trust you at all. That's why I'm going with you."

"No, you're not. You're getting your butt back aboveground pronto." Hawk didn't even bother to acknowledge the slur on his character. "The only piece of equipment we have is this flashlight. I'll bet money you've never even been in a cave before. I'm not taking you a step farther."

"You're right. I've never been in a cave before. But I won't hold you back. Consider me your backup." She tilted her head slightly to meet his narrowed eyes and set jaw. It was too dark to read his expression, even if his stony features did give anything away, but she knew him well enough already to imagine what he looked like. She was learning very quickly how to deal with J. C. Hawk. Never back down. Stand up and fight for what you wanted, and he could usually be made to see reason. Now that she'd formulated her plan of action for dealing with the master of Hawkslair, she saw no reason to change her approach, even though they were standing at the bottom of a twenty-foot hole in the ground. "If you fall and break your neck, I can go back and get help."

"Thanks a lot," he said in the husky voice that never failed to set Sara's nerves atingle. "Somehow that still doesn't convince me to change my mind."

"I won't change my mind, either. You can't make me leave." She hoped he didn't call her bluff. If he walked away and left her alone in the dark with only a pile of old bones for company, she'd be a basket case in a matter of minutes.

"Then you'd better keep up. If you don't, I'll leave you behind. I have no intention of ending up like that guy over there." He turned and started off into the darkness. "Understood?"

She'd already found one skeleton today. What more could happen? "Understood," she agreed and then called loudly over her shoulder, "Hang on a minute, El, I'm going exploring with Hawk."

"Be careful," Elliot hollered back. Poor El. She'd have to make sure sometime during this adventure that he got to be in on the fun stuff.

"No fair," she could hear Zack yell. "I want to go, too."

The sound of her nephew's voice faded abruptly as she squeezed past a sharp outcrop of sandy rock and entered a subterranean world where the only light came from the flashlight in Hawk's hand.

"Grab hold of my belt," he ordered. "And don't let go. One false step down here could get us both killed."

Sara did as she was told after only a moment's hesitation. For some reason she didn't care to name, she was reluctant to touch him. When she did slide her fingers inside his belt, she knew why she'd been so hesitant. Even through layers of fabric, the touch of his skin affected her as profoundly as the touch of his voice. The muscles at the small of his back were iron-hard, just like the rest of him, and the heat of his body radiated along her fingertips and up her arms. Once again the hair stood up on the back of her neck, and a little shiver of awareness ran along her nerve endings.

Hawk seemed completely unmoved by the disturbingly intimate contact. They walked in silence for what seemed like hours but could only have been a few minutes, at most. The walls of the passageway were narrow and rough. The downhill slope was steep but not too difficult. Roots and cobwebs brushed Sara's face and hair often enough to be unsettling, and now and then an occasional rustle in the mud and stones at her feet made her bite her lip to keep from crying out in alarm. It was bad enough knowing she shared the cave with a skeleton. She wasn't interested in meeting any of its living inhabitants as well.

"Do you think we can go all the way to the beach?" she asked, her voice muffled by the confined space and the heavy, wet air. Hawk stopped without warning. Sara took one more step and her nose bumped into his shoulder blade. She might as well have walked into the cave wall. "Ouch! What did you do that for?"

"That's why," Hawk said, drawing her forward. The touch of his hand on her arm raised goose bumps on her skin.

"My God." The path ended abruptly in a drop of ten or fifteen feet. It was hard to judge distance in the distorting illumination of the flashlight, but it wasn't hard to identify what was lying at the bottom. The goose bumps she felt now where anything but pleasant. "My God, another one." The bones of the second skeleton were stretched out among the rocks, as though their owner had prepared himself for death. They, too, looked as if they'd been there for a very long time. "Do you think they were together?"

"Probably."

Hawk hunkered down. Sara dropped to her knees also, heedless of the sharp stones at the edge of the drop-off. "I'll bet they were exploring together," she said, whispering, although there was no way she could disturb the slumber of the person below. "And he fell." She stopped talking abruptly, reaching out to Hawk without thinking. "They are men, aren't they?" she asked, horrified. "They aren't women or children?"

He shook his head. "No. And on second thought, I'd say they aren't Indians, either. The skeletons are too big. I'll bet if we did some investigating, we'd come up with some oil geologists, or banana-company surveyors, who disappeared back in the twenties or thirties. That's probably who these poor bastards are."

"Maybe he fell and was hurt too badly to continue. His companion kept on going, looking for a way out, but couldn't find one," Sara whispered, caught up in her speculations. In the excitement and unreality of the moment. "Elliot said the entrance Zack found is very new. It's probably only been there since the last rainy season. The poor guy was so close and yet so far away." She wasn't looking at the skeleton anymore. She closed her eyes, picturing the terrible emptiness of dying alone in the dark. "I wonder if this man knew why his friend never came back for him?"

"They might not have been such good friends," Hawk said dryly, breaking the spell. Sara's eyes flew open. She realized suddenly that her hand was still on his arm, and she snatched it back. "Why do you say that?"

"Look." He focused the beam of light on the skeleton's left hand. "There." Sara sucked in her breath. She didn't know how she could have missed seeing it the first time she looked.

"Gold." The word came out in a rush. "Is it gold?"

"Yes," Hawk said grimly. "My gold."

"Our gold," she said, so fiercely that he laughed. A real laugh, deep and rich and mellow. Sara felt gooseflesh rising on her arms yet again.

"Okay," he agreed, still chuckling. "Our gold."

Sara couldn't take her eyes off the sun-bright glimmerings almost hidden by mud and the remains of a small canvas drawstring bag. "He must have been holding on to it even when he died."

"Looks like it," Hawk said. "But you're right about one thing—this guy couldn't go on. Both his legs are broken. He probably sent his buddy ahead. But he had enough strength left to insist on keeping the gold."

"I wonder if it was any comfort at the end," Sara said, shivering. The cool damp atmosphere of the cave was suddenly even more oppressive.

"Let's get out of here." Hawk stood, then reached down and held out his hand. Sara took it and he pulled her to her feet.

"But the gold... We aren't going to leave it here, are we?"

He shook his head. "You and your one-track mind. It's been here for almost two hundred years without making it to the surface. It'll be safe a few more days. Let's go."

Sara held back. "If those two found Mary Hawk's gold, then they probably found Father Benedicto's journal as well. Do you think it's down there, too?"

"No," he said, not looking back into the black pit at their feet again. "There are only a few pieces of gold down there, nothing else. That's not Mary Hawk's treasure."

"How do you know?"

"Because if they'd found all of it, including Father Benedicto's journal, it would be lying down there along with those bones. If you'd found it, would you have left it behind?"

"No," Sara said, biting her lip.

"You're damn right, you wouldn't. You'd have dragged along every ounce you could carry."

"I suppose you're right. And if I were Mary Hawk and I wanted to keep people away from my real treasure, I might have planted a little of it where it was easy for someone like those two to find," she added thoughtfully, "to keep them from looking too hard for the rest of it."

"Why do you think she did that?"

"Because she was a woman. And so am I. And that's what I'd do," Sara said.

"That's a pretty long leap, but it makes sense." Sara couldn't tell if that was a faint note of approval in his voice, or if she was imagining it. Probably the latter. Hawk went right on talking. "We need the right equipment and a chance to find a way down to the beach without a lot of interested bystanders nosing around."

"How do you know this passage goes all the way to the beach?"

"I don't. But I intend to find out."

"And what about the bodies? I mean, shouldn't the authorities be notified? Those men must have had families somewhere."

"They've been here for sixty or seventy years, more than likely. They can lie here a few more days."

Sara didn't have an argument for that one. She was being too sentimental. Hawk was right. The two were long past caring.

"At least there isn't a curse," she said, trying to shake off the creepy feeling turning her back on the skeleton produced.

"There might as well be," Hawk said, preparing to head back up the slope the way they had come.

Sara reached out to stop him. "What do you mean by that?" Her voice echoed oddly in the heavy darkness. She sounded as scared and breathless as a little girl hearing a ghost story at a slumber party. "You never said the treasure was cursed."

"It isn't. But I'm beginning to think I am," Hawk said pointedly.

Sara had no doubt at all that he was referring to her. "I gave you my word I wouldn't interfere with your search," she said with wounded dignity. "I've done my best to keep my promise."

"Does that mean you're going to stay out of my way?"

"Absolutely not. I intend to be involved in every aspect of the search from this moment on. It's—it's my duty."

She heard him laugh for the second time. It was nearly as unnerving as finding the skeletons, but much, much more pleasant.

"Don't come on to me with that schoolteacher voice," he said, leaning so close she could feel his breath on her cheek, smell the warm male scent of his skin when she inhaled. "You are having the time of your life and you know it. Hell, I ought to be charging you for the privilege of tagging along."

"Well, of all the nerve." Sara stopped talking. She wasn't about to legitimize his accusations with a reply. Besides, she wasn't much good at telling lies. As much as she hated to admit it, she *was* having the time of her life. There was still no way she could justify Elliot's having contributed so much money to the scheme, of course. Even if they did retrieve the gold lying on the cave floor back there, it wouldn't come anywhere near to covering the loan. But she could see how easy it was for someone to get hooked on treasure hunting. Especially in the company of a bona fide pirate like J. C. Hawk.

"I'm right, aren't I?" he demanded. She was so close he could smell the shampoo she used to wash her hair. She looked good. Too good, damn it. There hadn't been a woman in his life for a long time. There'd never been a woman like Sara Riley, period. "You are having the time of your life. Admit it." For a moment he thought she was going to do just that, but he was wrong.

"Not fifty-thousand dollars' worth," she replied tartly.

"God, don't you ever stop thinking about money?"

"I feel re—"

"I know. And damn it, I am cursed."

"What the devil are you talking about?"

"Think about this. Not one of the villagers or the Indians from the settlement farther down the beach is going to set foot in this cave if they know there are bodies in here. It's going to cost a damn sight more to import some workers from Golfito than to use the local men. As far as I'm concerned, that's a curse. Especially with you looking over my shoulder to see where every colon is going."

"Then we'll do it ourselves," Sara said, hooking her fingers through his belt as he turned abruptly and started back the way they'd come. "We'll get Luke Wycheski to help. I'm sure he can be trusted."

Hawk grunted. Let her talk. It would keep her mind off the skeletons they'd found. And she just might come up with something useful. He liked her theory about his ancestor hiding a little of the gold where it could be found without too much trouble. That made sense. It was the kind of thing he liked to believe Mary Hawk would have done.

"We can get some bags. You know...to put the bones in." Her voice faltered a little, but picked up again. She was breathless from the climb and the pace he set, but she kept on talking. "We can leave them here until it's...convenient...to bring them out. We'll need ropes," she said. "And something to move rocks, if there are any in the way. What else?"

"Picks and shovels. Lanterns."

"Not flashlights?"

"The humidity's pretty hard on the batteries. Lanterns work better if you're using them for an extended period of time."

"I should have thought of that. Anything else?"

"That's enough for now." They were almost back to the spot where they'd started. The touch of Sara's fingers was burning a hole in his back.

"Don't worry, mister," she said softly, as Hawk directed the flashlight beam onto the skeleton so that they could bypass the remains. "We'll get you out of here soon."

The rope was waiting. Hawk gave it a jerk and Ben hollered, "Uncle El, they're back. What's down there, Mom? Swords and cutlasses and dead pirates? Did you find the gold?"

"We can't tell the kids yet," Hawk warned as he slipped the rope under Sara's arms and adjusted the knot.

"I know. But I feel like a stinker leaving them out of the fun."

"You are having fun, aren't you, Sara Riley?" he asked. Once more they were too close for comfort.

"Yes," she replied, laughing up into his face. There was just enough light from the opening above her for him to see the sparkle of pleasure in her green eyes. Eyes the exact color of the ferns lining the opening to the cave. Damn, he thought helplessly, a man could get lost in those eyes just as easily as he could get lost in the jungle. "I admit it. This is the most fun I've had in ages. I can't wait to get started on finding our way down to the beach."

"I don't remember inviting you along," he said gruffly, and was rewarded with the sight of the happy light in her eyes fading into shadows.

"So. We're back to square one." She eyed him warily as he yanked on the rope. He scowled back at her. This whole thing had gone far enough. Sweet-talking Sara Riley was a complication in his life he didn't need right now. He'd better remember that before it was too late.

"This is no place for a woman. Or an amateur."

She put her foot in his hand and her hands on his shoulders. For a moment they were eye to eye. "You know something, J. C. Hawk? You'd be a lot of fun yourself if you weren't such a royal pain in the butt."

CHAPTER SIX

A SERIES OF SHARP, barking howls fractured the heavy, late-afternoon silence. Sara was sitting in the lounge area of the dining porch with her sketchpad and colored pencils in her lap. She'd been trying for nearly an hour to capture the antics of three brown-faced monkeys, as they teased Hawk's big red macaw in the trees beyond the wall, but she'd given up. They were so much fun to watch that she couldn't concentrate properly on her drawing.

The eerie howls brought her to her feet, colored pencils scattered all around her. The little brown squirrel monkeys fled in fear as both boys came clattering down the path from the waterfall, running as if they were being chased by the devil himself.

"Mom! Aunt Sara! Did you hear that?" they yelled, galloping toward her.

"Something's after us," Zack screamed. "Help!"

Elliot appeared out of the radio room directly off the kitchen. He said something to the cook, Olivia, as she came onto the dining porch, wiping her hands on a towel. She responded in Spanish before vanishing back into her domain with a chuckle.

"Hey, what's up, guys?" he asked, shoving his hands into the back pockets of his shorts.

"That noise. What is it?" Zack hopped the low stone wall, to come to a skidding halt in front of Sara's chair.

"Is it a jaguar?" Ben asked in a voice composed of equal parts excitement and trepidation.

Elliot grinned. "Sorry, sport. It's not a jaguar."

"What is it then?" Zack demanded. "It was up in the trees right over my head, getting ready to jump down on me and bite right through my skull."

"Ben," Sara scolded as she bent to retrieve her pencils, "did you tell him that?"

"Yes," Ben said, unrepentant. "He wasn't running fast enough."

"It wasn't a jaguar," Elliot assured them both. "Where were you boys playing, anyway?"

"Just at the bottom of the waterfall," Ben told him.

"You must have been making enough noise to catch the attention of the scout for the pack of howler monkeys that live on top of the ridge. Pretty effective way to get rid of unwanted visitors, don't you agree?"

"Yeah," Ben said, collapsing into a chair and draping his arms over the table. "I'll say."

"They come down to the stream for water in the evening," Elliot continued, sitting down across the table from Ben. Zack stayed by Sara's chair, leaning over the arm as she settled back again. "Tomorrow afternoon, go back and just sit quietly, and you'll be able to spot them in the trees."

"Not me," Zack declared. "I don't care what they look like. They sound mean."

"I'll go along—"

Zack cut him off. "Can we go ask Olivia for some soda? I'm dying of thirst."

"Sure." Elliot had a puzzled frown on his face that made Sara's heart twist with sympathy. He just didn't seem to be connecting with his son. "But only one. Dinner's in less than half an hour."

"What'll we do till then?" Sara heard Zack ask his cousin as they went into the kitchen.

"Let's play catch. I'll get the drinks. You go get the ball and gloves."

"Okay."

"Olivia, *dos* Cokes, *por favor*."

Sara smiled. Zack had left his extensive collection of baseball cards at home, but he wasn't about to travel without his ball and glove. He'd even talked Ben into bringing his along.

Elliot hooked his arm over the back of the chair and watched them go. "Ben's picking up a lot of Spanish words."

"It's amazing how fast kids learn," Sara agreed. This was their fifth day in Costa Rica. In the twenty-four hours since they'd discovered the opening to the cave, Hawk had made himself scarce again. She assumed he'd radioed for the supplies and equipment they'd need to explore the cave, but the plane from Golfito hadn't delivered them yet.

Instead of treasure hunting, she'd spent the day lazing in her hammock, sketching and visiting with Elliot. When the boys weren't around, they'd talked about the discovery of the cave and the skeletons. When they were around, they talked about nothing in particular.

The inactivity was driving her crazy. Sara wasn't good at waiting. She never had been. Once or twice during the day, she'd caught sight of Hawk going about his work. He looked as if treasure hunting was the furthest thing from his mind. And it probably was. She envied him. Patience like that, focused and channeled, was a weapon in itself.

"I'm not making much headway with Zack." Elliot was asking for her advice on his relationship with Zack, she realized, and the change of subject was welcome. She spent entirely too much time thinking of Hawk.

"It's going to take a little time, El," she said, restoring her watercolor pencils to their box. She studied the sketch of the monkeys and the macaw critically, and decided it was worth saving to work on another day.

"A lot more time than I've got." Elliot rested his elbow on the table and propped his chin in his hand. "I need help, sis. I have nothing in common with my son. And no one to blame but myself."

"Maybe it's time you talked to him about his mother, how losing her affected you," Sara suggested.

"I'm not ready for that," Elliot replied in a tone of voice that convinced Sara he meant what he said. "Does he ever ask about her?"

Sara shook her head. "Only rarely."

"And what about me?"

"You haven't been there for him for a long time, El," Sara said, choosing her words very carefully. "It's only natural he doesn't turn to you for advice or companionship now. After all, we've only been here five days."

"I've tried everything I can think of to reach out to him. I even let him fiddle with my equipment, handle my specimens." He looked so perplexed, Sara couldn't help smiling.

"Oh, El. He's only nine. I'll bet Ben had a field day in your lab, but Zack..." She stopped, smiling abruptly when she saw the hurt look on her brother's face.

"Remember when you were a little older than Ben, and you and Dad couldn't seem to be in the same room together for more than five minutes without getting into an argument over something or other?"

"Yeah," Elliot said, frowning across the table at her, as though she were speaking gibberish. "What about it?"

"I know it's not the same situation precisely. Zack isn't a teenager yet, thank goodness. But the approach Dad took with you might help here as well."

Elliot continued to frown as he sorted back through his memories to try to make sense of what she was saying. "I don't know what the heck you're talking about," he said after a minute or two of silence, broken only by the excited chatter of the monkeys, celebrating the return of Hawk's macaw to his cage behind the kitchen. The big bird's retreat left them in unchallenged possession of the bananas Olivia had left on the stump.

"I think you must have played a thousand games of one-on-one that year. Mom used to joke that we'd have to have the driveway repaved before you graduated from high school."

Elliot finally smiled. "Yeah," he said. "I remember now. Dad's a pretty smart old bird. I never did figure out why everything he said, when he was beating the tar out of me at basketball, made a lot more sense than what he said sitting at the kitchen table every night."

"He kept your mind off your differences and focused your thoughts on what you had in common. You can probably accomplish the same thing with Zack by borrowing Ben's baseball glove."

"I haven't played baseball in years," Elliot said, looking doubtful again.

"You don't have to, El. Just catch for him. Zack's convinced he's the next Nolan Ryan. And talk to him, not at him."

"It's worth a shot," Elliot said. "I know he should be with me. I know you didn't take him to raise permanently."

Sara felt a sharp stab of pain around her heart. That's exactly what she did want and knew she couldn't, and shouldn't, have. "I love him as if he were my own, El," she said, but she didn't contradict him. For the first time since Mindy's death, Elliot was facing, however obliquely, his responsibilities as a father. "Don't rush him too much," she cautioned, giving in to her own need to keep Zack close as long as possible. "You'll have to be patient. Take it one step at a time."

"You're right." Elliot pushed away from the table, determination in his hazel eyes. "One step at a time. Playing catch is as good a place to start as any. After all, I don't have to talk about sports. All I have to do is catch the ball and listen."

HER TALK with Elliot gave Sara a restless night and drove her to the lounge area at first light the next morning. She'd just decided to go into the kitchen to help Olivia with breakfast preparations in return for a Spanish lesson when she saw Hawk crossing the clearing. He'd come from the path that led up to his house and he was heading for the steps to the beach. He was carrying a lantern in one hand. A pack and a coil of rope were thrown over his shoulder. He was wearing khaki slacks, heavy shoes and a long-sleeved shirt with the sleeves rolled up to reveal tanned and muscled forearms. The huge knife she'd noticed before was hooked on his belt. He was going to explore the cave. Alone.

But not for long.

Sara looked down at her shorts and faded coral T-shirt. She thought of the scrapes and bruises she'd sustained on her first trip into the cave and sighed. She was going to be a mass of black-and-blue marks before the day was over, but these clothes would have to do. Hawk would never wait for her to return to her cabin and change into something more durable. At least she was wearing running shoes instead of sandals. He couldn't refuse to take her along because of unsuitable footgear.

She opened her mouth to call his name, then changed her mind, grabbing a sheet of paper and one of her colored pencils instead. It was a fairly long walk to the opening of the cave. She wasn't about to give him any extra time to try to talk her out of coming along. She scribbled a note to Elliot and the boys and hurried after him. If this was the day J. C. Hawk was fated to find his pirate treasure, then she was determined to be at his side.

HAWK HEARD HER coming as soon as he left the stone staircase and headed into the trees. He must be getting soft. The peace and security of Tyiskita was a potent drug, dulling the instincts of a lifetime in a matter of months. She'd probably been following him since he left the clearing.

Sara Riley was a sharp-tongued, sweet-smelling pain in the neck, but he was almost getting used to her interference. She considered herself the guardian of her brother's interests in his search, and for that reason, entitled to poke her nose into every nook and cranny. She'd told him she'd be right beside him when he went into the cave again—if she got the chance. His own carelessness had given her just that opportunity. He might as well bow to the inevitable and let her come along.

He stopped beyond the trunk of a tree whose huge, buttressing roots stood out like bony knees, and waited for Sara to arrive. She was walking carefully, watching the ground for snakes, when he stepped out in front of her. She caught her breath in a sharp gasp and the color drained out of her face. For a moment he wasn't quite as proud of his little ambush as he'd thought he would be. But only for a moment.

"Oh sh—oot," she said, correcting herself right in the middle of the word. He had a pretty good idea that wasn't the word she had started out to say. He supposed she had to be pretty careful what she said, spending as much time as she did around other people's kids. "What did you do that for?" If looks could kill, Hawk decided, he'd have met his Maker by now.

"I don't like to be followed."

"I don't like to be left behind." The color was coming back into her face. Her cheeks were pink and smooth, her eyes bright, but there were faint shadows beneath them, as though she hadn't slept well the night before. "How did you get that stuff here without us knowing about it?"

"I had Luke Wycheski take the Jeep into Golfito yesterday to pick up these supplies. Everyone in the village would know what we were up to if I'd had it flown in. And it wasn't a secret. I told your brother yesterday."

"You didn't tell me."

"My error," he said. He almost smiled, but changed his mind. She was mad enough already. If he expected to get into the cave anytime soon, he was going to have to forgo the pleasure of sparring with her. "Who told you what I was up to this morning?"

"No one," she confessed. "I couldn't sleep. I was on my way to the kitchen to help Olivia with breakfast when I saw you."

"So you put two and two together."

She looked pointedly at the climbing gear. "And came up with four."

"Does anyone know you're here?" he asked, trying another avenue of attack.

Her thick but nicely curved eyebrows drew together in a frown. "I left a note in the dining lounge," she said. "I was going to tell Olivia, but you were walking too fast. I didn't want to take the chance of not being able to catch up before you got to the cave. And don't go getting any ideas about leaving me tied up to a tree or something," she added almost at once. "I'd scream my head off."

"Not if I gagged you," he said with just a touch of menace.

"I'm going with you, Hawk," she said, refusing to be silenced. "I'm going as Elliot's representative. Just like the other day. Remember?"

He let that one pass. "What about the boys?"

She was quiet a moment. She pulled her lower lip between her teeth, and this time it was Hawk who sucked in his breath. It was a very sensual gesture, totally unstudied and sexy as hell. "We won't be gone that long, will we?"

"I intend to stay in that cave as long as it takes to find a way to the beach."

"Oh."

He watched her consider that. "What's the matter, Sara Riley? Getting cold feet?"

She shook her head so hard, several strands of hair came free and curled around her cheeks. "No," she said. "I'm just a mother, that's all. It's a full-time, lifetime job. But so is being a father. Elliot's going to have to learn that sometime, too. Today's as good a time as any to start. He can be responsible for the boys until we get back. It will be a good opportunity for him to spend time with Zack."

"Fine. If you've settled everything to your liking, I suggest we get moving. I'd rather have you back up top before your brother decides to call out a search party."

"But I left a note." Sara had started walking when he did, but now she hung back once more. "You don't think...? No," she said suddenly, making up her mind. "He wouldn't do that. He knows I can take care of myself."

"Yes," he said, turning away so she couldn't see the smile he felt curling the corner of his mouth. "I imagine he knows you can take care of yourself."

Hawk secured one end of a rope to the tallest tree fern outside the opening to the cave. They needed a way out if there was no open route to the beach. He'd told Sara he intended to stay in the cave until he found a passage, but he wasn't so stupid he wouldn't leave himself an escape route. He tied several knots at intervals along the length, handed her an extra pair of gloves from the pack of supplies he carried on his back and dropped down into the hole.

"Move it, Sara," he said as she hesitated at the opening. "If you're having second thoughts, now's the time to say so." As he expected, the gibe was just the goad she needed.

"I'm not having second thoughts. These gloves are too big. I don't want to lose them. I imagine I'll have to pay for them if I do," she muttered, as she slithered down into the hole.

"Damn right," he said, grabbing her ankles as she prepared to drop over the lip of stone. He let go of her ankles and grabbed her waist. The flare of her hips beneath his hands reminded him suddenly of how long it had been since he'd had a woman. As soon as her feet touched the ground, he released her.

"Let's go," she said, sounding more breathless than the descent seemed to warrant. "We're wasting time. And money."

"Right." But he didn't move on. He handed her a flashlight, then knelt to take a canvas bag out of the pack and place it beside the skeleton Sara had discovered that first day.

"You remembered."

"We'll come back for him when we get the chance."

"Thanks," she said, touching his arm so quickly and so lightly he might have imagined the fleeting caress. "I couldn't sleep last night...for thinking about them down here. Alone. In the dark." She wasn't telling the truth. He didn't doubt the genuine concern in her voice, just the way she'd phrased the sentence. Something had kept her awake last night, but it hadn't been their two new friends. He'd bet on it.

"I told you he doesn't care anymore," Hawk said more harshly than necessary. He hadn't slept all that well last night himself, but it wasn't because of the two dead men in the cave, either. He'd been thinking about Sara Riley.

"I do. I really am glad you remembered."

"Let's go." They both had flashlights today, so there was no need for her to hang on to his belt. They made good time back to the drop-off where they'd found the second skeleton. Sara was silent most of the way. He could hear her breathing behind him, see her shadow dancing on the damp stone walls when they turned a corner.

"Here we are." She watched silently as he pounded a stake into the coral rock to hold the rope. She listened to his instructions for climbing down the sheer drop-off. She held the flashlight steady while he suited action to words, then tossed him the flashlight and took the rope herself. "That's how it's done. Think you can handle it?"

"I don't have any choice, do I? I don't see an elevator anywhere." She grabbed the rope and did exactly as he told her. Put her feet only where he directed the flashlight beam; didn't squeal or holler when a shower of loose stones rolled out from under her foot and left her dangling ten feet above him for a long, tense moment. She had to have scraped her knees and elbows, but she made no complaint when she finally stood beside him.

"You did fine," he said. "We'll leave the rope in case we have to come back this way."

For the first time that day, Sara looked at the second skeleton. "Are we going to leave the gold behind?"

"What do you think?" he asked, kneeling beside the remains to pluck the gold pieces out of the remnants of the drawstring bag. He held them in the palm of his hand.

"I didn't think so." She knelt at his side. In the reflected light, he could see there was blood on her knee. He felt a quick stab of remorse for bringing her along, then remembered he hadn't had a lot of choice in the matter. "Is there anything else in the bag?" she asked.

"No." He played the light beam over the area around the skeleton. "Nothing else. No flashlight or lantern.

No canteen. Just what's left of a couple of palm-wood torches.''

"No sign of Father Benedicto's journal?"

"Nada."

"I guess that's good, really. If it were here, it would be ruined. And that would mean that this was *all* the treasure." She touched one of the muddy doubloons still resting on his palm. "Why do you suppose they came down here so ill-prepared?" she asked, as he rubbed the gold pieces clean of mud.

"I suspect they weren't too bright."

"What if we get lost the way they did?"

"We won't. But it's a little late to start worrying about that possibility now, don't you think?"

"I suppose so."

"Here." He took her hand, turning it palm up.

"Oh no. I couldn't." She stared down at the half-dozen doubloons.

"Stop being polite." He stood up. "Consider it a down payment on what I owe your brother. A first installment on your share of the treasure. Besides, they'd be harder than hell for me to get out of the country."

She closed her fingers over the gold. "I should have known you had an ulterior motive."

He held out his hand and pulled her to her feet. "I've only got eight days left, remember." He took another canvas bag from his pack and laid it beside the skeleton. "Let's move on."

She didn't say anything else, but put the doubloons in the pocket of her shorts and followed him down the passageway. For the next ten minutes, the descent was dangerously steep. Then it began to level off. Passageways branched off in all directions. Hawk marked their way with a big piece of white chalk he'd brought along.

Abruptly the passage split three ways. "Which one do we take?" Sara asked, her voice barely above a whisper.

"You choose," Hawk said.

Sara studied the openings carefully, playing her flashlight beam over the walls and floors. "This is what happened to those two back there, isn't it? They were exploring. They came this far and got confused. Couldn't find their way back down the right passageway to the sea."

"Probably. As I said, it won't happen to us. Now, are you going to choose, or do I?"

"This one," she said, making up her mind. "It's the dampest."

"Good observation." It was the one he would have chosen also. "Let's keep moving."

They walked in silence another ten minutes. Then Hawk stopped to listen. "Congratulations, Sara Riley. I think you did it. Hear that?"

"Yes. It's the sea. And it's close. Hawk, we did it!" she said, and he could detect the excitement in her voice without turning around to look at her face. He didn't have to. He knew exactly what she looked like, eyes shining, her bottom lip caught between her teeth as she smiled. She'd been distraction enough when she was only determined to get her brother's money back. Now that she'd been bitten by the adventure bug, she was more of a problem than ever.

"I just hope we don't have to swim out."

That slowed her up. "I—I never thought of that."

"We'll cross that bridge when we come to it," he said, once again feeling as if he'd stolen her candy.

"I can swim. I'm just not very good at it."

"Don't worry about it."

The passageway dropped sharply once more, then leveled out. They hadn't gone a hundred feet when he noticed the walls were wet and water-dark almost to the level of his waist. Sara had noticed it, too.

"When does the tide come in?" she asked.

"Not for another couple of hours."

"Then we ought to have time to get out."

"We'll make damn sure we have time to get out." No sooner had he spoken the words than the tunnel opened into a large room. At least it felt like a large room. It was more a change in perception, in atmosphere, than anything he could see beyond the range of his flashlight that made him think that way.

"Son of a bitch," he said reverently under his breath. "Sara Riley, I think we've done it."

She stepped past him, playing her light across the walls. "Yes. Look." Beyond them, pale, milky daylight painted a thin slice of brightness against the wall. "There's a way out. We did it! We found Mary Hawk's cave."

"Maybe." He came up behind her.

"What do you mean, maybe? Of course this is the treasure cave. It has to be." She spun around so quickly, she came up hard against his chest. Without thinking, he reached out to steady her. She looked as young and excited as a girl half her age. Gone was the staid, disapproving schoolmarm of their first meeting, the suspicious older sister determined to see that her brother's money wasn't wasted on a fool's dream. In her place stood a woman who'd probably follow him to the ends of the earth if he asked her to, complaining all the way, but still ready and willing to take on whatever fate threw in their path. Still without thinking, or maybe because

he had been thinking about it too much, he pulled her
into his arms.

"If you say so, Sara Riley. If you're convinced this is
Mary Hawk's cave, then I'll believe you." He lowered
his mouth to hers before she could say anything else.
Her mouth opened in shock and surprise and, throwing all caution to the winds, he let his tongue delve inside. She was hot and sweet and still tasted faintly of
peppermint toothpaste. She felt good in his arms. And
the damnedest thing of all, after a moment of automatic, outraged resistance, she was kissing him back.

Good Lord, Sara thought, *I'm kissing a pirate. In a
treasure cave, complete with gold and skeletons. And
somewhere in the darkness beneath my feet, there's a
still-hidden treasure worth more money than I can
imagine.*

But none of that mattered at the moment. The only
thing that counted was the taste and the touch and the
scent of Hawk. His mouth was hard but not hurting.
His body was hard, too, but it felt good. It felt right.
She'd never liked kissing that much, but suddenly she
realized why. Wade hadn't been much of a kisser. Hawk
certainly was. She gave herself up to the expertise and
the wonder of it all and began to hope that it would
never end.

But it did. As abruptly as it had begun.

"We've got work to do," he said roughly, as though
nothing at all had happened between them. And sadly,
Sara realized, for him it most likely had not. She was
dealing with a man whose experiences were so far re-
moved from her own that she could barely even imagine what his life had been like. Finding long-dead bodies
holding Spanish doubloons in their skeletal hands;
working one's way through unexplored caves to the

possible hiding place of even more treasure; giving needy, middle-aged schoolteachers from Fort Wayne, Indiana, the kiss of a lifetime—it was probably all in a day's work for a man like J. C. Hawk.

"Sure. Of course. Let's get to work," she said, hoping it was too dark for him to see her blush.

"The tide will be coming in before we know it. We haven't even started to look around this place."

"Yes," Sara said. "Elliot and the boys will be wondering where in the world I've gone." It was time, past time, to start remembering who and what she was. Sara Riley, mother, teacher, bowling-league secretary. She wasn't Hawk's lover. She wasn't even his partner in adventure—not really. And certainly not for longer than the next eight days.

He struck a match and lit the lantern he carried with him. Its cold yellow light filled the room, but left the high ceiling in darkness. The floor was wet and strewn with sea wrack and small pieces of driftwood. The smell of the sea, now that Sara was no longer distracted by the scent of Hawk in her nostrils, was very strong. The walls, too, she noticed, were dark with water stains almost to the level of her head. Hawk caught her staring at the walls.

"My guess is, when we get outside, we'll find we're almost at the edge of the headland. The village will be to our left, my place to the right. We'll have to be careful no one sees us coming out."

"Is there any sign of the treasure?" Sara asked, wanting suddenly to get it over with, to be back outside in the sunshine and warm steamy air.

"There's no sign at all. But this is the cave. It has to be," he said, so roughly Sara felt a shiver crawl over her skin. This man was ruthlessly single-minded and she'd do well to remember that.

"We'll just have to come back and start digging as soon as possible," Sara said. "You'll have to hire some workers. After all, isn't that what you borrowed the money from Elliot for?"

"I figured we'd have to move a lot more earth to get into the place," he said, watching her from eyes as darkly shadowed as the cave roof.

"Then we're lucky so far," Sara said flatly. She was going to have to be very lucky to be able to put Hawk's kiss out of her mind any time soon. "Zack's tumbling down the rabbit hole was a blessing in disguise."

"Maybe," Hawk said, heading toward the faint sliver of light that marked the opening to the sea. "Let's just hope we don't have to swim out of here. C'mon. Give me your hand."

"Why?" Sara demanded, reluctant to touch him again.

"Okay. Have it your way. The sand's probably pretty unstable and we're going to have to wade through some water to get out. If you get stuck, you can dig yourself out on your own."

"Quicksand?" Sara swallowed hard. That would be the last straw, as far as she was concerned. She wasn't really much of an adventurer, after all.

"Close enough. Give me your hand," he said again, and this time it was an order, not a request. Sara did as she was told.

But the water ended up coming only to her knees. She didn't need Hawk to save her from the quicksand. The outside of the cave was just what she'd always dreamed a pirate cave would look like. Ferns and vines and the trunks of small wind-gnarled trees hung almost to the water's edge, concealing the opening. Sheltering rocks curved away on both sides, creating a tiny harbor barely big enough for a single boat to enter. On one side, waves broke against the rocks with a fine misting spray. On the other, it was calm water and sandy beach.

The opening itself was narrow and hard to negotiate. Twice she had to accept Hawk's help in clambering over the rocks. It would be no easy task to enlarge it if that became necessary. It would take a lot of men and heavy equipment. For the first time she had to admit treasure hunting might become a very expensive enterprise.

"Damn it," he said, and hauled her up into his arms. For a dazed, heart-stopping moment, Sara let her fantasies run free. The touch of her body had driven him wild. He couldn't control himself. He couldn't keep his hands off her. He was going to kiss her again. She closed her eyes, then opened them. Hawk wasn't staring down at her passionately, he was looking over her shoulder and he wasn't passionate at all, he was mad. "What damned lousy timing."

"What is it?" Sara turned, too, pulling herself free of his grip on her arms.

"Luke Wycheski and your boys. They've probably been out here on the beach all morning. It isn't going to take them long to figure out where we've been."

"No, it won't," Sara said. She started climbing over the rocky outcrop that separated the cave mouth from the beach. The faster she got away from J. C. Hawk, the better. She wasn't up to dealing with any more stray fantasies of pirate's kisses and making love on the warm golden sand of a deserted tropical beach. Especially not the same stretch of sand where her boys were playing catch with Luke Wycheski.

She looked back. Hawk was still on top of the rock, scanning the horizon. Sara saw the treasure ship off in the distance quite clearly, the small figures moving around on its decks, and realized for the first time how far they'd come. And how far she would have to walk back to the lodge. She was suddenly very tired. But then she felt the weight of the six doubloons in her pocket and smiled again. She had found gold, pirate gold, and no one could take that away from her. And as far as Hawk's kiss was concerned, well, she would consider that a bonus prize and not worry about it anymore.

"Mom!" Ben spotted them first. "Where did you come from?" He saw Hawk, the rope and pack on his shoulder, the lantern in his hand, in a flash. "You found it!" he yelled, so loudly the sound echoed off the hillside. "You found the treasure cave!"

"Quiet," Sara called back, putting her finger to her lips as the trio bounded over the sand toward them. "Yes, we found it. But you have to keep it a secret from everyone but your Uncle Elliot. No one else is supposed to know."

"Let's get moving," Hawk said, dropping down beside her. "If we're going to keep this place our little secret, we'd better get the hell away from here."

CHAPTER SEVEN

"WHAT DO YOU have planned for your day, Sara?" Elliot asked, as she helped Olivia set plates of freshly sliced mangoes and bananas in front of her brother and the boys before taking a seat at the long table on the dining porch herself. Olivia returned to the kitchen for toast and eggs, while Sara poured herself a cup of strong Costa Rican coffee from a carafe on the table.

"I haven't planned anything." She'd been hoping Hawk would want to go exploring in the treasure cave again. But yesterday he'd spent his day going about business at the farm and in the village. And today it seemed he was going to do the same. If he thought he could wait her out, stay away from the cave and the treasure until she returned to Fort Wayne, he was mistaken. She'd had one small taste of adventure and it was very heady stuff. She wanted more.

"It's going to be a scorcher," Elliot predicted. "But I imagine it will rain this afternoon. Before you know it, it'll be April and the rainy season will be in full swing."

"What do you do when it rains all the time?" Zack asked, forking eggs into his mouth with one hand and toast with the other.

"Zack," Sara said, "slow down and chew your food. It's not polite to talk with your mouth full."

"Sorry." Zack washed down his eggs with half a glass of juice. Olivia always had fresh juice on hand, but most of the time the fruits it was made from were too exotic to identify. This morning was no exception. "Do you have to stay indoors?"

"Not if you don't mind getting soaked. Sometimes when I'm going down to the village, I take a bar of soap and shower on the way." Zack didn't bother to smile at the small joke, but Elliot took it in stride. He was beginning to get the hang of dealing with a know-it-all nine-year-old. Playing catch every afternoon wasn't going to solve all the problems five years of separation had caused, but it helped. "It doesn't rain all the time," he explained. "But when it does, it rains very hard indeed."

"Like last night?" Ben asked. "It was awesome while it lasted."

"Just like last night. Only lots more of it."

"Last night it rained so hard, I bet if you'd been outside staked out on the ground for the fire ants to get you, with your face turned up, you'd drown. You know," Zack said, forgetting his breakfast for a bloodthirsty moment, "like Dad said the Mayans used to do to their prisoners." He grinned at Sara, devilish glints sparkling in his hazel eyes that were so like his father's. "Awesome."

"Not while I'm eating, Zack. El, what a thing to tell him. He'll have nightmares about it if you don't watch out."

"The Mayans were fierce warriors. The Spanish had a hell of a time trying to conquer them. In this part of the New World, they never completely succeeded."

"Uncle El has some radical books on the Mayan Indians," Ben broke in. "I'm going to do a book report while I'm here and take it back for extra credit."

"Such dedication," Sara said, rolling her eyes. "Doing homework on vacation."

"I'm wonderful, face it, Mom." Ben picked up a piece of fruit on his spoon and pretended to aim it, catapultlike, in her direction. "But first I'm going surfing with Luke and a couple of guys he met from the treasure hunter's boat."

"Benjamin Wade Riley, don't you dare throw that," Sara threatened, eyeing the piece of fruit poised for flight, "or you'll find yourself tied to that chair for the rest of the day."

"Surfing? Can I go, too?" Zack begged.

"That's up to Luke, pip-squeak," Ben said, making no attempt to hide his superiority at being asked to accompany Luke and his friends on their expedition. "He probably doesn't want to be bothered with a whiny little brat like you."

"Dad, Aunt Sara, make him let me go along."

Sara held up her hands. "Don't get me involved in this," she said, laughing. "Argue this one out with your father."

"Good morning," Hawk said, appearing almost out of thin air as he so often did. Sara had been facing the path that led to his house and still she hadn't seen him come.

"If I can't go surfing with Luke and Ben, can I go dig in the treasure cave with you?" Zack wanted to know.

"No," Hawk said, pouring himself a cup of coffee.

"Why not?" the youngster demanded. "That's what we came here for."

"It's too dangerous," Hawk said, adding milk and sugar to his coffee. Somehow, as strong as it was, Sara had expected him to drink it black.

"I don't care. I want to go in the cave."

"That's enough, Zackary."

Sara shut her mouth on the reprimand she'd been about to deliver herself. Zack looked almost as surprised at his father's scolding as Sara was.

"But Dad," he said, wheedling. Zack was working up to the masterpiece of his repertoire, a penetrating whine that had more than once driven Sara to the brink of madness. She wondered how these two child-ignorant men would handle that little scene.

"I said no, Zack." Elliot's voice was firm, but he looked as if he wanted to bolt for the familiar isolation of his lab. "When it's safe, I'll take you into the cave. And not before."

"Geez." Zack crossed his arms on his chest. Sara thought he ought to add a rider about Zack not sneaking into the cave on his own, but she kept silent. She didn't want to undermine Elliot's tenuous authority with his son. And she didn't want to put the idea of a clandestine trip into the cave into Zack's brain, if it wasn't already there. "C'mon, Dad."

"Zackary."

"It's not fair," Zack muttered into his eggs. "A real treasure cave that I found when no one else could, and I can't even go inside."

"You can help unload the explosives when they get here," Hawk said unexpectedly.

"Explosives." He had Zack's undivided attention. And Ben's as well.

"What kind of explosives?" her son wanted to know. "Plastique, like the terrorists use?"

"Sorry. Just plain old dynamite. I use it to blow up stumps."

"And now you're going to use it to blow a bigger opening in the treasure cave, aren't you?"

Hawk blinked. He hesitated only a fraction of a second before replying, however. "If necessary. But today I'm only going to blow up stumps."

"Can I watch?" Zack asked, bouncing up and down on his chair in excitement.

"That's up to your dad."

"Sure."

"Elliot." Sara couldn't keep herself from intervening. Dynamite and small boys in such proximity was every mother's nightmare.

"I'll be there to ride herd on him," Elliot said, laughing, and she knew he'd read her mind. "Don't be such a worrywart, Sara."

"Zackary's volatile enough on his own." She smiled to show she knew she was being overprotective. "And Ben's blown up the basement twice in the last ten months with his chemistry experiments. I'm staying as far away from all of you as I can get."

"That might be a wise decision, sister dear." Elliot laughed and pushed his chair back from the table, just as the sound of a motor heralded the entry of a beat-up red Toyota into the compound from the direction of the Golfito road.

"Who the hell is that?" Hawk said, standing so quickly his chair went skating backward across the concrete floor.

"Looks official," Elliot observed, exchanging glances with his friend, as a small, dark-skinned man in khaki climbed stiffly out of the car.

"Looks like trouble." The men walked toward the car, with Sara and the boys trailing behind.

"*Buenos días,* Señor Hawk," the man said, settling a military-style cap with an official-looking gold insignia on its brim onto his head.

"*Bueno días,*" Hawk replied. "What can I do for you?" he asked in English.

"I am Inspector Molinas of the Ministry of the Interior," the stranger replied with a flourish. "It has come to my attention that you are planning some... demolition... work." His English was very good. His smile was very oily. He looked just like every stereotype of the corrupt Latin American government official Sara had ever seen or read about. Except for the sparkle in his dark eyes and his charming and totally wicked grin. Was it possible he'd heard about the treasure cave already? Hawk said news would travel fast, but surely not already.

"I'm going to blow up some stumps, yes," Hawk answered politely enough.

If the small man he towered over heard the faint icy threat in his words that Sara did, he gave no sign of it. "*Bueno.* I have no problem with that. If you have the required permits."

"Permits? Since when is it required to have permits to clear brush on my own land?"

"Señor Hawk." Inspector Molinas looked as if he had been wounded to the quick. "It is my duty to see that all our laws are obeyed. Costa Rica is at the forefront of commitment to saving the rain forest. I can not stand idly by and see it destroyed."

"Allied Fruit did that years ago," Hawk said tightly, "with your government's approval."

"That was long ago. Things have changed. Today it is my responsibility to see that such a tragedy is not repeated." Molinas was polite but firm.

Sara saw a muscle tighten in Hawk's jaw, but his answer was equally correct. "I understand your concern. I'm in a hurry to get this taken care of. The rainy season will be here in a matter of days."

"That is something to take into consideration."

"I would appreciate any help you might be able to give me in expediting the paperwork," Hawk said.

"I am but a poor civil servant, Señor Hawk," Molinas replied with a sad smile and a twinkle in his eye that was hard to resist. He obviously enjoyed what he was doing. "The drive here from Golfito is long and hazardous. And I cannot afford to pay to be flown out to your most beautiful *finca....*" He left the words trail off. "But rules are rules. They must be followed."

"Yes," Hawk said cryptically. "The rules must be followed. Allow me to offer you some refreshments, *señor.* My home is farther up the hill. We can speak more comfortably there."

Sara felt a twinge of unreasonable jealousy. Why was he inviting that odious little man to his home when she'd been longing to get a glimpse of it since the day she arrived?

"*Bueno, señor.* An excellent idea."

"After you." Hawk gestured for the official to go ahead of him. "Elliot, you'd better stay here with your sister and the kids."

"Right." With a hand on each boy's shoulder, Elliot steered them toward the dining porch.

"He's probably going to offer the guy a bribe," Ben said, sounding worldly-wise and very blasé.

"You're kidding," Sara said before she could stop herself. "That's against the law."

"It's also how things get done in this part of the world." Elliot gave her a pitying look.

"Still . . . I mean, there's surely a . . . better . . . way to go about it."

"We don't have a lot of time left before the weather gets bad, sis. It's altogether possible we'll have to blow a hole in the cave wall sooner or later. Hawk knew how fast news would travel when he radioed into Golfito for that dynamite. Once the workers he's hired show up, it'll travel even faster. The last thing we need is a contingent of the *Guarda Nacional* showing up to put a stop to our project. Lighten up. Hawk knows what he's doing."

"It's illegal," Sara felt compelled to point out for the boys' sake.

"It's necessary." Elliot's tone of voice told her he wasn't going to argue about it anymore.

"I still don't approve." She'd never knowingly broken the law in her life. And if she ever did, she often suspected, she'd get caught at it.

Luke Wycheski, and two tanned and muscular young men who appeared to be about his age or a little older, drove into the compound from the direction of the village in an old Volkswagen bus with a number of surfboards tied to the top. Sara had been so engrossed in the conversation that she hadn't even heard the motor coming up the cliff.

"Hey, Ben, old buddy. Ready to go catch a radical wave?" Luke asked, crawling out of the driver's seat of the van.

"Bye, Mom. See you later," Ben said, trying to look as cool as Luke, and failing miserably. His voice broke audibly, as it did so often these days.

"Be careful," Sara cautioned. "These aren't the water rides at the amusement park, remember." Ben was an excellent swimmer, but he'd had no experience of ocean currents or riptides or any of the hundred-and-one other dangers she could envision him encountering.

"We'll take good care of him, Mrs. Riley," Luke promised. "I'd like to introduce you to some friends of mine," he said, recalling his manners. "They work for the treasure salvagers. Matt Benson and Terry Wheeler. This is Mrs. Riley."

"Hi," Sara said, smiling.

"Nice to meet you," they chorused with a casual wave and flashes of straight white teeth.

They might have been two of Megan's classmates, tanned and healthy and fit. "It's nice to meet you, too."

"I'm going with you guys," Zack announced suddenly.

"Mom." Ben's face was red with mortification.

"'Fraid not, squirt," Luke said.

"C'mon, Luke," Zack wailed.

"Sorry, old sport. You've never surfed before. I'll tell you what. If you behave yourself today, I'll take you down to the beach and give you a lesson, so that next time you can come, too. How's that?"

"I suppose," Zack said, clearly torn between putting up a fuss to get his way or taking it like a man and making a good impression on Luke and his friends. "I've got things to do on my own today," he added importantly. "But don't forget. We're only going to be here six more days."

"I won't forget," Luke promised. "Ready, Ben?"

"Ready," Ben said. "I've got my trunks on under my shorts."

"Then let's get going. We'll have him back in a couple of hours, Mrs. Riley. Don't worry."

"Have a good time," Sara said, waving as they drove off. "I wish," she said to no one in particular, "that they had asked me to go along."

SHE WAS WAITING for him just as he knew she would be. Her back was propped against one of the cypress poles that supported the dining-porch roof, her legs were crossed at the knee and she held a pair of binoculars in her lap. She was gazing up into the trees above her. The raucous cries of a pair of chestnut-mandibled toucans could be heard all over the compound.

"Birding, Sara? Or catching a little catnap?"

Her eyes flew to his face, wide and startled and as green as a jungle pool. The surprise lasted only a moment, but she didn't smile. He had expected a lecture and obviously he was going to get it.

"Good Lord, I wish you'd quit sneaking up on me like that," she said first.

"Sorry. It's a habit." He didn't elaborate, although she looked tempted to ask him what he meant by the remark. "Were you birding?" he asked again.

She narrowed her marvelous green eyes and gave him a long assessing look, trying to decide if he was actually interested in what she was doing or only trying to throw her off stride.

"Yes," she said, deciding he wasn't baiting a verbal trap for her to fall into. "There are two toucans in the tree above us."

"I heard them," Hawk acknowledged.

"Of everything I've seen here," she said, smiling a little now, despite her obvious displeasure with him, "of the parrots, your macaw, the monkeys and the iguanas, even the poison frogs—it's the toucans that signify the jungle to me. Exotic, wildly colorful and very, very different from anything I've ever known."

"I see. Is that all you want to talk about? Birding? Don't you want to know what happened at my place?"

"I suppose you're referring to Señor Molinas's visit," she said, suddenly very interested in the field glasses in her hand.

"Come on, Sara." He did nothing to suppress the faint curl of a smile at the corner of his mouth. "You've been sitting out here in the sun for nearly two hours, waiting to give me a piece of your mind. I made it easy for you. Here I am."

"I saw the inspector leave," she said, lifting her head to meet his eyes. "He looked very pleased with himself."

"He should be. The bastard drives a hard bargain."

She looked disappointed for a moment and he felt an unaccustomed twinge of self-doubt. Sara Riley's good opinion was becoming a lot more important to him than it ought to be.

"I wish you hadn't said those things in front of the boys. Benjamin, especially, is at a very impressionable age."

He leaned forward slightly, intimidating her just a little. She didn't flinch or shrink away.

"You don't give the kid enough credit. He knows right from wrong. He's also old enough to understand that bribery is a way of life in more parts of the world that you've ever dreamed of visiting, Sara Riley from Fort Wayne, Indiana. It's how things are done. It's what makes the world go 'round. Wake up and smell the coffee.''

"It's wrong," Sara said mulishly. He wanted to smile again, but he resisted the urge.

"In Fort Wayne it's wrong," he agreed. "Here—" he lifted his shoulders in a shrug "—it's a different world."

"That doesn't alter the fact—" Sara began, but he halted her lecture with a finger on her lips. "Shut up, Sara Riley, or I won't take you back into the cave with me, now that Señor Molinas has so graciously given us the go-ahead to explore and dynamite to our hearts' content."

"I don't want to see it destroyed," she said, a little breathlessly.

He was a little breathless himself. He leaned over and kissed her before she could say anything else. Her lips were soft and yielding against his mouth. She tasted of fruit juice and mint toothpaste and passion. Her hands lifted to his shoulders. Her breasts were inches away from his chest. He could feel the heat of her body, the softness of her skin, and he wanted her badly enough at that moment to take her there and then, beneath the hot, tropic sun with the toucans and the squirrel monkeys in the trees above witnessing their coupling.

She let his tongue into her mouth. She followed his exploration with her own. Hawk pulled her upright into his arms and she stumbled a little, holding the field glasses by the strap so that they banged hard against his thigh. He wanted to strip off her blouse and glory in the soft fullness of her breasts against his chest, kiss the rosy nipples until they were hard and pebbled and she could deny him nothing he demanded. But he knew she'd never allow that, so he settled for kissing her mouth thoroughly once more.

"Stop, Hawk. You're making me dizzy," she whispered with a quizzical little smile. She lifted her head, closing her eyes as a tiny frown appeared between her eyebrows. "I've always heard about kisses that make the earth move under your feet. This is the first one I've ever experienced, though."

Hawk kept his grip on her shoulders, but allowed her to move away from his body. He looked past her at the swaying light bulb on its cord above her head. The sound of breaking dishes came from the kitchen and he heard Olivia swear. "I'd like to take all the credit for that earthshaking moment but I can't." He spun her around. "It's an earthquake. A tremor, really. We're damn close to the fault line here. There've been one or two since you arrived. Didn't you notice?"

Sara shook her head. He felt a shiver of desire race across her skin, saw that her nipples had hardened beneath the soft cotton of her shirt, and had the satisfaction of knowing that he, not the earthquake, had caused her reaction. "This is the strongest one I've felt all year."

"An earthquake? I see." She stepped away this time, keeping her back to him. He didn't let go of her. She was still unsteady on her feet. She looked down at herself and crossed her arms over her chest. "I—I didn't realize what it was. We don't have many earthquakes in Fort Wayne."

"And I don't get many kisses like that one," he heard himself reply, because he knew she was embarrassed by her passion and he didn't want her to be.

"Thank you for the compliment," she said with dignity. A thread of pain underlay her words, as though he'd waited until the night before it was scheduled to ask her to the prom. "But I don't want it to happen again."

He'd felt uncharacteristically protective of her. Now he was mad. "Why the hell not?"

"I don't like mixing business with pleasure," she said, still very dignified.

"Damn it." He didn't have an answer for that one except to kiss her again and make her change her mind. He was considering the consequences of doing just that when Elliot came jogging into view from the direction of his cabin.

"That was quite a jolt," he said, not seeming to notice as Sara took two hasty steps away from Hawk. "Rattled everything in my lab. Is everything okay here?"

"Fine," Hawk said, moving to lean one shoulder against the porch support.

"Good. Have you seen Zack?" he asked. "He was playing outside the cabin a while ago." He glanced at his watch. "Well, an hour or so ago," he amended. "And then he disappeared."

"I've been here birding for quite a while," Sara said. "I haven't seen him." She frowned again, this time with apprehension. "You're sure he's not somewhere around the cabin? Did you check mine? He likes to watch the iguana."

"He's not there, sis. I made sure of that."

"He's got to be around here someplace," Hawk said. "I'll ask Olivia if she's seen him." He called out to the cook in Spanish, and without leaving the kitchen, she replied in the negative.

"Maybe he's building a dam at the waterfall?" Elliot ran a distracted hand through his auburn hair.

"Or maybe," Sara said, her voice dry with fear, "he went by himself to explore the cave."

CHAPTER EIGHT

"SWEET JESUS," Elliot said, his face turning pale. "I thought maybe he followed Ben and Luke down the beach."

"He doesn't have any idea where they went," Sara said. "But he might have gone to the village." She sounded doubtful.

Elliot dismissed the possibility with a curt negative. "He doesn't have any spending money, and he said that if he went down there, he was afraid Emily would put him in class with the other kids." He looked off in the distance, over Sara's head. "Do you really think he'd go into the cave on his own?"

"Did you ever specifically tell him not to?" Sara asked.

Elliot looked defensive, as well as scared. He shook his head. "It didn't occur to me. Do you think he could even find the opening onto the beach?"

"That kid could do anything," Hawk said darkly. "Get the Jeep, Carson. I'll get the flashlights and a rope."

"It might be better if we split up," Elliot suggested. "I'll take the opening on the hillside, in case he went that way. You and Sara can check out the beach entrance. We'll keep looking until we find him or meet up with each other."

"How will you find your way alone?" Sara asked, puzzled.

"Hawk and I went in yesterday. While you were napping," he added, when she looked surprised by the statement. "We put the skeletons of those two guys into sacks."

So much for her thinking she had figured out how to keep track of J. C. Hawk.

"I'm glad," she said. "I don't want Zack to see them." Sara didn't want to picture Zack stumbling onto the remains alone. She wanted even less to think of him lost in one of the unexplored passageways of the cave.

"Let's get moving," Hawk said shortly, as both Sara and Elliot stood lost in their thoughts. "The tide's on the turn already."

"Elliot." Sara reached out a hand and stopped her brother from leaving. "Did something happen between the two of you?" Even Zack, as impulsive and inquisitive as he was, would hesitate to enter the cave alone again, unless he felt driven to it. An altercation with his father, coupled with the disappointment of being left behind by the older boys, might have done just that.

He nodded. "I—I thought we were getting along pretty good, so I asked him if he wanted to come down here and stay with me all summer." Elliot looked confused and frightened, and Sara's heart went out to him. "He didn't say much, except mumbling something about missing his Little League season and going to Cedar Point."

Cedar Point was an amusement park on the shore of Lake Erie famous for its roller coasters. "I take the kids every year," Sara reminded her brother. "It's one of the highlights of his summer."

"I tried to tell him what a great place this was, how we could do things together, but it must not have been enough," Elliot said miserably.

"He just wasn't expecting it, that's all, El." *And she had done nothing to prepare her nephew for the possibility.* It was selfish of her, she knew. It was very, very hard to face giving Zack up, but that was no excuse for failing to back Elliot's attempts to reestablish a relationship with his son to the very best of her ability.

"It's too late to change anything now," he agreed. "I told him to think about it and he went outside to play. Damn, sis. When am I ever going to quit screwing up this parenting thing?"

"Probably never," Sara said, smiling to take the sting out of her words. "Just like the rest of us."

"You can discuss the latest child-rearing theories after we find him," Hawk interrupted, resting his hand on Elliot's shoulder. "I'll meet you back here in five minutes," he said to Sara.

She looked down at her half-healed knees. Again she wasn't dressed for spelunking, but she couldn't do anything about it now.

The drive down to the beach was precipitous and fast. Sara hung on for dear life. Hawk never touched the brake. He parked the Jeep in the corner of a grove of low-growing, spiky palmetto trees that hid it from the view of the village and the treasure salvagers in the bay beyond.

He didn't offer to take her hand as they clambered over the sharp coral rocks. Sara didn't expect him to. She was perfectly capable of negotiating that climb on her own. And he was carrying all the equipment.

"Move it, Sara. I don't want to take the chance of anyone from the salvage ship picking up on the fact that we've come out of this pile of rocks twice in the last two days."

He dropped onto the narrow lip of sand that fronted the hidden opening. The tide was turning, she noticed. Small waves were already lapping at the entrance to the cave. She'd have to wade through calf-deep water to get inside. This time she stopped to take off her shoes and carry them in her hand. Hawk didn't bother.

They threaded their way through the slim fissure in the rock and entered the cave. The contrast between the bright tropical day outside and the sepulchral gloom beyond was disorienting. Sara stopped, blinking in confusion. Hawk reached out and pulled her away from the small slice of brightness that penetrated the dark. It was an instinctive move for him, she realized, to blend in with the shadows and avoid the light. What kind of a life had he led before he came to live in Tyiskita?

She would probably never know him well enough to ask. The thought saddened her and she refused to consider why.

The sound of waves lapping into the cave through its narrow opening was magnified many times. Sara stood quietly, straining to hear, waiting for Hawk to make the next move. Searching for a strayed child on the safe and friendly tree-lined streets of Fort Wayne was one thing. Searching for one in a treasure cave that had already claimed two lives was something else all together. This was Hawk's world, not hers. She would let him take the lead.

"Okay," Hawk said in a rough whisper. "Let's go." Sara still couldn't see a thing. She stayed where she was until she'd turned on the flashlight he'd handed her. He played his own flashlight beam over the floor of the cave, looking for Zack's footprints in the wet sand. "The tide's coming in fast."

"How do you intend to look for him?" Sara asked, closing her eyes for a moment to speed their adjustment to the near darkness around her.

"We'll quarter this room first, then move up the passageway toward your brother like we planned." He stepped away from her, swinging the light beam along the wall, looking for openings large enough for a small boy to hide in.

"That will take too long."

"You have a better idea?"

"There's an easier way than that," Sara said, deciding J. C. Hawk might have been a great spy, or mercenary, or whatever, but he didn't know anything about finding lost little boys. "Zackary Elliot Carson," she called, using her best out-of-patience mother's voice. "If you are in this cave, you had better let me know where, or you are going to be in big trouble when I get my hands on you."

Hawk spun to face her, as though threatened by some unseen foe. He looked lithe and lethal and taken completely off guard by the words echoing off the coral walls.

She couldn't help laughing at his consternation, despite her worry over Zack. "Sorry. I didn't mean to startle you. With nine-year-olds, threats sometimes work best."

"I was a nine-year-old, too, once," he said, the deadly menace in his dark eyes replaced by a reluctant smile. It was Sara's turn to be surprised. "Listen." The single word was a command Sara had no intention of disobeying.

She heard it, too, faint, but not too far away. It was
Zack calling to her, his voice echoing, distorted and
shrill with pain. Sara's heart began beating so hard in
her ears, she couldn't hear. Hawk headed unerringly for
a darker fissure in the rock wall.

"This way," he said, but Sara was already on his
heels.

Once Sara stuck her head inside the short, sloping
passage, she could see the pale glow of a very small
flashlight, but there was no sign of the child. "Zack?"
she called, softly so the echo wouldn't distort his reply.

"I'm stuck," he sobbed. "My leg is stuck and it
hurts." The last word rose to a wail.

Sara slid past Hawk, brushing off his restraining
hand. "Let me go to him," she insisted. "He needs
me."

Zackary seemed to be trapped behind a large fall of
sharp-edged stone. Sara couldn't tell if it was recent,
maybe even caused by the tremor that morning, or if it
had been there since the beginning of time.

Hawk held her still, his grip just less than hurtful.
"I'm going first. There's no telling what we're getting
into. That rockslide is new. The floor in this part of the
cave is unstable as hell. That kid picks the damnedest
places to get himself stuck in."

She had felt it, too—the uncomfortable sensation of
her feet sinking into the sticky sand even when she was
standing still.

"Aunt Sara!" Zack's voice sounded more frightened than ever.

She almost bolted, but Hawk's words made sense.
She squeezed back against the wet rock wall. "Talk to
him," she ordered. "Don't just come leering over those
boulders at him with no warning."

"Leering?" He raised one dark, arched eyebrow. "What the hell does that mean?"

"Never mind," she said, giving him a push in the right direction. "You're not in the Marines anymore. Just don't scare him."

Hawk edged past the fall of stone. Or tried to. It was simply too narrow for his height and broad shoulders. He backed off. "Hang on, Zack," he said, in a straightforward, man-to-man voice that was bound to appeal even to a scared nine-year-old. "Sara's coming to get you."

"Bring a flashlight," he sniffed. "Mine's almost burned out."

Hawk turned back to her, his face in shadows, his expression stone-hard and completely unreadable. "If you can move him at all, then get him out."

"We shouldn't move him until we know how badly he might be hurt," Sara whispered back, remembering her first aid.

Hawk lifted her chin with his hand so that there was no way she could miss what he had to say, although his voice was little more than a rasping whisper, as dark as their surroundings. "In an hour this place is going to be under three feet of water. If we don't get him out now, it won't matter how badly he's hurt or not hurt, do you understand?"

Terror beat at her mind with numbing wings. The only thing that kept her knees from buckling and collapsing her onto the wet, sandy floor of the cave was the touch of Hawk's fingers against her skin, hard and reassuring, and the absolute certainty in his eyes that they would succeed.

"I understand." She brushed past him, holding the big flashlight he'd given her in one hand, and squirmed past the narrow opening into Zack's dark prison.

"Aunt Sara," Zack sobbed.

"This is absolutely the last time I'm coming into a place like this to get you out," Sara said in her best exasperated-mother voice. "If you do anything like this again, I'll—I'll lock you up in your room for a year. With no television!" She dropped to her knees in the sand beside him. "Oh, Zack, honey. Are you all right?"

"My leg's stuck," he sniffed against her shoulder. "And my flashlight's almost burned out. Get me out of here and I promise I won't ever do anything bad again. Ever."

"It's okay, honey." She held him tightly, and rocked him back and forth, just as she had so many nights after he'd first come to live with her. "Why did you run away from your dad and me? Why did you come in here by yourself?"

"'Cause I wanted to be like the big guys. I wanted to do something awesome, too."

"Sara." Hawk didn't raise his voice, but Sara's head snapped around as if he had. "There's no time for chitchat. Can you get him out by yourself?"

"I...I don't think so." She played the flashlight over the fall of stone pinning Zack's legs to the floor. "No," she said, with a sinking heart. "There's no way I can move a rock that big by myself." A shower of small stones and shale covered almost the entire lower half of Zack's body. He'd worked his right leg free, but his left leg was pinned between two large boulders. Sara's heart skipped a beat. The rockslide was sizable. Zack could have easily been killed. As it was, except for possible damage to his leg, he seemed to have suffered only a few cuts and bruises.

"I was digging," Zack explained, propping himself up and wincing as his elbow came down on yet another sharp piece of rock. *"Ouch!"*

"Here, let me do that." Sara brushed back a strand of damp brown hair and then started moving rocks, throwing them into the darkness, where they landed with a splash that sent more chills up and down her spine.

"Look what I found." Zack uncurled his fingers. Two shiny doubloons shimmered warmly in the light. "It's Hawk's treasure. I found it!"

"Sara!" Her name was a command.

"Yes, Hawk."

"What do you need to get him out?"

"I need you. Or Elliot. I can't manage by myself."

"Then we're going to have to move this stuff to get to you." She could tell by the strain in his voice he was trying to move one of the obstructing boulders from his side. "Damn it," she heard him mutter under his breath. "Sara."

"Yes?"

"You're going to have to stay here while I go get your brother. I think with Elliot's help we can get through to you."

Dear Lord, she hoped so. Sara smiled at Zack. "We know you can, Hawk."

"And when my dad gets here, I've got something to show him," Zack added, his voice still full of tears.

"Don't worry, kid. I'll be back with your dad in just a minute or two."

"Good," Sara said. "It's awfully wet back here. I think there's water coming in from somewhere behind us." She made a face at Zack to show she only mentioned the fact because it was such a nuisance. "Hawk? Did you hear me?"

"I heard you." His tone didn't betray her. "Hang on, Sara. I'll be back."

"We'll be here."

After he left, the noise of water gurgling into the cave was very loud. She was already sitting in several inches of seawater. She moved behind Zack, propped him up against her shoulder. "There. Is that better?"

"My leg hurts," he complained, snuggling his wet sandy body closer, as though he were trying to fuse himself to her.

"Can you move your toes?"

"Yes," he said, after a moment of trying. "But I can't move my leg because my shoe is stuck."

Sara felt the water rise around her hips with each sighing rush of waves onto the shore beyond. She had no idea how long it would take Hawk to find Elliot and return. She couldn't sit here, idly waiting to drown. She didn't need to swing the flashlight beam up the walls of the cave to know that the waterline would be several feet above their heads if they remained seated on the floor. Her first terrifying fears that Zack's leg was crushed beneath the massive rock had proved ungrounded. But the danger they were both in was still very real. She was going to have to do something to free Zack, even if it meant digging underneath the boulder with her bare hands. After a few moments' thought, she decided to do just that.

"Zack, honey," she said, smoothing her hand across his hair, "I'm going to try to scoop the sand out from under your leg. Maybe we can get you loose on our own."

"I wanted to try that," Zack told her with a sniff and a swipe of his T-shirt sleeve across his eyes. "But I couldn't sit up straight. I couldn't reach my leg. I want out of here," he wailed, starting to cry again.

"Shh, stop crying," Sara urged. "Help me pick out a good rock to dig with. There are some nice flat ones here, I see."

Zack was momentarily distracted. "I wish I had a bigger flashlight," he muttered.

"I'll buy you the biggest one they've got at the hardware store when we get home," Sara promised, hefting a piece of coral rock in her hand. "How about this one?" She wanted to keep him talking, keep him from noticing how fast the water was rising around them.

"Fine. I'll hold the flashlight." He moved into a sitting position. "You dig. I think there's more water in here than there was when you came."

"Just a little," Sara said, as though she hadn't noticed. "I'll bet we have you already loose when your dad gets here."

"I hope so." He sounded lost and scared once more. From the corner of her eye, Sara saw him watching the water ripple around them and surge away into the darkness beyond the opening of the small antechamber.

"Tell me how you found your doubloons," Sara said, making it an order, not a request, by using her best schoolteacher voice. "I would have been much too scared to come into a dark, spooky place like this all by myself."

"I wasn't," Zack insisted. "At least not until everything started to shake and these crummy rocks fell on my leg. *Ouch!*" he yelped. Sara was up to her elbows in water, scooping sand from beneath his leg, praying she wouldn't hit bedrock before she had enough room to work his shoe free of the imprisoning rocks.

"What's wrong? Did I hurt you?" she asked, her heart beating like a trip-hammer in her chest from reaction and fear.

"No," he said sheepishly. "I was just afraid you were going to."

"Where did you find the gold?" Sara asked. She was digging as fast as she could, but the water washed the sand back into the depression beneath Zack's leg almost as fast as she scooped it out.

"Right here." He tightened his grip on the two doubloons. "The gold was lying there shining in the light. Just like in the pirate stories. Only I didn't come in here right away because I didn't want to find some nasty old pirate skeleton back in the corner. You know, with a sword sticking out of his ribs or something creepy like that. You don't think there is one, do you?" he asked, swiveling his head and the flashlight in that direction.

"No," Sara said, thankful once more that Zack hadn't seen the remains of the two lost explorers. "Swing the light back here. I can't see what I'm doing. Can you move your foot yet?"

"A little." He pushed at the rock with his free leg. It didn't budge. "Hurry, Aunt Sara. The water's getting higher."

Sara redoubled her efforts, listening all the while to the rush of the surf through unseen openings. But what she was really listening for were sounds of Hawk's return. She bit her lip to hold back a sob of fear and frustration as she worked her way farther under the rock. Her fingers were numb and stiff, and it took several moments for her to realize she was no longer scraping sand, but something harder, less yielding—and man-made.

"Zack! Is that your shoe?"

"I think so. I can move it a little now," he said, shifting his weight from one hip to the other. The water was already past his waist. His face was pasty with fear in the reflected beam of the flashlight.

"Try. Try harder. Maybe we can wiggle your foot out of your shoe." For the first time in her life, Sara was grateful for Zack's annoying habit of not lacing his shoes. It was possible, just possible, that she could wiggle him free. She stretched out full-length beside him, working away at the depression she'd struggled so hard to create. Stretching her fingers, she managed to close them around his ankle.

"Yikes, something's got my foot."

"It's me, silly," Sara said, laughing, almost giddy with relief. The taste of saltwater was on her lips. A few more inches and her face would be underwater. "When I say to, pull. Try to work your foot out of your shoe. Can you do that?"

"Yes. I want out of here bad!"

"Okay. One, two, three, *pull!*"

Sara closed her fingers tightly around his ankle. It felt slender and fine-boned, but amazingly strong. She worked frantically to scoop sand out from under his heel, and was blinded by a wave of saltwater as Zack, freed at last, surged backward.

He disappeared for a moment, completely submerged. The flashlight flew out of his hand and hit the wall of the cave. The sound of breaking glass was loud in her ears as darkness dropped over her like a shroud. Zack was still backpedaling. Sara grabbed for his foot, fearful suddenly that she would lose him again now that he was free. The danger hadn't passed. They were still virtually trapped in a dead-end passageway that would soon be filled with water.

"Zack!"

He came up spluttering, grabbing for her with two wet, cold hands. "I lost the flashlights."

"That's okay. We can get out of here without them."

"I can't see anything. What about my shoe?" he asked as Sara pulled them both upright. The water was above her knees. Fresh panic beat at the edges of her brain, but she didn't give in to its pull.

"I lost both my shoes," she laughed. "You've still got one. C'mon. Move your hand along the wall. This way is out." *Dear Lord,* she thought, *let me be right.* She couldn't be certain she hadn't gotten turned around while she was hauling Zack out of the water, but if the water got deeper, she'd know they were heading farther into the cave, toward the hole where it was gaining entrance from the sea. If that happened, she'd turn them around and head in the other direction. At least they were upright and moving. For the moment, that was even more important than being able to see.

"*Yeouch!* I stepped on something." He was limping badly but walking without her help.

"It's okay, honey. We're almost out." Sara had one arm outstretched, one holding on to Zack. Her right shoulder brushed against the cave wall. Her left fingers touched stone. They were in the narrow opening leading into the main area. "You'll have to crawl over some more rocks," she coached Zack. "Then stay put until I get over them, too. I don't want to lose you again."

"I'll stay put," he said fervently, already starting to climb. Sara curled her fingers around his belt until he was above her reach and over the last of the rockslide.

"Wait for me," she called breathlessly, starting to climb. The coral rock was sharp and she was barefoot, but she barely felt the scrapes and bruises. Now what she wanted more than anything else was to be free of Mary Hawk's treasure cave. "Wait for me!" She scrambled over the top and landed beside Zack in water above her knees. The pull of the tide was strong. The opening to the beach seemed infinitely far away.

Suddenly indecisive, Sara pulled Zack against her and held him tightly. She didn't know what to do next. She remembered Hawk's warning about the unstable sand at the cave's mouth and shuddered. But the thought of heading off into the darkness of the passageway up the hillside was equally unappealing.

What if she missed Hawk and Elliott in the darkness?

What if she got the two of them hopelessly lost?

She wanted fresh air and sunlight and a chance to examine Zack more closely to see that he was really all right. She wanted a shower and dry clothes and a good stiff drink. She was Sara Riley, schoolteacher and mother, not Wonder Woman. She had had just about all the treasure hunting she could take. She held Zack closely and tried not to cry.

"Sara! Zack!"

It was Elliot's voice, but Sara knew instinctively the man behind the flashlight on the far side of the cave was not her brother, but Hawk.

"We're here," she called out, shielding her eyes from the light as Hawk swept it over their disheveled forms.

"How the hell did you get him out of there?" he demanded, as Elliot splashed past him, heading for his sister and his son.

"We got tired of waiting," Sara said with a shrug that turned into a shiver. Now that the danger was almost past, she began to realize how close to death they both had come. The pull of the advancing tide as it surged in and out of the cave made it hard to stand. The noise, too, increased as the water level rose.

"Are you all right, son?" Elliot asked, running his hand over Zack's head and shoulders. His eyes sought contact with Sara's, asking for reassurance. He reached out and touched a raw spot on her cheek. "You're hurt." She winced, but brushed aside his concern.

"It's nothing. We're cold and tired and soaking-wet. But we're fine."

"Zack? Why'd you run away from me?"

"I wanted to do something radical like the other guys. And I did. I found it!" He stuck his hand in the pocket of his shorts and pulled out the two doubloons. "I found the treasure. I'm rich. I'll split it with you, Dad, and then you won't have to stay here. You can come back to Fort Wayne and do your research. We can all be together there."

"Zack...I can't—"

"You look like you're out on your feet, Sara," Hawk interrupted. "Let's get the hell out of here."

"Which way?" Sara asked, ignoring his unflattering comment. It was the truth, and she was too tired to take exception to it.

"This way." He gestured toward the opening. Sara looked there in dismay. Water foamed and surged around the entrance as the tide gathered momentum.

The terror she'd managed to keep at bay in the dark antechamber as she worked to free Zack's leg from the sand returned with even greater intensity. "I don't think I can make it," she said to Elliot, averting her eyes from the darkly powerful man beside her. "I'll go back the other way. I'll—I'll meet you at the top of the hill."

"You'll never make it without shoes," Hawk growled, reaching out to turn her slightly so that she had to look at him. "You have lost your shoes, right?"

"Yes," Sara confessed. "I forgot all about them."

"Then we're going this way."

"But the quicksand..." Sara shuddered despite an attempt not to.

"It's not a problem if you know what you're doing." Hawk gave her a hard, assessing look. "Let's go, Sara." Before she quite knew what he was doing, he had covered the small distance between them and scooped her up in his arms.

"Put me down!" Sara demanded. She'd never been carried in a man's arms before—never, not once.

"Be quiet, Sara Riley. Let someone rescue you for a change."

She didn't have an answer to that one, and to tell the truth, once she got over the shock of it, she found she liked being held against his chest. She was soaked to the skin and his shirt wasn't much drier. In the bright light of the tropical sun, she knew she would be embarrassed by the transparency of her cotton blouse. But for the moment, she responded only to the touch of his skin against hers, to his scent, his strength—sensual pleasures long denied. Right up until the moment he shifted his weight and threw her over his shoulder.

"Uhh," Sara grunted as the breath was knocked out of her, along with the fantasy.

"This passageway isn't wide enough for the both of us," Hawk said, and he didn't even sound out of breath.

He moved through the opening with seemingly little effort, although Sara felt the strain of rock-hard muscles against her belly and beneath her hands. Elliot followed with Zack in his arms. By the time they'd negotiated the hazardous passage into sunlight and fresh air, Sara was back in control of her emotions and her libido.

"Put me down," she said, squirming a little in his arms in her haste to be free. Hawk only tightened his grip. "Someone will see us," she insisted, struggling just a little bit harder. She had enjoyed being held by him entirely too much for her own good. "They'll be able to locate the entrance to the cave." She was beginning to feel ridiculous, arguing with the man while she was upside down.

"It's too late for that." He shifted both hands to her waist and let her slide down the length of his body until her feet met sand. The touch of him from thigh to shoulder was enough to make Sara lose the power of speech for a few moments.

"What do you mean?" she managed after a couple of quick deep breaths.

"We have company." He pointed off along the beach.

Emily Wycheski and about a dozen youngsters of all shapes and sizes were walking toward them, playing tag with the incoming tide. But that wasn't what caused a shiver to race up and down Sara's spine. Beyond Emily and the oblivious, happy children was a far more sinister figure: the snake doctor, Ian Carter-Stone. And it was more than obvious that he knew exactly where they had been—and what they had found.

CHAPTER NINE

"Is ZACK ASLEEP?"

Sara spun around, her arms crossed over her chest, her heart missing a beat, as it so often did at the sound of Hawk's voice.

"Both boys are asleep."

"No bad dreams? No side effects from being caught in the rockslide?"

"Just a few bumps and abrasions, that's all." She smiled, a proud mother's smile. "And he's never been prone to nightmares, thank goodness."

"And what about you?"

"The same thing. A few more scrapes and bruises to add to my collection. I'm not used to this kind of life. My main form of exercise is walking back and forth to school carrying fifteen pounds of books and art supplies."

"Where's your brother?" Hawk asked, changing the subject.

"He went down to the village."

"To the cantina?" He moved into the circle of candlelight on Elliot's veranda. She'd been standing in the shadows, watching the moonlight on the sea.

"I don't know. It's possible. This afternoon shook him up pretty badly. I think he needed to get away from all of us." She should have seen Hawk coming down the path from the dining room. She might have if he'd used a flashlight. Obviously, he hadn't. She knew he had eyes like a cat, a sleek jungle predator more comfortable prowling its domain at midnight than at noon. She didn't think she'd ever get used to him appearing out of thin air the way he so often did, but it no longer frightened her enough to make her jump out of her skin.

"And Mother Sara stayed home to baby-sit?"

If he meant to hurt her, his gibe missed its mark. She was too tired to argue with J. C. Hawk. She was almost too tired to remain on her feet. But in the end she couldn't resist making a reply. "I didn't feel like making the trip down to the village on foot, in the dark, just to drink a lukewarm beer or two." She shuddered. "I like mine cold."

"You're right. The beer *is* lukewarm at the cantina. And very few of the village women ever set foot in the place."

"No," she said thoughtfully, "I suppose they don't."

"Ticos view their man-woman relationships differently than folks do in the States."

"Men are still lord and master here, you mean."

He gave a grunting half laugh. "Different drummer," he admitted, sidestepping a confrontation as adroitly as she had.

"Elliot told me it was a different world down here," she said musingly. The night was warm and humid, but she felt the cooling touch of a sea breeze on her cheek and stepped into the moonlight to let it caress her still more. She rested her head against the cypress post that held up the roof. "Everything I see, everything I hear, everything I feel makes me realize how true that is. Even the stars are different. See, there's the Big Dipper, tipped over on its side, and so low in the sky it's almost as if someone is using it to try to scoop water out of the sea. It's so familiar and yet so strange. It makes me wonder what I'm doing here.''

"You're here to ride herd on my profligate waste of your nephew's inheritance, remember?''

"I remember." She also remembered the cache of eight doubloons in Elliot's cabin. She had shown hers to Zack and Ben as they were getting ready for bed. She'd also told them about the two skeletons, in hopes of instilling a little prudence into her nephew's adventuresome soul.

But Zack hadn't been frightened off by her cautionary tale. Now that he was safe once more, his courage had returned. He wanted to see the skeletons for himself. And so did Ben. Elliot, sitting at the edge of his son's bed, had looked at her helplessly.

Zack's near brush with disaster had had a profound effect on her brother. He'd faced the possibility of losing Zack just as he'd lost the boy's mother, with no warning, with no chance to say goodbye, and he was handling it badly. He'd withdrawn again into his own restricted, emotionless world and had shut her out, as he had Zack.

What progress father and son had made during the week was wiped away, as though carried off by the tide. They were almost strangers again. Zack was too tired to notice, Sara hoped. But she had sensed the change in Elliot right away.

And, selfishly, she couldn't help but feel a small, swift burst of happiness at this new estrangement, because now she knew she wouldn't have to leave Zack behind.

"What nefarious schemes are you hatching now, Sara Riley?'' Hawk asked, lifting her chin with his fist, bringing her world back into focus, then narrowing it in the space of a heartbeat to the two of them.

"Nothing," she said, hurriedly, guiltily.

"Yes, you were."

"I'm tired, nothing more." She felt treacherous tears stinging the backs of her eyelids. "It's been a very long day."

"You're a trooper, Sara. But you're also a liar. You've been thinking about Zack and his dad, haven't you?"

It was lucky she had to spend less than a week more in this man's company. She doubted you could hide anything from him if he wanted to know what it was badly enough.

"Yes. They were getting along so well. And then... this afternoon. After we got Zack out of the cave."

"After *you* got Zack out of the cave, Sara. Don't try to make me the fall guy for this one."

"What do you mean?" she asked, pulling away from the touch of his rough hand on her skin. His thumb had been smoothing the line of her jaw and she'd been within a breath of snuggling her cheek into his palm.

"You saved Zack's life. You're the heroine. You made Elliot look bad."

"I—I couldn't just sit there and let Zack drown." She could barely squeeze the word past the lump of renewed terror in her throat. She would hear the sighing rush of incoming waves, feel the water moving inexorably up over her hip and thigh till the day she died.

"Of course you couldn't. Elliot knows that. At least the thinking, reasonable part of his brain knows that. But Elliot's a man. And honey, as much as you'd like to pigeonhole us, civilize us, it won't work. Men aren't the same. They don't think the same. You took something away from Elliot by digging Zack out of the rockslide before we got there. Something that he's afraid he can't get back. His manhood.''

''That's ridiculous!''

''Maybe it is to you. But Elliot hasn't got a great track record as a father. It's eating at him. It has been, even before Zack insisted you go down into the cave to rescue him the first time. Today didn't make it any better. And deep down inside, Sara Riley, I think you're just a little bit glad Zack and his dad are back at square one.''

''I ought to—''

''What, slap my face?'' he asked, with just the slightest curve to his lips.

''No,'' she said, not smiling at all. ''I ought to punch you right in the mouth.''

''For telling the truth?''

''For making it sound as if I don't want Zack and his father to be together, to be a family.'' She was appalled that the tears she wouldn't let fall could still be heard in her voice. ''I'm doing everything I can to bring them together.''

He reached out and caught her shoulders. ''That's just the point. You try too damn hard, Sara. You can't work miracles in two weeks' time. Especially when your heart isn't in it.''

''My heart *is* in it,'' she insisted, not fighting his touch as she ought to. ''He belongs with his father.'' She said it as much to convince herself as to convince him.

''You never do anything by halves, do you, Sara Riley?''

''What do you mean?''

"You can't undo years of benign neglect in the space of a few days. Slow down."

"I'm not a saint, Hawk." Again she wasn't certain why, but she was compelled to tell him the truth. "If I don't give Zack up now, I'll never be able to let him go."

"I'm not saying you're a saint." Hawk's voice was harsh and uncompromising. "Far from it. You're selfish, Sara. You want all of Zack or none of him. What you don't want to do is share. If you scare Elliot off, reinforce all his doubts, you can take Zack back to Fort Wayne with a clear conscience, can't you? After all, you tried. You did your best."

She closed her eyes at the searing pain in her heart the words caused. Why did he have to force her to look at her actions with such merciless honesty? Zack wasn't her child. He was Elliot's son. They belonged together. Elliot was a good man. He would be a good father—if he had Zack with him, alone, without her interference, however well-intentioned.

"I hate you, Joseph Hawk. You're a bastard, an unfeeling, unprincipled bastard. What do you know about raising a child, loving a child? What do you know about loving anyone?"

Her words didn't hurt him. The set, hard look of misery on her face, mirroring the pain he'd inflicted on her, did. But he didn't let it stop him. What he was telling her was the truth. But the reason he had for doing it was his own. He'd accused her of being selfish. He was being selfish as well. If she didn't succeed in bringing Zack and his father together this time, she'd be back to try again. Maybe as early as the summer, to stay as long as it took for Zack to establish a real relationship with his father. That's what he wanted—to have Sara

Riley in his world, at least long enough to get his fill of her.

"I know what's best for Zack," he said. "And for his father. Do you?"

"Yes."

"You never back down, do you, Sara?" This time he did smile. He was tired of arguing with her. She wasn't going to change her mind, not tonight, not now. Maybe later, after she'd cooled down, had time to think about what he'd said, she'd begin to see there was truth in what he'd told her. But tonight she was not a thinking rational being, she was a woman, an incredible mixture of fact and fancy, logic and emotion, ice and fire.

"No. I . . . never back down."

She did back away, however, or try to. He still had his hands on her shoulders. He tightened his grip, just enough to keep her from moving, not enough to hurt her.

"And I truly do have Zack's best interests at heart. And El's. Not my own."

"I know, Sara. I didn't mean to hurt you," he heard himself say. Maybe it was the sheen of tears in her eyes. Maybe it was the call of a nocturnal bird in the tree-tops, the smell of flowers heavy on the damp air. Or was it the scent of her hair, the softness of her skin that made him want to apologize for his harshness and plain speaking? It had been so long since there had been a woman in his life that he'd forgotten what it was like dealing with one.

"You don't play fair, Hawk," she told him, a wistful note in her voice. "I should have expected that."

Was she comparing him to that two-bit philanderer she'd been married to? Elliot had told him before she'd arrived that her husband had left her for a younger woman. "Are you telling me your ex did play fair?"

She closed her eyes and he realized he'd hurt her again. He regretted it, but it was too late to recall the words. In all his adult life he'd never had anyone to please, anyone to rely on but himself. For more years than he cared to remember, considering another human being's feelings before his own had been a luxury he couldn't afford. "No," she said finally, in a very small voice, "he didn't."

"And now you don't trust any man?"

She shook her head, but opened her eyes to look at him. His gut tightened painfully. Her eyes were the color of green velvet in the flickering light of the candles on the table behind him. "I know there are men out there who can be trusted. But I no longer trust myself to be able to pick them out of the crowd."

He wanted her to tell him she trusted him, even though he knew she didn't. How could she? He'd done everything in his power to keep her from learning what his real purpose in finding Mary Hawk's treasure was. He still wasn't going to tell her. If word got around that he wanted to buy as much of Allied Fruit's abandoned banana plantation as he could get his hands on, the price would skyrocket. And when she found out that he intended to do nothing at all with the land if he did get it, she'd think he was a madman, as well as a crook.

"Do you do a lot of crowd-watching back in Fort Wayne?"

"No. I'm much too busy raising my children and doing my job to give much thought to dating again. My daughter Megan's the champion dater in the family."

"Is she as pretty as you are?" Hawk asked. He liked keeping her off guard. Her green eyes widened with shock and surprise as they did whenever he caught her unaware. Her mouth firmed into a straight line and she worried her lower lip between her teeth.

"She's beautiful and she doesn't look anything like me," she said, frowning at the personal level of the conversation.

He shook his head. "You're wrong. She looks exactly like you."

"But you just asked me what she looked like."

His smile was slow and broad. "I wanted to hear what you'd say about her, about yourself. I've seen her picture."

"Where? Of course, her senior-class photo. Elliot has one taped above his computer station, doesn't he?"

"I knew what all of you looked like long before you got here."

"And I knew absolutely nothing about you." She had stood quietly within his grasp, but now she made a small, determined effort to be free. He didn't let her go. She stopped struggling, lifted her eyes to his, watching him, searching for knowledge he was unwilling to give. "I still don't."

"And I'm not going to tell you." If he wanted to play it smart, he'd turn around and walk away. The trouble was he didn't want to play it smart. He wanted her. A hell of a lot more than he'd wanted a woman for a long time. The need had snuck up on him like a tiger in the night and there was only one way he knew to cure himself of the unwanted infatuation. He intended to have her before the week was out.

"Why not?" She wasn't struggling to be free anymore. She lifted her arms to his shoulders. What he saw reflected in her eyes now was neither lust nor hate, love nor anger. It was compassion and caring, and it was nearly his undoing. "What is so awful about your past that you don't want anyone to know about it?"

"Nothing," he said huskily, although that was a lie. There was plenty awful about his past—terror and death and dying. So much of it she could never begin to comprehend the horror of it all. But the things he had seen, the things he had done had kept her and her family, and countless others just like them, safe and secure in their midwestern paradise. "I told you I was in the Marines. Then I worked for the government. I did what I had to do, that's all. My folks are dead. I don't have any brothers or sisters. There's only me. And this place." He'd said more than he'd intended to say. She'd managed to turn the tables on him with just one look, one softly murmured plea for intimacy of thoughts and words. She shifted slightly in his arms, bringing her body closer, so close her breasts brushed his chest with each breath she took.

"And the gold?" she whispered.

"And the gold." He lowered his mouth to take hers in a long hard kiss. She didn't flinch or pull away. Her mouth opened beneath his. Her tongue flicked out to meet his as he explored the moist darkness of her mouth.

"Tell me what you'll do with the money when you get it," she said, her breath hot against his mouth when the kiss ended. "Somehow I don't see you as the type to go running off to Monte Carlo or the south of France."

He grunted a reply. He was only half listening to her words. He wondered what she'd do if he pulled her down with him into the hammock on the other side of the porch. Would she fight to be free? Or would she open her legs and her body to him as readily as she opened her lips to his kiss?

"I'm right, aren't I?" she demanded, but her voice was so breathless the words were a mere thread of sound against his cheek.

"You talk too much," he growled, kissing her jaw, her neck. Her throat, the skin softly golden in the faint candlelight, was as slender as a reed. He could span it with one hand, feel the wildly beating pulse beneath his fingers. "Maybe I'm going to start my own little country down here. What do you think? Hawk the First. I kind of like that." He brushed his palm over her breasts. She wore no bra again tonight and he felt her nipples stir and harden beneath his touch.

She caught her breath on a sigh of pleasure but kept right on talking. "Whatever you are, you're no megalomaniac. You don't keep going back into that cave, into that danger every day just for the money. Admit it."

"I'm not admitting anything." He pulled her closer, determined to stop her questions the only way he knew how. He traced a line of kisses across her collarbone, pushing aside the soft cotton of her blouse, unfastening the buttons with one hand while he held her mouth still for his kiss with the other. "I want that treasure. I'll do whatever is necessary to get it. Don't try to make a hero out of me, Sara Riley. It won't work."

"And this won't work," she said, her voice breaking as he touched her hard, pebbled nipple with the tip of his tongue. Her hands were in his hair, smoothing, caressing, pressing him closer. She wanted him as badly as he wanted her—he was certain of that. Until she spoke.

"Hawk, please. Stop." She was no longer straining against him. She began pushing at his chest with both hands. She wasn't being coy. She wasn't playing the tease to lead him on. She meant what she said, although there was reluctance in her voice. He stepped away. She pulled the open edges of her blouse together. Even in the near darkness, he could see her face suffuse with color, see her struggle to bring her breathing under control. "Thank you," she said, with as much dignity as she could muster. Her voice trembled and so did her hands.

"I wouldn't have hurt you, Sara," he said roughly. The blood was pounding in his ears and in his sex. He still wanted to pick her up in his arms, carry her to the hammock and make love to her, bury himself in her until she melted in his hands, climaxed around him. But he'd never forced a woman in his life and he didn't intend to start with Sara Riley.

"I know that. And I'm not afraid of you, if that's what you're thinking," she added. "What just happened was my fault as much as yours." She stopped fiddling with the buttons of her blouse. She'd left the top two undone. He wanted to reach out and run his finger along the soft, shadowed cleft of her breasts. He shoved his hand into the pocket of his slacks.

"It's no one's fault. We're two consenting adults, as they say back in the States, answerable to no one but ourselves. Don't apologize for being a woman, Sara."

"I'm not." She lifted her chin, looked him straight in the eye. "But I'm not the kind of woman who's a slave to her hormones, a moonstruck divorcée living out a jungle fantasy with a real-life pirate. I know when I'm making a mistake. I wasn't just spouting psycho-babble when you asked me about trust a while ago. It's a very real and basic need. I have to trust the man I make love to, Hawk. Most women do. But more importantly, he has to trust me." She reached up, touched his cheek, gently, fleetingly. "That's the problem, you see. You

don't trust me. Good night, Hawk.'' She turned and
went into her brother's cabin before he could say a
word.

She'd turned the tables on him.

She didn't trust him, because she'd been hurt and
humiliated by the man she should have been able to rely
on, come hell or high water. She wasn't about to make
the same mistake twice. He didn't blame her. It was just
Hawk's bad luck to be the next man to come along.

He heard her moving around inside Elliot's cabin,
answering a sleepy question from Zack or her son.
Hawk turned and moved down the steps onto the path,
gliding away into the dark, tropical night. The smile was
gone from his lips. Sara didn't trust him, because she'd
been hurt and humiliated by her bastard of a husband.
His refusal to confide his past and reveal his future
plans seemed to her to be just such another betrayal.

He couldn't afford the luxury of telling her.

The reason he couldn't trust her with his plans for
Tyiskita's future was a lot less complicated and emo-
tional than Sara's. If he told her what he really dreamed
of doing with this place and the wrong people found
out, it could get her seriously hurt. It might even get her
killed.

CHAPTER TEN

"Hey, Aunt Sara, where're ya going?"

Sara halted at the top of the stone steps leading down to the beach. She'd thought she'd left Ben and Zack sleeping in the cabin when she went to breakfast. Elliot, too, was still in his bunk. She had no idea when he had returned last night.

She'd sat in the dark in the tiny, crowded main room of his cabin for what seemed like hours, trying to regain her equilibrium and still her rapidly beating heart after Hawk had left. She'd told him she was no moonstruck divorcée, ruled by passion and her hormones. That much was true. She hadn't dated seriously since her divorce. Celibacy had become a way of life. It shocked and surprised her that five minutes in the arms of J. C. Hawk was more than enough to make her forget all the rules she lived by.

Infatuation was too simple a word to describe what she'd felt last night. Surrender was closer, complete and total capitulation to the fire and excitement that he ignited inside her with just a kiss, a touch. Desire so strong and insistent it made her toes curl and her chest and stomach tighten with pleasure so intense it was almost pain. She'd never felt this way before in her life, but it didn't mean she couldn't recognize what was wrong with herself. If she wasn't careful—and she intended to be very careful in the future—she was going to fall in love with the man.

The thinking, rational Sara knew that was an impossible dream.

Sara the woman, desiring and desired, wished it were not.

"Aunt Sara! Didn't you hear me? Wait up," Zack called, impatient as always.

"I'm waiting," she called back, smiling as he bounded up to her. "I thought you were still asleep." If the events of yesterday had any untoward effects on him, they didn't show. His hands and knees were scraped raw, but so were hers. There were no shadows of pain or fear in his clear hazel eyes. He'd fallen asleep in shorts and a T-shirt. He still had them on. Sara decided to forgo a lecture on personal hygiene and simply enjoy the pleasure—and distraction—of his company.

"It's too hot to sleep. You going swimming?" he asked, following her down the steps.

"Nope."

"You going back to the cave?"

"No. I'm going for a walk," Sara told him, forestalling any more guesses as to her destination. "I'm going to visit Emily's classroom. Still want to come along?"

Zack paused, considering. Sara continued down three more steps, then turned to see what he was doing. His forehead was wrinkled in thought, curiosity warring with a nine-year-old's natural aversion to entering a classroom, any classroom, on such a beautiful day. "School? Bummer."

"So, are you coming with me?" she asked. "You know, it might be interesting to see how other kids learn. Maybe you could even tell them a little about your school.''

"Yeah," he said, still not completely convinced. "I suppose I could. Manuel and Jorge go to school there."

"Who are Manuel and Jorge?"

"Some guys I met. Luke introduced us. They're okay. You aren't going to stay long, are you?"

"Only a little while. I promise."

"Okay," he said, and began skipping along behind her once more. "I wish Ben would've let me bring my pieces of eight. I could have showed them to the guys and the other kids in the village. He said I couldn't carry them around, though. He said I couldn't tell anyone about them or Hawk would slit my throat."

"He didn't."

"Well, not exactly." Zack looked chagrined at being caught in a lie. "But almost. He was getting ready to take a shower this morning. He's as bad as a girl." It was the ultimate insult. Then he bounced back to the original subject. "Why can't I show anyone our treasure? It's ours—yours and mine. Hawk said so last night."

"There are other people looking for the treasure as well, remember," Sara said, wondering suddenly if the jungle might have ears.

"The bad guys." Zack nodded, very serious as he moved alongside her when they reached the beach. "Maybe it's those guys out on the boat. Maybe some creeps from Golfito. Or even the village." *Or your friend the snake doctor,* Sara added to herself.

"And we only found a little bit of it, right? There's lots more down there in the cave somewhere. Enough to make us rich for ever and ever."

"It is worth a great deal of money."

"I want to help you and Dad and Hawk find it."

"You're not afraid to go back into the cave?"

"No." He turned his head to look at her. "Not me." He thumped his chest.

Oh, dear, Sara thought. The child was afraid of nothing, it seemed. "We'll wait for your dad and Hawk next time, okay?" she cautioned, deciding not to make an issue of it at the moment.

"Okay."

"I hope we find the gold and stuff before it's time to go back home."

"What if we don't find the treasure, Zack?" she asked, stumbling into the subject she didn't want to pursue, but unable to let the chance to speak to him about staying on at Tyiskita drift away. "Would you like to stay here longer, and help your dad and Hawk find it?"

"Nope," he said, skipping away from her toward the stepping stones across the creek. "I don't want to stay here all by myself. There's no one to play ball with. And there's no TV."

At least, she thought, clinging to one small ray of hope, he hadn't said he didn't want to stay with his father. It wasn't much, but it was all she had.

"Hi, Sara. Welcome to Tyiskita school. Such as it is." Emily had seen them coming up the beach and stepped into the doorway of the big corner room of the village building that housed the school. *"Buenos días,"* she added more formally in Spanish. *"¿Cómo está usted?"*

"Muy bien. ¿Y usted?" Sara replied, equally formal.

"Bien. Hi, Zack," Emily said, smiling.

"You could have asked me in Spanish, too," he told her with what might have been the beginning of a pout. "I know that much."

"Good. Then you can say hello to the class in Spanish," Emily replied, still smiling.

"*¡Atención, clase!*" She switched to English, speaking slowly and clearly. "This is Zackary Carson. Please make him welcome."

"*Bienvenido, Zackary,*" the children, two dozen or so of assorted ages, shapes and sizes, replied with shy smiles.

"*Hola,*" Zack said, looking as uneasy as Emily's students.

"Have a seat." She waved them to two empty, rickety desks at the back of the room. Sara looked around the big airy room as she sat down. It was a bare-bones operation: no TV monitors, no computer consoles. There was only a blackboard and an outdated map on one wall, a bookcase with a small assortment of books, a box holding scissors, glue, colored paper and other odds and ends. Emily began chalking a multiplication problem on the board.

"We're just about to have a math lesson."

"Oh great," Zack muttered, catching Sara's eye. "My favorite subject."

"Zackary," Sara said warningly.

"I'll behave," he muttered, sliding into his seat. "But remember, this is supposed to be my vacation."

He did sit quietly, even taking the quiz of multiplication tables and long division that Emily gave the older children to do. But he was more than happy to be released with the others when Emily called a recess twenty minutes later. He raced out into the sunshine on the beach with the village children as though he'd known them all his life.

"Don't wander too far off," Sara called, helping Emily gather scattered papers and pencils left behind by the mass exodus. "Olivia's expecting us for lunch in half an hour."

"Okay," he called back with a wave, and went racing off with two boys about his size and age. Manuel and Jorge, Sara guessed, who, it seemed, spoke just slightly more English than he did Spanish.

"They're off to the stream to find skipping stones," Emily explained. "They won't go far."

"After yesterday I'm almost afraid to let him out of my sight," Sara confessed.

"I heard," Emily continued, straightening the pile of quiz papers on her desk.

"From Elliot?" It wasn't really a question. Sara was almost certain it wasn't Hawk who had confided in the younger woman.

"Yes. He stopped by to see me last night."

"I—I knew he had come down to the village." Sara chose her words very carefully.

"He told me everything that happened yesterday, including the reason why Zack went into the cave alone."

"I see. I'm glad Elliot has someone here he can talk to. He's taking it so hard," Sara said. "He's barely seen Zack since he was four. Now he's trying to establish a viable father-son relationship in a little more than a week." She wasn't sorry to have someone to confide in herself, although she didn't know how much of her family history it was appropriate to tell Emily. "It's going to be almost impossible to bring about. And it's my fault. I should have realized it would be too difficult."

"It's a pretty common human failing to follow our hearts instead of our heads," Emily said, shoving pencils, papers and books into the drawer of her packing-crate desk. "The hardest thing to do sometimes is let others set their own pace.... By the way, my mom sent down a carton of books for the kids. It arrived yesterday on the plane. Would you like to help me unpack them?"

"Of course." Emily was right. Sara had done all she could for Zack and Elliot at the moment. She couldn't manufacture situations to bring them closer. And she couldn't keep blaming herself for being reluctant to have Zack return to his father. She loved him as if he were her own and that wasn't going to change.

Somehow she'd have to find the strength to do what was best for all three of them. She just wasn't sure right now what that was.

"I'm using these children's books for English lessons," Emily was saying as she tore open a small cardboard box of colorful toddler books. "They're great for words and numbers. I wish I could get a lot more just like them in Spanish. Our textbooks are woefully outdated. And pretty boring, if you want to know the truth. The kids learn so much more quickly with the picture books. And it's a lot easier on me," she confessed with a grin. "My Spanish isn't all that great, either."

"Then why are you doing this?"

"There isn't anyone else," Emily said simply. She spoke without conceit and without censure, but Sara felt terrible just the same. She should have known without asking why Emily was doing what she did.

So that the children could learn.

After all, it was why she'd become a teacher herself.

It was easy enough to forget that sometimes, in the stress of trying to wear so many hats. She'd earned her degree between pregnancies and part-time jobs. She'd taught first grade for two years, then had taken the art teacher's job at Lewis and Clark when he retired three years later. She'd been there ever since.

Sara liked what she did, but, like most art programs, her classes were considered easy credits. Not that she didn't have talented, committed students; she did. But she also had her share of bored jocks and troublemakers. In fact, if she were honest, there were so many students just marking time in her classes that she was in real danger of becoming jaded about her profession herself.

This morning, seeing Emily work with these bright and eager youngsters who lacked all but the most basic educational tools reminded her of her own youthful enthusiasm for teaching, a fire and intensity she was ashamed to admit she had let wither and lie dormant. She would do her best to renew that commitment when she returned to Fort Wayne, she decided.

"Aunt Sara!" Zack came skidding to a halt just outside the classroom. "Can I ask you something special?"

"What?" she asked, smiling at him and the two boys with him, their big brown eyes filled with excitement and expectation.

"Can I have my birthday party here? Before we go home?"

"Your birthday isn't until next month."

"I know. But I want to have a party here, with these guys. This is Manuel and Jorge," he said, pointing to his new friends. "Their dad lived in California for five years. They speak English pretty good. A lot better than

I speak Spanish, anyway," he admitted with a grin.
"They said they always have big parties for their name
days. That's what they do instead of birthdays. I
learned that in school."

"You did?"

"Yeah. I'm not stupid, Aunt Sara. I listen in school."

"That's not what your teacher tells me."

"Aunt Sara, I'm trying to talk birthday party, here."

"Okay," she said, holding up her hands in surrender. "Go on. I'm listening."

"We'll have a big party. You can ask Olivia to bake
a cake. I don't care about presents," he insisted, with
what sounded like only a little regret. "But we can play
ball. Or go surfing with Luke or something neat.
Please. Let me have a party before we go home."

"We'll think about it," Sara said. "You must ask
Olivia yourself if she has time to bake a cake. And you
must ask Hawk if it's okay to have a party on his property."

"Okay. I'll do that. How about day after tomorrow?" Zack said.

"I'll have the children make a piñata in activities
class," Emily offered, smiling at the three boys chattering away in a mixture of Spanish words and English
phrases that almost defied translation. "I've been saving up a sack of hard candy from one of my mother's
care packages for the next village fete."

"I'm not certain Hawk—"

"I'm sure he won't object," Emily said. "Name days,
holidays, holy days are all important to Tico families.
The children will be very happy to help Zack celebrate
his birthday."

"Okay." Sara still wasn't convinced Hawk would
welcome an invasion of village children into his cliff-

top retreat. "If Olivia is too busy to bake a cake, I'm sure I can manage something for refreshments."

"I'll help, if you like," Emily offered.

"Thank you." Sara laughed. "I wonder if Olivia has any cake mixes in the kitchen? If not, I'm going to have to figure out how to bake a cake from scratch with a Spanish cookbook. I think Zack and I had better get back up to the lodge. Translating the recipe might very well take me until the day after tomorrow."

"It'll be a piece of cake." Emily giggled and made a face. They both laughed at the terrible pun.

"Thank you for inviting us into your classroom. I think I found something here today I had lost."

Emily looked puzzled, but didn't question her further. "Are you sure you don't want to stay for history class?" she asked Zack, raising her voice to be heard over the trio, whose conversation had been getting steadily louder.

"No!" He glanced in Sara's direction. "I mean, no, thank you," he added hastily.

"Come down later when you decide on a time for the party so that I can tell the children."

"Okay."

"Okay. 'Bye, Zack."

"*Hasta la vista,* baby." Zack grinned, heading off toward the beach with a wave.

"Zackary Elliot Carson!" Sara threw up her hands. "He's incorrigible. And he's one of Arnold Schwarzenegger's biggest fans."

"He's a great kid." Emily picked up the hand bell, preparing for class to resume. "You're lucky to have him."

"I know," Sara said. "Goodbye."

SARA AND ELLIOT were sitting alone at one end of the big dining table when Hawk arrived at the top of the cliff steps. They were watching Zack set out bananas for the monkeys. Elliot looked as if he'd had a bad night, he noted. There wasn't much he could do about the problems between Elliot and his son. He couldn't imagine what he'd do with the kid here all the time, anyway—unless Sara stayed to take care of him, and that was about as likely as a snowstorm in the jungle. It wasn't any more likely that Elliot would give up his research and head back to the States. It was stalemate, as far as he could see. And damn well none of his business. He had his own fish to fry.

"Gunny Escobar is flying the stuff in from Texas this afternoon," Hawk told Elliot, as he slid into a chair beside Sara's brother. He accepted the cup of coffee Olivia offered with a grunt of thanks. "I don't want the stuff coming down on a commercial plane."

Elliot whistled. "What kind of strings did you have to pull to get clearance for a shipment like that to cross the border?"

"Let's just say we have friends in important places these days and leave it go at that," Hawk said. He didn't care if Sara knew he had a shipment of very sophisticated explosives ordered to help clear the cave. He just didn't want to have to sit here and argue about the cost with her.

"You've pinpointed the place where you want to start looking for the treasure, haven't you?" Sara asked, as she watched Zack hop back onto the porch to grab his ball and glove from on top of the bookshelf. He walked around the side of the building and began throwing the ball against the wall. The sound was rhythmic and repetitive, until the macaw took exception to the noise and set up a fuss. Then it was just plain annoying.

He might as well tell her the truth from the beginning. If he didn't, she'd keep at him until he did. He nodded. "I think Zack's little cul-de-sac looks like the best place to start."

"Then I assume this shipment you're alluding to is more explosives."

He nodded again. He was ready for her next question.

"Why can't you use the dynamite you already have? Surely it would be far more economical. It must be costing a fortune to fly explosives all the way from Texas in a private plane."

"You're right." He didn't let the smile he felt tugging at his mouth show.

"Then why?"

"I want to excavate Zack's little cubbyhole, not blow the whole damn cave and myself with it to kingdom come."

She took a sip of her coffee, shivered and added more hot milk from the pitcher on the table. "Okay," she said at last, grudgingly, as far as Hawk could tell. "I suppose you're right. When do you intend to start the excavation?"

"The first low tide after Gunny gets down here."

"Are we going to have to pay him extra to do the demolition?"

Hawk almost laughed aloud. She never gave up. Not for a moment. "No. I'm going to do it myself."

"I should have known," she said and changed the subject. "Would it be all right if we had a party here for Zack before we go back to the States?"

"A party?" Damn, what would she think of next? If he lived to be a hundred, he'd never figure this woman out.

"A birthday party."

"Zack's birthday is next month," Elliot said.

"I know. But he has his heart set on a party here. He wants to invite the children from the village. Evidently he's made friends with a few of them while we've been here. Emily offered to have the school children make a piñata. We could bake a cake, if Olivia's willing to help me translate the recipe from a Spanish cookbook. Maybe they could play ball here in the clearing. Or soccer..." She let the words trail off into silence. She took another swallow of her coffee, watching Hawk over the rim of the cup.

A kid's birthday party. God, he'd forgotten such things even existed.

"No problem," he said. "Just keep the kids out of my hair. I'll tell Olivia to give you all the help you need."

"Thank you."

He kept watching her. He could see her breathing quicken beneath the soft cotton of her pink T-shirt. It was a good color for her, he decided. She looked good in soft colors—peach and blue and bright spring greens that darkened and intensified the color of her eyes. And she couldn't hide the physical reaction his scrutiny caused. She wasn't indifferent to him, he knew that. But she wasn't going to let him catch her off guard the way he had last night.

"That baseball banging against the building is driving me nuts," Elliot said, standing up. "Maybe Zack can be persuaded to play some catch. What do you think, sis?" Elliot was so preoccupied by his own problems with Zack, Hawk was positive he didn't register Sara's flustered look as she pulled her gaze from his and transferred it to her brother's face.

"What?"

"I said, do you think a game of catch might help put me back on the right track with Zack?"

"It can't hurt, El. Just don't try to rush him into anything this time, okay? And don't worry. He's a tough little kid. He can take a few bumps and bruises. But we can't ever let him know how scared we were for him down in the cave."

"I don't want to lose him, sis. He's all I have left of Mindy in the world. How can you get through a day without being worried stiff what they'll do next?"

"You can't," Sara said with a smile that made Hawk catch his breath. "But don't let him know you're scared." She smiled again and this time it was filled with devilishness. "Never show weakness. He'll be onto it like a shark sensing blood in the water, okay?"

"Okay." He gave her a sheepish grin. "I'll get the hang of this yet."

"Sure you will."

"See you later, Hawk." Elliot got up to leave.

"Right." He'd only been half listening to what they said. His attention had been focused on Sara. He couldn't stop thinking about what she'd felt like in his arms last night. He kept wondering what color her nipples were, the skin of her stomach and the small of her back, the tight nest of curls at the juncture of her thighs. Damn it, in a minute he'd be getting hard, and when he stood up she'd be sure to see. He set his cup down with a bang.

She looked at him, startled.

"I've got work to do."

"Of course." She bit her lip.

He could read her face like a book. She wanted to ask him if he was going back to the cave, but after what had happened between them last night, she didn't have the nerve. He turned to go.

"Hawk."

He didn't think anyone else would have noticed the slight hesitation in her voice. "Yes?"

"Thank you for letting us have Zack's party here. He hasn't celebrated his birthday with his father for three years."

"De nada."

"Did I mention it will be the day after tomorrow?"

"I don't think you did, but that's fine with me."

"Two days after that, we'll be leaving." She was standing, too, watching him closely, as though for some sign. Of caring or indifference, he didn't know which. He couldn't afford to find out.

"I haven't lost track of your deadline, Sara. Ten days. Wasn't that the amount of time you gave me to find the treasure?"

"Well, yes. But—"

"Are you going back on your word?" he asked harshly not letting her finish. He didn't know any better way to break the tenuous thread of desire between them than to slice it cleanly in two, then cauterize the wound.

She looked as if he'd thrown a bucket of cold water in her face. His hand curled into a fist. God, he hadn't known how hard it would be to keep from wanting to take her in his arms and tell her he was sorry. But she was a growing addiction he couldn't afford to indulge. Someone had been nosing around the cave entrance— the upper one, just off the cliff path—and he didn't

want Sara tagging along with him the next time he went
into the cave, because he had no idea if someone would
be there, lying in wait. He could have told her all this,
asked her to give him her word not to follow him down
there, but she would have refused. It was easier just to
make her so mad she wouldn't come near him if her life
depended on it.

"No. No, of course not."

"Then let me get to work."

She didn't give up without a fight. "What's this all
about, Hawk? Has it got something to do with last
night?"

"Yes," he said, figuring he might as well be hung for
a sheep as a lamb. "You'd be a hell of a lay, Sara Riley.
I'm not going to deny I wanted you last night. And
don't bother trying to deny you wanted me, too. But
you told me to go away. I did. And I'm staying away.
Now all I ask of you is to do the same. Stay the hell out
of my way."

For a moment she looked as if she wanted to cry. It
was almost his undoing. Then her eyes darkened and
flashed with green fire. She picked up her coffee cup
and he tensed, waiting for her to throw it. She didn't.
She set it down again, very carefully.

"I gave you my word, Hawk. Including today, you
have five days left."

He held up his hand to stop her next words. "I know
what you're going to say next." He smiled, a mere upward curve of his mouth. "After that you're going to
make my life a living hell."

She called him a name he figured she'd never called
anyone before in her life and marched out of his sight.

Hawk slammed his fist into the table.

She was gone. Out of his hair. He'd be lucky if she said a civil word to him in the next five days. Which was exactly what he wanted.

Wasn't it?

CHAPTER ELEVEN

THE NEXT DAY, Elliot took Ben and Zack into the cave, but Sara stayed behind. With Olivia's help she translated a chocolate cake recipe from a dog-eared Spanish cookbook. The chocolate she grated into the batter was from cacao trees growing on the property. So were the other spices, as well as the honey she used for sweetener. The process to extract the chocolate from the cacao nuts was long and involved, according to Olivia's explanations. Sara was sorry she wouldn't be around at harvest time.

She had no idea if Hawk was in the cave with her brother and the boys or if he was somewhere nearby, waiting for his planeload of deadly explosives. She didn't know and didn't care, or so she told herself. She didn't want to have anything else to do with Elliot's mysterious landlord or his buried treasure. She wasn't going to set foot in that cave again, ever. She had no business traipsing around, acting like Kathleen Turner in *Romancing The Stone*—especially with a man like Hawk.

Sara slid the heavy metal cake pans into the bottled-gas oven and slammed the door, so firmly that Olivia turned from the sink, where she'd been cleaning potatoes for lunch, with raised eyebrows.

"Perdón," Sara said, wondering if the Tico woman could guess the reason for her sudden attack of ill temper was her boss.

"Está bien," Olivia replied and turned back to her vegetables.

Damn the gold, Sara thought to herself. Ever since she'd decided to come to Costa Rica, her life had been out of control. She didn't even feel like herself. Sometimes, if she took the shiny, rough-edged pieces of Spanish gold out of the box on the shelf in Elliot's cabin, held it in her hands and let it warm to her touch like a living thing, she even *felt* like a heroine in a movie or book. And she wanted this adventure, this fantasy time, to last forever.

It had to be something in the water or the air that made her feel so strange. There was no other explanation for it. Something that made her want to be the one to unearth the rest of Mary Hawk's treasure; made her wake in the night to slip into the hammock on her porch and watch the Big Dipper slide into the sea while she dreamed of a dark-haired pirate's kisses and his touch, when she should have been sound asleep. And damn it, that same nameless something made her hurt badly deep down in the center of her woman's soul, because she'd been rebuffed by a man the likes of J. C. Hawk.

Sara set the big crockery bowl she'd used to stir up the cake batter on the wooden counter with a thump.

"¿Señora?"

"I'm sorry, Olivia," Sara said in English. "I have a headache."

"¿Quisiera una aspirina?" she asked, pointing to the cupboard above Sara's head with the tip of her paring knife.

"Gracias." She did have a headache, she discovered. "I think I'll go sit on the porch until the cake is done."

"Bueno." Olivia went back to her vegetables, and Sara left the hot steamy kitchen for the slightly cooler porch, where she could be alone with her thoughts and her regrets. But not for long.

"Hi, Mom. We're back," Ben hollered, appearing at the top of the cliff steps. He bounded across the clearing, startling the bright little green-and-yellow parrots in the trees overhead. They flew away, screeching a warning that was immediately taken up by the small brown monkeys that played in the branches in the cool of the morning, before disappearing into the deeper jungle higher up the cliff in the heat of the afternoon. In the distance, a howler monkey took up the challenge, its barking cry echoing among the rocks and trees. Ben never even looked in that direction, paying no more attention to the exotic sights and sounds than he would to a dog chasing the neighbor's cat across the yard back in Fort Wayne. It never ceased to amaze Sara how quickly youngsters could adapt to new surroundings.

"Back so soon?" she asked, sipping the glass of fruit juice she'd used to wash down the aspirin.

"Zack got a case of the willies when he saw the skeletons in the cave," Ben told her. "Even though they're in those bags, it's pretty gruesome." Sara looked past him to where Zack and Elliot were coming into view at the top of the steps.

"Did they frighten him very badly?"

"Nah," Ben said, then qualified his answer. "Well, sorta. You can't really see anything, you know. And Uncle El wouldn't let him look inside the sacks. Zack's mad about that. He's such a little ghoul."

"Oh, Ben." Sara couldn't help but laugh at her son's cynical, worldly-wise tone. "Don't call your cousin a ghoul."

"It's the truth. Who do you think those guys were?" he asked, only to be interrupted by Zack.

"Aunt Sara," he cried, rushing up to her. "Why didn't you tell me you found those dead guys in the cave?"

"I didn't want to frighten you." Sara brushed his unruly brown hair back from his eyes.

"But that's where you got your pieces of eight. You should have told me."

"I don't like to think about it," Sara answered truthfully enough. "I didn't think you would, either."

"You wouldn't let that happen to me," he replied with so much trust Sara felt her throat grow tight. "And I think they really *were* pirates and killed each other in a fight over Hawk's treasure. But Dad says not." He was silent a moment, digesting those facts, spinning them around in his busy little mind until they came out more to his liking. "But he can't be sure," he said, grinning from ear to ear as he brandished an imaginary cutlass in one hand and fended off opponents with what was obviously an invisible dagger in the other.

"Settle down, wienie-brain," Ben ordered.

Zack ignored him. "If we could only find a sword or something, then I could prove they were really pirates and not just some poor dumb guys that got lost in the dark."

Sara smiled at Elliot over the boy's head. "I'm not so sure your object lesson about not going back into the cave alone hasn't boomeranged."

Elliot looked rueful. "I was thinking the same thing."

"I didn't realize the skeletons were still in the cave," she said, a slight frown between her eyes. "I thought Hawk said he would have them moved . . . somewhere more appropriate."

"There hasn't been time," Elliot explained.

"C'mon, Dad. I'll go get my glove and ball and we can play a game of catch before we eat," Zack hollered.

"You go get it. I'm going to sit here and talk to your aunt."

"Come with me, Ben," Zack ordered.

"Nope. Get it yourself." Ben had flopped down backward on the chair next to Sara's. He folded his arms across the top and rested his chin on them. "I'm stayin' here with Mom."

Zack stuck out his tongue and was off like a small T-shirted whirlwind. The silence that followed in his wake was deafening. Sara sat with her elbows on the table and her chin in her hands.

"Lord, sis. How have you put up with all that unfocused energy all these years?" Elliot asked, watching his son disappear up the path to the cabin.

"I had plenty of practice with Megan and Ben."

"I never acted like that," Ben defended himself. "I was the sweetest baby and a great little kid. I've heard you say so yourself."

"I must have been delirious," Sara said, making a face. "You were every bit as ornery as Zack. And just too smart for your own good."

"Yeah. That's me. The whiz kid of Lewis and Clark Junior High." He didn't sound all that pleased with the title.

"Ben, I thought you liked school."

"Yeah, well think again." He wouldn't look at her directly, but his eyes, behind his thick glasses, were full of misery.

Sara didn't know how to answer. This was a side of her son she'd never seen. "Why didn't you say anything about this before?"

"Because none of the rest of the guys were bigger than me before. This year I'm too small to play football, too slow to play basketball and too much of a dork to get a date with a girl. Wake up and join the real world, Mom. Being on the *A* honor role isn't enough to make up for being a computer nerd."

"Honey, you'll grow. You'll probably be as tall as your Uncle Elliot someday."

"Someday's too far away. I wish I could trade places with Zack. I'd rather be here than home any day. I could study with Uncle El, surf and snorkel with Luke. Go treasure hunting with Hawk. This place beats Fort Wayne all to—" he caught himself just in time "—pieces." He got up, flipped his chair around and left.

"Good grief," Sara said, caught between laughter and tears. "My son has entered adolescence with a vengeance."

"It would seem so," Elliot agreed, staring after him. "Do they always go off like that? Like a rocket going up?"

"Not always." Sara frowned. "But often enough. I thought after Megan I'd notice the signs. Obviously, I was deluding myself." She sighed. "I had no idea he was unhappy at school. His grades are excellent. He's in all the gifted programs. I know he was disappointed that he didn't make the football team last fall, but..."

"But this was totally unexpected, eh, sis?" Elliot looked at her, his head bent slightly to the side as though he were studying her, the same way he might study a specimen of flora or fauna in his lab.

"Yes, it is." She steepled her fingers, tapping her fingertips against her lips. "I guess Mom was right when she said she figures just about the time you get the hang of parenting, your kids up and leave for college or get married."

Elliot laughed. "We're a pretty sorry pair right now."

Sara laughed too. Not because she was feeling all that much better about Ben's sudden blowup, or the fact that she'd obviously been too preoccupied with her own problems this past year to notice how unhappy he was, but because Elliot was able to laugh at his own blunders as a parent as well. That was what was important at the moment.

In a few days she'd be home. They would all be home, back in their own world, safe and secure, and she could give her full attention to Ben's first faltering steps into adulthood. She would put aside the doubts that had gnawed away at her self-esteem since the divorce. She'd concentrate on her work and on her children. And she certainly wouldn't have the twin distractions of a treasure hunt and a modern-day pirate to take her mind off what mattered most. Everything would be fine again.

As soon as they were home.

The old-fashioned, wind-up timer in his kitchen went off with a chime.

"The cake's done," Sara said, relieved to be taken away from her thoughts. "Olivia and I made two so there'll be enough for everyone."

"Chocolate, I hope," Elliot said, rising from his seat when she did.

"What else? Zack's as big a chocaholic as you were at that age."

Elliot had just started commenting on the complicated process of extracting chocolate from the cacao bean when the radio crackled into life in the next room. An American voice with a nasal Texas twang sputtered angrily over the airwaves, demanding to be recognized. "Where's Hawk, damn it?" the voice yelled. "Yo there, Tyiskita. Do you read me?"

"Loud and clear," Elliot responded, grabbing the microphone as Sara followed him into the small, bare room that housed the radio receiver. "Go ahead."

"You ain't Major J. C. Hawk, are you?"

"No. I'm Dr. Elliot Carson. Major Hawk isn't here right now. Over."

"Well, you dang well better git him," the voice came back. "This here's Gunny Sergeant Willie Escobar and I got somethin' the major wants real bad."

"I'll take that," Hawk said, appearing suddenly at Sara's shoulder. "I'm here, Gunny. What's the holdup? Over."

"I'm still in San José, Major. Seems there's some gentlemen here that don't cotton to me bringing the cargo on down to Tyiskita. Leastways, not without a real hefty security fee, if you know what I mean."

"I know what you mean." The look on Hawk's face made Sara feel like running for cover. "How much more does Inspector Molinas need to satisfy the authorities?"

Willie named a sum in colones that made Elliot whistle and brought a curse to Hawk's lips. "That son of a—" Hawk thumbed the switch on the receiver. "Did you bring your gold card, Sergeant?" There wasn't a trace of anger in his voice, but there was tension and fury in the rigid muscles of his jaw and in every line of his steel-hard body.

"Never leave home without it, Major. Over."

"Pay the man, Gunny. I'll make it right when you get down here."

"Yes, sir. Don't look like I'll make it today, though. The weather here's just about as uncooperative as the *guarda*. I'm socked in. I'll try to get out first thing tomorrow morning, the good Lord willin'. Over."

"Roger. We'll look for you when we see you. Keep in touch."

"Yes, sir. I will. Over and out."

Hawk set the receiver down without making a sound. He might as well have slammed it to the floor. His face was completely expressionless when he turned around.

"You assured me Inspector Molinas wouldn't bother us anymore," Sara reminded him, unwisely.

"I was wrong." Hawk's voice was low and deadly. "And he's not the only one meddling where he doesn't belong."

"What do you mean by that?"

"Why did you take the boys back down to the cave?" Hawk asked, turning on Elliot so quickly her brother jumped. Sara remained standing in the same spot, almost directly between the two men.

"I thought if I showed Zack the remains, showed him how really dangerous that place is, it might curb his tendency to explore on his own."

"It sure could have." Could that be genuine concern Sara heard beneath the gruffness in Hawk's voice. "Someone's been in that cave besides us. The signs are everywhere," he continued.

"I didn't see a thing."

"I did." The words were a flat statement of fact. There was no contradicting them. Elliot didn't even try.

Sara had heard the boys come onto the porch. Now, even though she didn't turn around, she sensed they were standing behind her, listening.

"But what did you see? Who?" Elliot questioned.

"If I knew who it was, I'd have done something about it by now."

"Sorry, Hawk. You're right. Taking the kids in there was a foolish thing to do."

"Don't let it happen again."

"Perhaps you've forgotten whose money you just guaranteed to pay Señor Molinas's latest bribe," Sara said, just as quietly as he had spoken.

"I haven't forgotten."

"Good. Then you won't mind apologizing to my brother for being completely out of line."

Hawk remained very still.

"Sara, there's no apology necessary," Elliot cautioned, but she was on a roll.

"Are you threatening me, Sara Riley?" His voice was the whiskey-rough growl that rasped along her nerve endings like cold fire.

Sara could smell chocolate cake burning in the kitchen. She didn't move a muscle. "I'm just reminding you who's bankrolling this little expedition, that's all."

"Your brother is my partner, Sara, not you. And remember I'm in charge here. Everyone takes orders from me. Is that understood?" He looked as if he wanted to strangle her. If they were alone, perhaps he would have tried.

Or would he have kissed her instead? He had that same fierce light in his coal-black eyes, that same dark passion on his face she'd seen reflected in the moon-light the night he'd almost made love to her on her veranda.

Sara didn't know which option she dreaded more.

CHAPTER TWELVE

THE PARTY WAS a great success, but somehow the plans had gotten out of control and it snowballed into a village fete. By mutual consent, the location was moved from the lodge to the beach. Zackary was treated as one of Tyiskita's own. Sara was awed and humbled by these friendly, simple people who had so little but who shared it so graciously and so completely. Everything needed for the party was transported to a grove of palm trees on the beach near the creek. Chairs and tables were brought out of houses, covered with threadbare but spotlessly clean linen and plastic cloths. Chairs appeared from the school and the cantina. Children ate on blankets spread on the sand. Plates and glasses and silverware showed up from a dozen different homes.

Everyone was there—the mayor, the schoolchildren and their parents, Luke's young friends from the treasure salvage ship in the bay. Even the snake doctor, Ian Carter-Smith, put in an appearance. There was grilled fish and sweet potatoes roasted over open fires, black beans and rice with bits of chicken and beef—the staple diet of many Tico families. There was fresh fruit, juice and beer, and homemade liquor that was so strong it burned like fire going down and landed in your stomach with a rush of sudden heat.

After the second shot, Sara stuck to fruit juice.

The birthday cakes were a great success, even though one of them was a little overdone and the frosting was a sticky concoction of tinned marshmallow crème and coconut milk. The candles were a couple of sparklers donated by Zack's new friends, the Ramirez brothers. The children sang "Happy Birthday" in Spanish while Zack grinned from ear to ear.

One of the youngsters, a little girl, had just managed to break the piñata, and all the children were scrambling to get their share of Emily's candy, when the sound of a plane engine became audible above the surf. In the blink of an eye, half the village was headed for the airstrip.

Sara and Emily, as well as most of the village women, stayed behind, watching as the small plane taxied to a standstill about a hundred yards away. Sara recognized the plane that almost two weeks ago had brought them from San José. She pushed a strand of sea-blown hair out of her eyes and glanced across the clearing to where Hawk and Elliot were sitting on the porch of the cantina with the mayor and some of the other men, observing but not participating in the children's games. She had been uncomfortably aware of Hawk's presence at the gathering all afternoon. She could sense the tension in him, invisible to the others, who weren't aware of his every movement, his every gesture, as hour after hour passed and his friend did not arrive with the explosives he needed to begin the excavation of the cave. Perhaps the man wasn't coming today, either. In another hour it would be dark, too late for him to fly back to San José if Escobar didn't arrive soon.

Hawk stood up. His gaze was intent. Something about the unloading of the little plane had caught his interest. As so often before, Sara couldn't help but think of some great jungle cat sighting its prey. She turned her head to see what he was looking at.

A jaunty little man in Levi's, cowboy boots and a Harley-Davidson T-shirt had jumped out of the plane. He was carrying an ordinary nylon duffel in one hand and a faded Stetson in the other. He was short and round and nearly bald, only a monk's fringe of dark hair remaining above his ears. The top of his head was tanned as darkly as his face. Laugh lines spread out around his eyes and mouth. He looked a little like a Latino Santa Claus, except for his eyes, which were dark, intelligent and hard as agates. The eyes of a man who had seen and experienced far too much of the hidden, dangerous places at the edge of the world.

"You made it, Gunny," Hawk said, holding out his hand.

The smaller man handed him the duffel. "Not without a hell of a hassle." He grinned. "It's good to see you, Major."

"You too, Gunny. Where's your plane?"

"That damn Molinas upped the ante," Willie growled. "I told him to hell with it and walked away. Found this young guy willin' to bring me out here. For a lot more reasonable price. I'll pick up my plane tomorrow and head back home."

"Don't underestimate Molinas," Hawk warned.

Willie laughed. "Don't worry about that, Major. There ain't nothing about that plane that ain't in order down to the last little detail. You trained me better'n that."

"Thanks, Gunny."

"Don't mention it, sir."

They both turned to watch the little plane take off again. So did Sara. Luke's friends from the salvage ship

were on it, returning to San José to catch a flight for the
States, on their way back to school, Emily had said.
They'd been let go because the treasure salvagers were
running out of money and had found nothing of con-
sequence so far. Luke's friends hoped to be back for the
summer—if the dive was still in progress. Sara noticed
that Ben watched them go with wistful eyes. He'd enjoyed being included in the young men's activities.

"Let's put this stuff into the Jeep," Hawk said. "I
don't want anyone getting their hands on it."

"I saw the salvage ship in the bay," Gunny said.
"Not too many marker buoys floating, though, that I
noticed. Must mean they hadn't come up with much."
He was referring to the fact that if the treasure hunters
had found the wreckage of the *Mary Deere*, they would
most likely have attached floating buoys to the artifacts to mark their positions. Elliot had explained the
procedure to her several days before. Twice since then
Sara had climbed the ridge with her binoculars to watch
the activity onboard from the bench above Hawk's
house. Both times she'd seen no markers.

Hawk nodded once. "Looks that way. They're a
pretty tight-lipped bunch, but there doesn't seem to be
a lot of activity going on out there. They've been moving around a lot the past couple of days. They're out in
pretty deep water now. That's a bad sign. I'd say it's
nearly a bust."

"Too bad," his friend said, and chuckled. "Too
damn bad."

Hawk's mouth twisted in a reluctant smile. "Yeah,
it's too bad. Let's go."

"Sure thing. Ladies. At your service." He lifted a
finger to the brim of the big Stetson he'd put on as soon
as he'd cleared the wing of the plane.

"I'm Sara Riley," Sara said, offering her hand. "And this is Emily Wycheski."

"You a friend of the major's?" he asked, giving her a quick once-over that left no doubt in Sara's mind he cataloged everything about her physical appearance that he wanted to know.

"I—"

"You might say she's the treasurer of this operation," Hawk replied before Sara could answer. She got the feeling he hadn't introduced her himself not because he harbored a grudge from their argument the day before but because he was focused so completely on the business at hand. "And Emily is the village nurse. And schoolteacher."

"At least until the education ministry gets around to sending someone more qualified. Hi." Emily held out her hand.

"Pleased to meet you both." Hawk's friend folded his meaty hand around hers, gave it one quick shake and let go.

"Move it, Gunny. It's getting dark. I want this stuff safely stowed away before sunset."

"Aye, sir."

"Wow. He sounds like a bear with his paw in a trap," Emily said, shaking her head. "What set him off this time?"

"I did," Sara muttered. "As usual."

"Sounds interesting," Emily said, offering an opening.

"It's not." Sara just wasn't ready to confide in anyone about her contradictory feelings for J. C. Hawk. Teenage girls blew hot and cold about their affairs of the heart, not thirty-seven-year-old women with three children to raise. The less time she spent around Hawk, the sooner she'd be cured of her infatuation for him. It was as simple as that.

"If there's anything you want to send up the hill in the Jeep, you'd better be getting it over there," Elliot said, walking in their direction. He was carrying a baseball bat with a glove hooked over the end by its strap. Sara noticed a pickup game was getting underway on the beach. "Hawk won't be wanting to make many more trips down here tonight. I imagine he's got plans to discuss with Gunny Escobar."

"Do you know him?" Sara asked. If it weren't for his eyes, Sara might have been fooled into thinking Gunny Escobar was no different from the men she had known all her life, men like Wade and Elliot and her fellow teachers at Lewis and Clark. But his eyes were battle-weary, and they gave little away that he didn't want you to see.

Like Hawk's eyes.

"He was in the Marines with Hawk." Elliot slipped the glove on his hand and pounded his other fist against it, testing its feel. "Special forces, both of them. They've been friends for years. He's been down here once or twice since I've been here. He usually flies his own plane. Never stays long. Pretty mysterious fellow."

"Most of the men that come here looking for Hawk are that way," Emily observed. "Lost souls."

She was right. Veterans like Gunny Escobar, with no kith or kin or country to call their own, would come looking for Hawk. A natural leader, the kind who inspired loyalty in others, he would draw them like a magnet. The men who served under him would follow him to hell and back. They would die for him, if necessary. She thought of the dark shadows of regret that sometimes haunted his eyes. In the past, some of them had died, Sara realized with sudden, blinding insight. Some of them had.

And if the force of his personality inspired such loyalty in the men who had served under him, what chance did a woman have against that dark, dangerous pull, if he wanted to make her his?

Not much, Sara thought, feeling the familiar, unwelcome tug on her own heartstrings. Not much.

GUNNY ESCOBAR had come through for him again. But Hawk didn't like the risk his friend had taken just to help him out. Gunny had a wife and three kids back in Houston. He had a good job, a house, a mortgage. All the things they'd dreamed about and denied themselves all those years.

This whole thing was getting out of hand. He wouldn't be a bit surprised if Gunny got back to San José and found out Molinas had confiscated his plane. The war was long over and behind them—all the wars, both little and big. He couldn't ask Gunny to risk his neck or his plane again. But he had. The siren call of Mary Hawk's gold was just too strong. He had to have it. He needed it to save and restore his own little corner of paradise.

And the sooner, the better. He didn't like the signs he'd noticed of someone snooping around the cave. One or possibly two men, who were either too dumb to cover their tracks or so sure of themselves they didn't have to. Either way spelled trouble.

Once they got up to his house, he would brief Gunny in detail. But not here, in front of half the village, with enough explosives in the duffel to take out everything and everybody in a hundred-yard radius. The back of his neck tingled, a sign they were being watched. He spun around. Sure enough, they were being followed.

"Who's back there?" Gunny asked, his hand going casually to his pocket.

"Just about everyone in the village who can walk," Hawk replied in disgust.

Gunny turned also. It wasn't half the village following them, but close to a dozen men, women and children. Sara Riley led the way, with what appeared to be a box of cooking utensils and other assorted paraphernalia from the picnic.

"Hawk, wait a moment, please."

Gunny laughed. "We're losin' our touch, man. How'd we let them sneak up this close?"

Hawk gave him a look that shut him up. For about ten seconds.

"Looks like your lady friend is in charge."

"She's not my lady friend. She's about the most aggravating female I've ever met."

Gunny gave a low whistle. "That bad, huh?" He grinned.

Hawk did too. "She's that bad."

"Hawk?"

"Yes, Sara." He waited. Her remarkable eyes narrowed slightly and he realized with a small but distinct shock to his nervous system that she saw through his mask of outward calm. She sensed the roiling impatience, the need for action that ate away at his gut. He knew, as well, that she didn't understand what drove him, but that she was aware of its urgency all the same.

"Would you please take these things back up the cliff with you in the Jeep? They're heavy and would be hard to carry up the steps."

She pulled her gaze from his and smiled at Gunny Escobar. "Have you eaten?"

"Yes, ma'am. In San José."

"Call me Sara, please."

"Thank you, Sara." He touched the brim of his Stetson once more.

"There's plenty of food left," she offered a second time. "You're welcome to it."

"That's very neighborly of you—"

"Gunny." Hawk's voice cracked like a whip. "We have work to do."

He touched the brim of his hat again. "Some other time."

"Dad, come on. We're waiting for you to start the game." Zack joined the small crowd around the Jeep, pulling impatiently at Elliot's arm. "*Vámonos!* Hurry up."

"Just let me help your Aunt Sara get this stuff into the Jeep."

"Thanks, El." Sara handed over the box, a little relieved to be rid of its weight. The afternoon was warm and sultry and thunder rumbled off in the distance, promising one of the quick drenching showers that came more and more frequently as the days went by and the rainy season drew closer.

"Here, I'll take that." Hawk put one foot on the side of the Jeep and slid the duffel containing the explosives onto the seat. He turned back to take the box from Elliot and froze in his tracks.

"*Terciopelo,*" someone hissed.

Sara's throat closed on a scream.

On the floor at Hawk's feet, not one but two small snakes lay coiled around the accelerator. Though only a little more than a foot long, they were marked with the same pattern of velvety black and yellow, light and dark, as the adult snakes whose pictures Sara had seen in one of Elliot's books, except for their tails, which were yellow at the end.

"Don't move, Major." Gunny might as well have saved his breath. Hawk had turned to stone. One snake was only inches from his shoe. Not the heavy work-boots he usually wore around the compound, Sara noted with a sinking sensation of dread in the pit of her stomach, but ordinary running shoes that left his ankle and calf unprotected. One of the small heads lifted as though scenting the air. The yellow tail vibrated against the floorboards of the Jeep.

"*Rabo amarillo*—yellow tail," someone whispered and the children took off running for the beach to tell the others.

"What'll I do, Major?" Gunny asked, in such a low voice that Sara, standing only inches away, had to strain to hear his words.

"Nothing." Hawk's reply was softer still.

Elliot stood quietly, but he was no longer holding the box of kitchen supplies. Instead, he had his hand curled around Zack's new baseball bat.

"I've got my knife." Gunny's hand went to the top of his boot.

"You can't kill both of them," Elliot pointed out.

"I kin try."

"No." Barely above a whisper, Hawk's voice still demanded obedience. "I've seen a severed head chase a man a hundred feet into the bush."

"Jesus," Gunny said reverently.

Sara closed her eyes on the nightmare image, one she was sure would haunt her dreams for weeks to come.

"Get Ian Carter-Stone."

"The snake doctor?" Sara couldn't believe what she'd heard. Surely Hawk wasn't going to trust his life to a man who was for all intents and purposes his enemy.

"Don't argue, Sara. Bring him here."

Zack was hanging on to her arm like a vise. "Let go, honey. We've got to find the snake doctor," she said.

"He's right there." Zack pointed with a shaking finger. "He's coming right now."

Sara looked over her shoulder. The small black man was making his leisurely way toward the Jeep, surrounded by a cadre of village men and women.

"So, Hawk, you got yo'self in bad trouble, hey mon?"

"You could say that." Hawk hadn't taken his eyes off the two snakes. Now they were both awake, heads moving restlessly.

"You want I should charm dem away, hey?"

"Do it, damn you," Gunny Escobar growled, unsheathing his knife, deadly and slim, from his boot.

"Hey mon. No knives, okay? Hawk here, he might get bit 'fore I can do somet'ing about ol' Tommgoff, hey."

"Don't hassle me, man."

"Gunny." Hawk's voice was as quiet and deadly as the snakes.

"Yes, sir." The knife disappeared. Ian Carter-Stone looked pleased.

"*Silencio!*" he said, throwing up his hands. The murmur of the crowd died away. Here and there a child sniffled in fear and was shushed by its mother. Ian Carter-Stone was carrying a big stick, gnarled and carved, polished to a smooth dull sheen. He brandished it in large circles that grew progressively smaller.

His words were a hypnotic singsong mixture of Spanish, English and Carib.

What he said made no sense to Sara. The only reality for her was Hawk—the tension in his arms and shoulders, visible beneath the soft white cotton of his shirt; the corded muscles of his forearm and hand on the roll bar of the Jeep.

The snakes grew still. One had actually draped itself across the toe of Hawk's shoe. Gunny Escobar moved like a small dense shadow until he stood behind Hawk. He reached out, curling his hand around Hawk's belt, as though to jerk him backward, away from the danger. No one moved. No one spoke. Everyone seemed as intent on willing the snakes out of the Jeep as Ian Carter-Stone.

Everything grew dim. Sara blinked and realized that the sun had dropped below the horizon. The short tropical twilight had descended while they waited. One snake now began to move, crawling over its brother, across Hawk's shoe, dropping down onto the sand, where it coiled, still watching, or seeming to watch, the snake doctor's stick. Sara held her breath. Zack's grip on her arm hurt, but she didn't move a muscle. Slowly the other snake followed suit, lingering, to drape itself with deadly grace over the running board of the Jeep, swiveling its head to look first at Hawk, then at Ian Carter-Stone. Then slowly, fluidly, it dropped onto the sand—to its death.

Gunny's knife flashed between Hawk's legs, pinning the lance-shaped head to the sand. Moving faster than she'd ever seen him, Elliot killed the coiled snake with Zack's baseball bat. It was over before anyone could speak or move.

"Good," Ian Carter-Stone said finally, breaking the silence. "You have killed dem. Good. Now de big ones will not blame me. Dat is as it should be."

Hawk lifted his head from the death throes of the second snake. "I'm in your debt."

Ian Carter-Stone laughed, a sound much larger than the man himself. "I know dat, Hawk. And I won't forget."

"I ain't from this part of the world," Gunny said menacingly, totally unimpressed by Ian Carter-Stone's performance. "But where I come from, snakes don't naturally crawl into vehicles."

"*Terciopelo,* he ain't just any snake," the snake doctor replied, unperturbed. "He likes peoples, mon. Plenty of rats and mice 'round where people be. Good eatin'. Easy pickin's." He shrugged. "Who knows how dem little ones got where dey was? Hawk, mon, he just lucky I be here. And I be in a charitable mood." He signaled one of his followers to put the limp bodies of the two snakes in a bucket and carry them back to his house. "De more trees dey be here, Hawk, de more little yellow tails dey breed. Puttin' trees back where dey ain't none now—it not always be for de best, maybe." He laughed again, but there was no mistaking the warning in his voice. "Be careful where you walk, mon." The gathering darkness cloaked him in shadow before he'd gone twenty feet.

"What the hell did he mean by that?" Gunny asked, kneeling to clean off the blade of his knife in the sand.

"Let's just say the good doctor and I don't see eye to eye on the future of Tyiskita and leave it at that."

"Leave it at that?" Sara couldn't believe her ears. What he'd told her before was the truth. There were others after the treasure who would stop at nothing to get what they wanted. "Gunny's right. Someone may have just tried to kill you. How can you stand there and do nothing?"

"What do you suggest I do?" Hawk asked, looming over her in the near darkness. "Beat a confession out of the snake doctor? Round up a few of the village men and slice off an ear or two until one of them spills his guts?"

"Crude but effective." Gunny saw the look of horror Sara directed at him and looked sheepish. "Just jokin', ma'am."

"Don't be ridiculous." Sara was acutely aware of Zack and Ben listening, enthralled by the conversation. How could these two men talk so casually of violence and attempted murder in front of children? Hawk's face was as hard and set as a mask carved of granite. He looked absolutely feral in the lurid light of the sunset, as deadly as the snakes someone might have placed in his Jeep. Surely it was only her imagination that made her believe she saw regret, mixed with anger, in his midnight-dark eyes.

"C'mon, Sara. That's what you're thinking I'd like to do, or what Gunny and I *would* do if we had the chance—murder and torture innocents, rape and pillage, rob old ladies and defile children. Men like us with no conscience and no soul."

"That's not true! I never said such a thing!" God, could the man read her very thoughts?

His next words made her blood run cold. "You don't have to say it, Sara. You only have to think it and I can see it in your eyes."

CHAPTER THIRTEEN

MOONSET. The stars overhead were brighter, closer than ever. There had never been stars like this in Indiana. Sara had no idea what time it was or how long she'd been awake. She sat on the low stone wall of the veranda, a long-sleeved, cotton shirt covering her nightgown to ward off mosquitoes, and waited for dawn. She'd never been prone to insomnia, not even the first few miserable weeks after Wade had moved out of their bedroom and out of her life. But since she'd met Hawk, it was almost a permanent condition.

But tonight her dreams had been different. There were no dark, exotic fantasies, no misty, sleep-world fulfillments of urges and desires she denied herself in the bright hot light of day. Tonight her dreams had been frighteningly real and filled with blood and danger. Was someone trying to kill Hawk?

She shivered in the warm night breeze. Somewhere in the trees below the cottage, an early rising parrot squawked a tentative greeting but got no reply. A few invisible creatures rustled in the grass at her feet, and Sara thought once more of the beautiful and deadly ferde-lance—a night hunter, Elliot had said, silent and lethal. She drew her knees up to her chin and wrapped her arms around her legs.

Surely she was mistaken in her assumption. Why would anyone want to kill Hawk before he found the treasure? It was possible the snakes in the Jeep had been only a bizarre accident. And if not, it was likely the incident wasn't even connected with the treasure hunt, but had to do with Hawk's opposition to the coming of the big hotels along the beach.

She wasn't so naive and sheltered that she couldn't understand that in this part of the world these things happened. People were less restricted in their actions and in their use of violence to resolve a dispute. They didn't file lawsuits and go to court at the drop of a hat. Men settled their differences one-to-one, *mano a mano*, some more directly, more honorably than others. It was simply the way things were done.

Joseph Hawk certainly didn't need her to watch out for him. The prudent thing to do was stay out of his way. But in the morning, she'd talk to Elliot, make sure Hawk didn't go into the cave alone if it could be helped. Just to be on the safe side.

Sara smiled to herself. She could easily imagine what Hawk would think of her appointing herself his bodyguard. He was the last man on earth who wanted or needed a woman to look out for him. And he wouldn't be grateful to her for siccing Elliot on him. Elliot had enough trouble looking out for himself.

Poor El. She had to talk to him about other things than the possible attempt on Hawk's life, his future with his son foremost among them. She'd been overoptimistic about their relationship, expecting too much too soon. She'd flown off the handle with Hawk when he'd pointed that out to her, because it hurt so badly to think of Zack leaving her. But pain, no matter how excruciating, didn't alter the facts. Zack belonged with his father.

Maybe she could come back to Tyiskita in the summer. She'd read somewhere that the rains let up for a few weeks in late July or August every year. Little League season would be over, football practice not yet underway. Zack would be ready for a new adventure. She could bring him back then....

Sara dropped her head onto her knees. She could feel tears burn behind her eyes but blinked them away. Zack did belong with his father; it was as simple as that. She wasn't selfish, as Hawk had accused her of being. She loved her nephew and wanted what was best for him, that was all. But Hawk had been right about one thing. She was the one who would have to make most of the sacrifices if Zack was to have a chance to learn to love his father. She would have to step back and let him choose between them. And she would have to very subtly tip the scales so that Elliot would win. Again, just as Hawk had said she must do.

Hawk. Why was it that no matter where her thoughts took her, they always came circling back to him? Sara lifted her head and rested it against the cypress post at her back. Why did he have to haunt her darker musings, as well as her fantasies? She was far too vulnerable to him. She would have to work very hard on strengthening her defenses against him if she planned to return to Tyiskita in the summer. She couldn't afford the distraction he presented to her senses and her reasoning.

She had no choice in the matter, really. Because she probably would come back to Tyiskita. For Elliot and Zack's sake, not her own.

The first faint glimmer of the false dawn made pencil streaks across the horizon. Pale phosphorescence tipped the slow curl of waves far below, along the beach. Sara turned her head toward the darkness at the top of the ridge where Hawk's house stood. *Hawkslair.*

Two more days and she would be gone, back to the cold rain and slush of the tail end of a long Indiana winter. She had no intention of standing by her threat to disrupt the treasure hunt—she'd decided that sometime during the long sleepless night. She would tell Hawk so this morning at breakfast. And she would tell him one more thing more before she left: the whole truth. That she wished more than anything else that she could be with him at the end of the search.

She was staring directly at Hawk's house when the explosion occurred. A ball of red-and-gold fire lit up the night like a small sun. The concussion rolled across the ridge like a wave, shaking the very foundation of her cabin. The sound was deafening. Sara was on her feet and running before the echo had died away. It looked as if half the cliff top was on fire. Smoke billowed and rolled above the trees.

She thought of the dynamite Hawk had stored up there. She remembered the innocuous green duffel bag full of sophisticated explosives that Gunny had arrived with yesterday. Some or all of those explosives had just detonated. There was no other explanation.

She ran as fast as she could in the half light of the breaking dawn, her heart in her throat. What would she find when she reached Hawk's house? Flaming debris and his lifeless body trapped in the rubble? No one in the vicinity could have lived through such a blast.

The ghastly light of the fire failed to penetrate the darkness beneath the great trees that formed a high archway over the path to Hawk's house. "Damn it!" Breathless, Sara retraced her steps to the dining porch, to pick up one of the flashlights kept there for forgetful guests. She stubbed her toe on the leg of a chair and only then realized she wasn't wearing any shoes.

She didn't have time to go back for them. She refused to think about what might be lurking along the edges of the path. On she went, half running, half walking, a stitch in her side making each breath she took an agony. Below her she could hear shouts from the village, and when she paused for a moment at an opening along the cliff's edge, she noticed lights go on in the salvage boat offshore.

She looked back down the path and saw bobbing lights. Elliot. And the boys. She didn't wait for them to catch up. Fear drove her forward at a dangerous pace along the steep path. Twice she slipped and almost fell. She barely noticed the pain in her feet. She had to get to Hawk. That was all that mattered.

She saw him almost at once as she reached the clearing near his house. He was standing with his back to the flames, a dark shape against the remains of a still-burning building that looked suspiciously like an outhouse. He was wearing jeans and shoes and nothing else, and he looked blessedly whole and unharmed as he directed the spray from a garden hose onto the smoldering thatched roof of his house. It wasn't a big house, Sara realized as she hurried toward him, but it was situated to take best advantage of the sea breezes and the spectacular views of forested shoreline and the Golfo Dulce beyond.

The greatest damage appeared to be at the back—the kitchen and bathroom, she guessed. There were a couple of holes in the thatch, and the roof of a small porch had collapsed on one end.

"What the hell are you doing here?" Hawk yelled over the sounds of the fire and the small gasoline engine pumping water up the hill from an invisible source of supply.

"What do you mean, what am I doing here?" Sara hollered back, her fear for his safety instantly transforming into anger at his aggrieved tone. She'd all but killed herself getting to him and he acted as if she were the last person on earth he wanted to see. "I couldn't sleep. I was sitting out on the porch and half the hillside blew up in my face." She looked around. "Where's Gunny?" Her fear returned in a dizzying rush.

"Almost to San José, I hope. He hitched a ride on a fruit truck late last night. The road to Golfito's a bitch after dark, but Miguel is a good driver. I want Gunny on his plane and headed back to the States before Molinas even knows he's gone."

"Thank God. I thought..." Sara didn't finish the sentence, only stared at the remains of the outhouse.

"Don't worry. No one was inside." Hawk turned the hose on the still-burning building. Thankfully, the flames seemed confined to the small clearing behind the house. The trees and the undergrowth at the top of the cliff, even at the end of the dry season, were too green to burn easily.

"What was inside?" Sara asked, her voice still raised to carry above the noise of the pump and the flames.

"Don't be dense, Sara. What do you think was inside?"

"The explosives Gunny brought for excavating the cave?" A fine mist from the hose drifted down around her, wetting her hair, her nightgown and her shirt until the damp cotton clung to her like a second skin.

Hawk gave her a long, hard look. His face was all angles and shadows in the harsh glow of the dying fire.

His chest and arms were smudged with soot, his skin bronzed by heat and light.

"It was the dynamite. The other stuff's still in the duffel. Under my bed."

"But shouldn't you get it out?" His house could be a smoldering time bomb if the explosives were still inside.

"No need." The words were barely more than a growl. "It's pretty much harmless without the detonators, and they went up with the shed."

"Hawk, I'm—"

"Where the hell are your shoes?"

"What?"

"Your shoes, woman. Don't tell me you climbed all the way up here barefoot." He dropped the hose, grinding out a string of curses the likes of which Sara had never heard before in her life. "You're lucky you didn't fall and break your neck. Or worse."

Sara didn't even want to think of what he meant by "worse." "I didn't have time to think about shoes. I told you, it looked like you and your house and everything else for a mile around here blew up."

He was advancing on her like a relentless, half-naked demon from some fiery corner of hell. "That's no excuse for pulling a harebrained stunt like that. Did it ever occur to you that there just might be more of those yellow tails loose up here? Fer-de-lances have very large litters. Fifty or sixty of the little devils at a time." Sara took her eyes off him for just a moment and glanced at the ground, though she knew it was a foolish thing to do with him so close. She was right. In the space of three heartbeats he'd covered the space between them.

"More snakes?" she asked in a half squeak, half moan, and he knew he had her full attention at last. He scooped her up in his arms and swung around, looking for a safer place to set her down. She had come charging up here to do battle with his enemies just as she would if he were one of her own. It was a seductive thought, to belong, to be one with another human being. He could feel her breasts move against him and realized she was naked beneath the thin cotton shirt and nightgown. And aroused, although she'd deny that fact with her dying breath. She was very much aware of him as a man. And God help him, he was just as aware of her as a woman.

"Who's doing this, Hawk?" After the first few steps, she stopped struggling to be put down. She wound her arms around his neck, but leaned a little away from him. He wondered if she realized the tips of her breasts brushing against his skin with every breath she took was even more erotic, more tempting, than having their soft weight pressed fully against him. She looked over his shoulder at the remains of the old outhouse. Then she looked at him, frowning. Her stubborn expression and the fear and anxiety in her gorgeous green eyes demanded a response. "Who wants you dead?"

He had his suspicions, but he wasn't about to tell her what they were. She was as brave as a she-tiger defending her young, but that didn't make her any more qualified to cope with a man, or men, bent on destroying another human being. He could fight his own battles. He'd been doing that for twenty-five years. Keeping her in the dark, until she flew back to San José with the kids, shouldn't be that difficult. As it turned out, he didn't even have to make up a lie. The words were no sooner out of her mouth than Elliot and the two boys burst into the clearing.

The fire was dying quickly. The outhouse had been the first permanent structure he and his father had built at Tyiskita, the summer before he graduated from high school and went into the Marines. Those weeks had been the last significant time he'd spent with his father, who had died the following year. They had built the outhouse of stone and wood and had made it to last. But even it couldn't withstand a half-dozen sticks of dynamite.

"Hawk! Sara?" Elliot pulled up short and looked around. "What happened? Are you all right? Where's Escobar?"

"We're fine. And Gunny's on his way back to San José to claim his plane before Molinas gets the bright idea to impound it for one reason or another."

"Aunt Sara, what's Hawk carrying you around in your nightgown for?" Zack demanded. "Are you hurt?"

"I'm fine," Sara assured him.

"How'd you get up here so quick, Mom?" Ben asked.

"She came running up here without her shoes on," Hawk growled, depositing Sara on a picnic table in the middle of the yard. "There's nothing you two can do here. Go back and get her some shoes. Now." He wasn't in the mood to explain everything to a couple of kids.

Ben stared at him from behind owlish glasses, but he didn't look scared. He also didn't make a move to obey.

"Move it!" Hawk barked out the command just as he would have in the military. And he was obeyed just as readily.

Sara started to climb down off the table, her mouth open to protest. At his growled "Stay put until they bring your shoes," she sat down with a muffled word or two that didn't sound very schoolteacherlike and gave him a dirty look.

"The next time your life's in danger, count me out," she said mutinously. "And stop ordering my boys around as though they were in boot camp."

Hawk didn't smile, but he wanted to. What a hell of a day. And night. Sara looked as if she'd been dragged through a hedge backward, but she still had a lot of fight in her. She was a trooper, he had to give her that. And sexy as hell. Still, the last thing he needed was a barefoot avenging angel on his hands when he didn't know whether whoever had blown up his outhouse had also dumped a bucketful of snakes with bad dispositions in his yard as well.

"Go home, Sara," he said, surprised to hear the softness, the indulgence, in his own voice.

"You told me not to get off this table without my shoes."

His amusement, if not his respect for her, vanished in a spurt of familiar irritation. She was absolutely the most obstinate woman he'd ever met. If he gave her an inch she demanded a mile. He wondered if she was that way in bed—giving everything she had and demanding everything her love could give back in return. Making love to Sara Riley should have been the furthest thing from his mind just then, but it wasn't. His awareness of her was always there, right below the surface. Like an itch that needed to be scratched. It took a hell of a lot of willpower not to let her see that need.

He'd begun to have the sneaking suspicion over the last few days that she might be able to read his mind. It was a disconcerting notion, one whose implications he didn't want to deal with at the moment. It put him at a disadvantage, something he didn't like. In dealing with

Sara Riley, he'd vowed always to keep the upper hand, so he didn't give her the satisfaction of a reply. He turned to her brother instead. "There's nothing much more we can do up here. I'll get Manuel and Olivia's husband and a couple of others up here later to fix the roof. There's nothing else we can do now."

"Sure thing," Elliot said, gazing at the glowing embers of the outhouse. "First the snakes and now this. It isn't a coincidence. We need to do something about whoever's behind it. And fast." He turned on his heel just as the boys reappeared in the clearing, breathless and disheveled, with a pair of sandals for Sara.

Ben handed the shoes to his mother, who bent to put them on. "Luke and Emily and Olivia and about half of the village are on their way up," the boy gasped. "Is the fire out?"

"Yes," Sara said.

"C'mon, boys," Elliot said. "Come with me. We'll head them off. There might be more snakes around. Let's not take any chances. Sara, are you coming?"

"As soon as I get permission," she said, not quite looking Hawk in the eye, still frowning mutinously.

Hawk sighed. His arms and shoulders stung like hell from the burns caused by sparks from the burning outhouse. His throat was raw from breathing in the acrid smoke, and he was dead-tired. Yet he was more than ready to do battle with his self-appointed guardian angel. "She'll be along in a minute, Carson."

Sara must have heard the private challenge in his voice. Her head came up. Their eyes locked and after a brace of heartbeats she looked away.

"If that's the way you want it." Elliot glanced up at the dawn-pink sky. "It'll be daylight in a few minutes. I'll have Olivia get breakfast started."

When he'd left, Hawk walked over and shut off the water pump. Its steady, pulsing beat died away. Suddenly they were alone again, with the scent of smoke and cordite heavy in the air and the sound of disturbed birds and monkeys coming awake all around them. It was almost daylight. Sara could see Hawk very plainly now. His chest and arms were streaked with soot. His dark hair, like hers, was wet from the mist of the hose. She shivered a little in the dawn chill. She was wet to the skin and she knew her hardened nipples were plainly visible beneath the thin cotton shirt and gown.

"You'd better get something on those burns," she said gruffly because she didn't want him to know how much the thought of him in pain affected her. She wanted to go to him, kiss the hurts away, hold him close against her and keep him safe.

Hawk. The victor of a thousand battles, big and small. The last man on earth who needed a woman to protect him.

"I'll take care of them later."

"Get your first-aid kit and I'll do it for you." He was suddenly standing very close. She could smell the smoke in his hair, the musky scent of his sweat, feel the heat of his body on her arms and legs through her clothes. Frustration and desire washed over her in a suffocating wave. Couldn't he see that she wanted to help?

"Later," he said, moving even closer.

"Aren't you in pain?"

"Yes. But you get used to it." He was so close now, her knees touched his chest. She put both hands on the picnic table, resisting the urge to curl up in a ball to escape his pull on her senses.

She closed her eyes. If she lived a thousand years, she'd never understand the life he'd lived, the dangers he must have faced. Was that what attracted her to him? That he was so completely beyond the realm of her experience? That he was exciting and dangerous and the sexiest man she'd ever met?

"Sara."

"Yes?"

"You'd better leave." His voice sounded rougher, even more sensual than usual.

She opened her eyes, willing into submission her longing to be held in his arms. "I'm staying. I don't like the idea of you being up here alone. You'd be a sitting duck if someone was up on the top of the ridge with a gun."

"You're a bloodthirsty woman," he said with one of his rare smiles. "No one's going to shoot me in my own backyard."

Sara's breath caught in her throat. When he looked at her like that, she could almost believe he cared.

"Someone tried to blow you to smithereens in your own backyard," she reminded him, her hands on his shoulders to keep him from leaning closer.

"Point well taken. So you're willing to stay and be my personal guardian?" he asked, levering his body forward so that his mouth was mere inches from hers.

"I . . ." She had no idea how to answer.

"I'd like nothing better than to go inside, take a shower and a long nap. Want to come with me?"

"No." Her brain refused before her heart could say yes. "I mean . . ."

"You mean you'd never think of doing such a thing with a man you barely know and don't trust, is that it?"

"No. I wouldn't do that with any man when there was the possibility of my children walking in on us."

"That's no excuse, Sara." His hands on her hips were firm and hard. "The boys won't come back up here without permission. You know that." He pulled her forward. She raised her knees to keep him at bay, but he parted her legs and pulled her against him before she could complain. She wasn't wearing anything under her nightgown. It was pushed up high on her thighs and she was pressed intimately to him, the denim of his jeans shockingly, arousingly rough against her skin.

"Hawk, don't," she said, but he ignored her half-hearted plea. In reality she didn't want him to stop. She wanted to feel his hands against her breasts, his erection against the softest, most intimate parts of her body. She wanted to know, once in her life, what it meant to be desired and possessed by a man who didn't play by the rules, who took life by the throat and shaped the world to his liking.

He kissed her, his mouth demanding, his tongue thrusting past her teeth to seek the hot moistness inside. She kissed him back, her tongue dueling with his, her breasts crushed against his chest, her hands curled possessively into his thick dark hair to hold him even closer.

He groaned low in his throat and strained against her, his hands holding her tightly, his body hard and exciting against her softness. "Damn it, Sara. You're driving me crazy." He pushed at the shirt she was wearing, then the straps of her nightgown, baring her breasts. He took one rosy nipple in his mouth, and Sara's back arched responsively as she strove to be closer still. He rocked back and forth against her, slowly, rhymthically, a promise of what was to come.

She opened her eyes. A flock of brilliant blue-and-yellow parakeets flew by on their way to feast on the fruit trees in the orchard. A half-grown monkey had come to investigate the fire and stayed to watch their lovemaking with curious black eyes. Hawk transferred his mouth to her other breast, and for a moment Sara lost track of time and her surroundings. She clung to him as though he were the only solid reality in the universe. She wanted him to lay her down on the table and make love to her, under the pink-and-gray dawn sky. It didn't matter that he wanted only her body and nothing more. That was all she required of him in return.

Wasn't it?

She felt his hand on her inner thigh and shivered. It made no difference that this would be a one-time thing. That back in Fort Wayne she would never for a moment consider giving herself to J. C. Hawk, almost a stranger, a hard and dangerous man. It only mattered that his hands and his mouth and his sex were driving her to madness.

As if from a long way away, she heard the sound of his zipper being lowered. She closed her eyes again, allowing the multitude of sensations whirling through her body to assume control of her actions.

"Sara?" She didn't let herself hear the hesitation in his voice. He leaned back from her. Warm, humid air swirled between them, feeling chilly on her sensitized breasts and the soft hidden places of her body.

"Don't stop, Hawk. Please." She tried to pull him close once again, to recapture that sense of being completely and totally in his power, unable to save herself, unwilling to try.

"No." This time there was no hesitation in his voice. "Look at me, Sara." He framed her face with his hands, demanded her obedience with no more than the slightest inflection of his voice. She opened her eyes reluctantly. "If I'm going to make love to you, I want you to look at me."

She couldn't pretend any longer. She had thought for one glorious moment that she could give herself to him with no thought for the future or the past. She'd been wrong. "Is that what we'd be doing, Hawk? Making love? Or having sex?"

"Does it matter what you call it?"

"Yes," she said wearily, feeling the sensual beat of need and desire in her veins drain away, fade into reality. "It does make a difference to me."

"Why?"

"I—I'm not the kind of woman who can take pleasure from a man and walk away afterward without a backward look. I need . . . a connection."

"But you don't want a connection to me, is that it, Sara Riley?"

Again he'd come right to the heart of the matter. She could not allow herself to even dream of loving him. It was impossible.

"Yes."

"But you want me so bad you can taste it." He hadn't made any move to release her.

"Yes. But that doesn't make it right."

Their lower bodies were still pressed intimately together. He still wanted her—that was obvious—but he held himself deadly still, already sealed away from her into a steel-hard shell of his own making.

"What will make it right, Sara? If I tell you I love you? That I can't live without you? Pretty lies—is that what you need to hear?"

She wouldn't allow herself to believe she might have hurt him. She would only be projecting her own emotions onto his. She'd seen that kind of self-deceptive behavior among friends back in Fort Wayne who were having trouble in their relationships. She wasn't going to fall into that trap.

"No. That would only make it worse when I wake up in the morning and have to look at myself in the mirror. I don't want to complicate our relationship even more than it already is."

He looked as if he wanted to shake her. "At least tell the truth. You won't make love to me because you're afraid. Afraid you might not be able to hold yourself back. That you might just lose control. That you might like it so much you'll never want to leave, go back to your safe and ordered little world in Fort Wayne."

"You're a bastard, Hawk," she said, pulling her nightgown back into place. She didn't even have the satisfaction of shoving him away from her. He stepped back, yanking up his zipper, his dark, unreadable eyes burning holes into her skin.

"No. I'm just Hawk," he said, his voice as insolent as his stance. He watched as she tugged the hem of her nightgown down around her knees. She was too preoccupied to notice the muscles bunching and knotting in his jaw, the tension in every line and angle of his body. "I still want you, but I'm not going to beg you for it. And I'm not going to make you any promises I can't keep. Don't expect them."

"I never asked for any." Sara hopped down off the picnic table. She was tired and humiliated, and her body still thrummed with desire so strong it made her heart hammer in her chest. No woman wanted to be treated like a sex object. She couldn't fault Hawk for feeling the same. "I'm sorry," she said, humiliation and frustration staining her cheeks. "I shouldn't have behaved the way I did. I'm sorry if I came on too strong. I'm not very good at physical relationships. The only man I've ever slept with in my whole life was my ex-husband. And frankly, he wasn't the world's greatest lover."

"And you think I might be?" he asked, looking slightly mollified.

She'd gone this far; she might as well keep telling the truth. "Yes," she said, already moving backward, away from the picnic table and away from him. "I think you might be."

She turned and almost ran out of the clearing, not looking around once. What had happened back there? Hawk had offered her his body, the pleasure they could give each other and nothing more—exactly what she'd indicated that she wanted from him. The kind of relationship he would understand—no strings attached, a short, intense love affair, the makings of memories to last a lifetime. But in the end, she couldn't go through with it. She'd ended up embarrassing herself and insulting him.

The sad, miserable truth was she wanted so much more than he could give. She wanted all of him, his heart and soul and his body. She was dangerously close to falling in love with J. C. Hawk. That was why she'd pulled back from his lovemaking at the last moment—not because she couldn't make love to a man she had known so briefly, but because she knew with every fiber of her being that if she gave herself to him, she'd be lost for the rest of eternity.

She wanted him to be part of her life—for the rest of her life.

Her life.

Safe and secure and predictable. Even if by some miracle he grew to love her as much as she loved him, it

would make no difference. He didn't belong in Fort
Wayne, Indiana, any more than she belonged here in the
middle of the jungle.

He couldn't change and neither could she.

CHAPTER FOURTEEN

WHAT THE HELL had gotten into him that morning? Hawk wondered as he headed down the hill to the dining porch. And more to the point, what had gotten into Sara? He'd been within a heartbeat of taking her on the picnic table beside his house. As hard as it might be for her to believe, he wasn't in the habit of making love so indiscrimately. Especially when less than an hour before, someone had tried to blow him to smithereens in his own house, as she had so bluntly phrased it.

He wished to hell the two of them had gone through with it, so he could get her out of his mind. What was it about the woman that made him act so rashly, so stupidly? It certainly wasn't only her looks—not that she was bad-looking. But she wasn't the kind of woman who made you forget who and where the hell you were. At least she shouldn't have been.

And it certainly wasn't her personality. Shy and retiring she was not. She gave as good as she got. Life with Sara Riley would be anything but dull.

Life with Sara. That's what was wrong with the whole scenario. That's what he'd seen in her eyes that had made him stop, step back, distance himself both physically and mentally: a need for commitment, for sharing himself. Maybe even love.

No, not maybe. She'd looked at him with love in those damnably beautiful green eyes that were crystal-clear windows to her soul.

She was falling in love with him, a man who had no love to give in return. And when he'd realized that, he'd turned on her like a cornered cat. He had a plan for the rest of his life, damn it, a dream he'd held on to through hell and back, and it didn't include the things that Sara wanted to do, the places she wanted to be. His life was here. In Tyiskita. In a country at peace, with no stand-ing army and no desire to police the world. He wanted peace and quiet and a lot of hard work, and maybe at the end of it being able to look out over the wasteland Allied Fruit had made of the rain forest and seeing it healthy and restored. Maybe even knowing that once again the great and small jungle cats he so admired had a toehold on survival, in a place he'd helped create.

But only if he found Mary Hawk's gold. It all came down to that. In just over two days, Sara Riley would go back to Fort Wayne and he would still be here with his dreams. And no way of financing it. Even if he was foolish enough to think he could make her change her mind and stay here with him, he didn't have time to make the effort.

The days of kidnapping a woman and keeping her tied up in a tower somewhere until she did what you wanted her to do were long past. Now relationships played havoc with your heart and your brain. Emo-tional involvement was a luxury he'd never been able to afford. He still couldn't.

He'd been on the verge of falling in love before, once or twice, but he'd managed to get over it, turn his back and walk away, just as he had this morning. Falling in love was for fools. Falling in love with a woman you

could never have was tantamount to emotional suicide.
He'd ride this one out like all the rest. And with any
luck, in thirty or forty years he'd forget all about her.

He paused in the shadows of the forest at the bottom
of the path. He moved his shoulders restlessly, trying to
relieve the discomfort from the thin cotton of his shirt
rubbing against his recent burns. But it wasn't the
slight, annoying pain, or even the sight of Sara and her
brood gathered on the porch for a late breakfast, that
stopped him in his tracks. It was something else, something not quite right. Something that raised the short
hairs at the nape of his neck, made him pause to sniff
the air like a hunting cat scenting its prey.

Something was wrong. Very wrong. He didn't know
what, only that it was suddenly quiet, too quiet. There
wasn't the sight or sound of a bird or a monkey anywhere. Only the velvety black wings and flashing purple throat of a hummingbird, feeding on a pink
hibiscus, disturbed the static scene around him.

Even the air was still, heavy with humidity—and
something else. He swiveled his head, to watch the
ocean move restlessly along the shore. Then, farther
out, he saw the waves begin to dance and tremble, as
though stirred by an unseen hand. Movement beneath
his feet followed so closely on the sight that they were
forever fused in his memory.

Earthquake.

Hawk started to run, crouched low to the ground,
staying on his feet from blind instinct and years of ex-
haustive physical training. He reached the porch just as
Zack began to scream excitedly. Both he and Ben were
on the railing side of the table with Elliot. Sara was sitting with her back to the kitchen doorway, frozen, her

hands flat on the table, her eyes as big as saucers as she attempted to fight her way to a standing position.

"Get the boys out from under that roof," Hawk yelled, and Elliot reached out and grabbed Zack by the neck of his T-shirt, lifting him over the wall with one hand. Ben half dived, half fell over the stone wall and rolled free.

"Sara, move your butt. Get out here."

She shook her head. "I can't."

"Why not, for God's sake? Move it!"

"C'mon, sis." Elliot held out one hand to her, clutching a swaying cypress post with the other, then lost his balance and toppled out into the yard.

"No." The light bulb above Sara's head swung in a dizzying arc. "Olivia. I heard her cry out. She might be hurt." Sara put out one arm to steady herself against the wall. "I'm going to see if she's okay."

"Not now, dammit!" It was more important to get Sara out from under the poorly reinforced roof, which could come down at any second. Olivia, hurt or not, was far safer in the kitchen. He didn't have time to explain before Sara, too far away for him to grab, lurched to her feet and into the kitchen. Hawk took three steps and grabbed a support post, intending to step over the low wall. Elliot put out a hand to hold him back, but as quickly as it began, the earthquake ended. Except for the ominous rumble of a rockslide somewhere off in the distance, everything was deathly still once more.

Quiet and deceptively peaceful. And then all hell broke loose. Birds flew up from trees and bushes in every direction; a troop of frightened, chattering squirrel monkeys raced through the treetops, around the miraculously undamaged porch. With a crash, the aquarium holding the poison frogs slid off the table, where it had balanced precariously for one long moment, and landed on the concrete floor, breaking into a hundred pieces.

Zack squealed like a little stuck pig. Hawk dropped into a crouch, instinct and training taking over even before his mind registered the source of the noise.

"Oh hell, not the frogs," Elliot groaned.

"Get a pair of gloves and a jar out of the back room and round them up, will you, Elliot?" Hawk asked, coming to his feet. "I'll check on Olivia and your sister."

"Right. Guys," Elliot directed, "check out the aquarium and keep track of where those frogs head to. Don't try to pick them up. And stay away from the broken glass."

"Right," Ben said, nodding.

"I'll bet the frogs are sliced to ribbons," Zack predicted, laughing excitedly. "An earthquake, Ben! A real earthquake! No one back home will believe we lived through a real earthquake."

"Shut up, dummy, and just be glad we did," Ben scolded. "Let's get those darn frogs rounded up so we can go see if everyone's all right down in the village."

"Yeah." Zack suddenly looked very sober and ashamed of himself. "I didn't think of that. I'm sorry, Ben. I—I just never had anything like this happen before. Do you think there will be another one, Dad?" Hawk heard the frightened youngster as he headed into the kitchen.

"Sara?" The place was a mess. Jars and boxes and bottles had fallen from the open shelves. There were broken dishes and spilled food everywhere. He smelled gas and went directly to the stove to turn off the valves. "Is she all right?" he asked, turning to drop to his knee

next to Sara and the cook. Olivia was holding her head.
A lump had already formed above her right eye, but the
skin wasn't broken and she answered his questions
about what had hit her lucidly and with no apparent
loss of memory. "Let's get her outside. There'll probably be aftershocks, and this is the last damn place to be
when that happens."

"What?" Sara looked a little dazed herself. "Oh yes.
Aftershocks. Can you stand, Olivia?" She obviously
didn't trust her Spanish, so Hawk repeated the question in Olivia's native language.

"*Sí,*" the cook replied, sounding stronger already.
"*Madre de Dios. ¿Qué pasó?*"

"It was an earthquake," Sara said, patting her hand.
"Can you walk?"

"*Sí.*"

Together she and Hawk helped Olivia to her feet. Not
once did Sara look directly at him. There were mauve
shadows under her eyes, he noted, and she looked pale
and tired beneath her sunburn. He figured she hadn't
fared any better than he had in the short while since the
outhouse blew up.

"Is everyone okay?" she asked, as they walked Olivia between them to a seat on a tree stump near the
monkey's feeding station.

"We're all okay. Damn it, Sara. Why didn't you listen to me when I told you to get out from under that
porch? You wouldn't have done Olivia any good if the
whole damn roof came down on your head."

She looked at him as if she'd never seen him before
in her life, as if he were a stranger. There was sadness
and resignation in her green eyes. "I'm not like you,
Hawk. I can't weigh all the pros and cons in the blink
of an eye and always do what's expedient, take the ac-

tion that promises the best odds. I follow my heart. For better or worse. I'm sorry."

"Oh hell, Sara, don't apologize." He looked as distant to her at that moment as he had when they first met. Sara's head was still reeling from adrenaline and fear. She'd never experienced such an earthquake. The small tremors she'd felt now and again since their arrival were nothing compared to what had just occurred. Hawk was wrong about one thing. She *had* thought about what might happen if the roof collapsed on her, but that hadn't changed her mind. She hadn't been about to leave Olivia trapped in the kitchen, and deep down, she didn't think Hawk would have, either.

But he'd have been smarter about getting her out.

And he was right—she had to quit leading with her heart. She'd get sucker punched again for sure.

"We'd better be getting down to the village and see if everyone's all right down there," Hawk said.

"I wonder where the epicenter was," Elliot said, breaking off a leaf from a certain plant and crushing it between his fingers before pressing the pulpy green mess to the lump on Olivia's forehead. "If it was inland, we're okay. If it was out to sea . . ." He didn't finish the sentence. He didn't have to. Just because she'd never lived through an earthquake until five minutes ago didn't mean Sara didn't know what devastation they could cause. Landslides. Mud slides. Tidal waves.

Elliot was already striding toward the cliff steps, looking out to sea. "Everything seems pretty calm right now. The villagers will be smart enough to move uphill. But the salvage boat . . . hope they've got the sense God gave a duck and move off till the danger's over."

"Elliot, what about your lab?"

"My lab?" Elliot blinked. "To hell with the lab, sis." He gave her a sheepish grin. "I'll have plenty of time for a fit of the vapors later. Let's get Olivia home now and get down to the village. I imagine Emily and Luke will need some help. I'll get the Jeep."

"Sara, there's a first-aid kit in the radio room. We'll make a recon sweep through the village and come back up here to radio Golfito if we have to," Hawk said.

"I'll get it. You guys ready to help?"

"Sure. Just let me get rid of these frogs," Ben replied, glancing around for a safe place to deposit the big glass jar that now held the four surviving frogs from the aquarium. Sara wondered briefly where they'd managed to find a glass jar that wasn't smashed to pieces, but didn't take the time to ask.

"Then let's get moving."

She hurried back across the porch to the radio room to do Hawk's bidding. At least this time she was dressed for rough work, she thought gratefully. There'd been a quick, heavy shower just after dawn, which had put out the embers of the outhouse fire and cooled the air. She'd put on a pair of thin cotton slacks and a loose V-necked blouse with wide sleeves she'd rolled up to her elbows. Her feet were tender and sore, and she'd used up most of the adhesive bandages she'd brought along to patch up her wounds. Luckily, her remaining pair of running shoes were roomy enough to allow her to walk without too much discomfort.

"Let's go, Mom," Ben called.

She grabbed the big first-aid kit from the low shelf where it stood and hurried back outside. She was surprised to see everything looking so normal, almost as if the earthquake had never happened. If it weren't for the mess she was leaving behind in the kitchen and on the porch, and for Olivia looking pale and shaken in the front seat of the Jeep, she might have thought it was all a dream.

The village, amazingly, seemed to have suffered little damage, due mostly to the fact that the houses had no electricity, and only small bottled-gas stoves for cooking and heating water. The two most badly damaged homes, one of them belonging to Ian Carter-Stone, were closest to the bluff, where a small landslide had buried several outbuildings and knocked one house off its foundation. They found most of the villagers standing on the first rise above the town, women close by their husbands, holding shaken and crying children in their arms. It had already been determined that no one was missing and no one seriously hurt. Almost everyone, except Emily, who was busy patching up cuts and bruises, was watching the sea for any signs of a disturbance that might presage a tidal wave.

The sea was calm—and deserted except for several small shrimping boats out of Golfito heading homeward as fast as they could go. The salvage boat was nowhere to be seen, vanished as though it had never been there. Luke Wycheski jogged up to the Jeep and took the big first-aid kit from Sara with a nod of thanks.

"The treasure hunters headed out to sea as soon as the tremors stopped," he told them without being asked. "I imagine they didn't want to be trapped in the bay if there's a wave." He hadn't shaved, his hair was a tousled mess and his left cheek was scraped and bruised.

"Is someone monitoring the radio?"

"The mayor and one or two others. As soon as we hear from San José about where the epicenter was, we'll be able to move people back down to the village and start cleaning up."

"Right now, why don't you tell us what we can do?"

The next two hours went by in a blur. Sara stayed by the Jeep with Olivia until the woman's husband and son could be located. Then she began to help Emily treat the injuries caused by the quake, the most serious of which seemed to be an old man with a broken leg. By the time they had the limb set and splintered, the all-clear sign had been given to return to the village. The quake, they learned from the shortwave radio in the post office, had been centered in an uninhabited region near the Panama border. It had only rattled windows in Golfito and been barely felt in San José.

In twos and threes and larger groups, the villagers started down from the ridge to assess the damage to their homes and livestock. No sooner had most of them returned than a substantial aftershock jolted the ground. Children cried and old ladies lifted their hands and voices to heaven, but it was over in a matter of seconds. Twenty minutes later, work parties had been organized, lost chickens and pigs rounded up, fires lit to cook rice and beans, and life among the coconut palms at Tyiskita went on.

Early in the afternoon, Sara looked up from where she was replacing school supplies on the shelves to notice that the treasure hunters' ship had returned. There was much activity and scurrying around on the deck, but not a single boat was lowered over the side to make the short journey ashore to check on the villagers and their needs. Sara marveled at the greed that must drive them to the exclusion of all else. They hadn't even bothered, so far, to get on the radio and inquire if anyone in the village needed their help.

From the corner of her eye Sara watched Ben and Zack race up to the mayor's house, where Hawk and

Elliot were helping to repair the porch. The boys spoke earnestly, Zack jumping up and down with excitement. Sara's curiosity was piqued. Olivia had sent them down the beach with her son, in the direction of the cave, to check on her house. Evidently they'd found something very interesting on the way. The two men shook hands with the mayor and headed for the Jeep, the boys half running along behind. Something was up. She made her excuses to Emily and followed them.

"If you think you're going to check on the treasure cave without me, you're sadly mistaken," she announced to the four of them piling into the Jeep. Sara hoped her show of bravado would hide the awkwardness she felt in Hawk's company.

"Furthest thing from our minds, sis," Elliot assured her, but Zack's comment put the lie to his words.

"Gosh, Aunt Sara. I'm sorry. We forgot about you." He scooted over so that she could join him in the back seat. "Ben and I saw the cave when we were going to Olivia's place to see if her goat and chickens were okay. Guess what?" His eyes were wide and incandescent with excitement. "There's been another rock slide. There's a great big hole in the cave and water a long way inside."

"You didn't go in alone, did you?" Sara asked, as Hawk turned the Jeep around and headed off down the hard-packed sand. She looked back over her shoulder. Emily was standing outside the schoolroom watching them leave, a hand shading her eyes. In the distance a boat was being launched from the treasure ship, and Sara noted the event distractedly as she listened to Zack's excited recitation of what had happened at the cave.

At least they're finally sending someone to help, she thought, and turned her attention to the boys.

"I just went a little way inside," Zack assured her.

"Only because I wouldn't let him go any farther," Ben added.

"I was careful. I remember what Hawk said about quicksand." Zack looked pleased with himself. He put his hand on Sara's arm. "We saw something, Aunt Sara."

"What?" She caught her brother's eye. He looked as excited as his son, but it was Hawk's reaction, the stone-cold, leashed tension in his back and shoulders, his white-knuckled grip on the steering wheel, that set her own heart to jumping around in her chest. "What did you find?"

"A chain," Ben interrupted, unable to bear letting his little cousin take all the glory and all the credit. "A big chain, jutting out of the wall. It disappeared under the water," he said, disappointment evident in his voice and in his expression. "We couldn't budge it and we didn't want to get caught in another rockslide. We figured there'd be more aftershocks like the one awhile ago."

"We couldn't move it at all," Zack squealed as Hawk braced the Jeep, making no attempt this time to keep their presence a secret. "Know why?"

Sara shook her head.

"Because there's something fastened to the end!"

CHAPTER FIFTEEN

THE ROCK SLIDE caused by the earthquake had widened the cave opening considerably and made it easy to see from the beach, Sara noted in a glance. The tide was on the turn, heading back out to sea.

They piled out of the Jeep, and Hawk grabbed a flashlight, lantern and shovel from under the back seat. The boys raced ahead, but stopped obediently at the bottom of the fall of rocks that had previously blocked the entrance of the cave. The boulders, big and small, were scattered at the water's edge. Sara took one look at her shoes, hesitated for just a moment, and then stepped into six inches of foaming water along with all the rest.

They hugged the wall of the cave, avoiding the area of dangerously shifting sand. The larger opening allowed so much more daylight to enter that the flashlight wasn't necessary, but Elliot paused at the mouth of the cave long enough to light the lantern. "Just in case."

"There it is," Ben said, pointing to a spot about a foot up from the floor near the cul-de-sac where Zack had been trapped. A small section of wall, almost a slice of rock, had broken away, revealing a huge old chain embedded in the stone, exactly as the boys had described.

"We told you, we told you," Zack chanted, jumping up and down in agitation. "Hurry! Pull it up. See what's hooked on to the other end."

Hawk moved forward and the rest followed, as though tugged by some invisible string. Sara's heart was beating fast and hard, high up in her throat. Mary Hawk's treasure had to be attached to the other end of that chain. It had to be.

"Aunt Sara." Zack tugged on her shirt sleeve. "We had to have crawled right over that chain when I was stuck back there." He glanced into the still-dark recesses of the cul-de-sac.

"You're right, Zack," she said, squeezing the hand he placed in hers. "Imagine. We were that close and didn't even know it."

"Dad and Hawk would have found it, though, even without the earthquake. Right?"

She chanced a look at Hawk. He was completely absorbed in examining the heavy chain in the light of the lantern Elliot held. "Yes," she said without a doubt in the world. "They would have."

"But we probably wouldn't have been here. I know it's not a good thing to have an earthquake. But it was a good thing for us it happened today. So we can be here when they find the treasure."

"Where does it lead?" Sara asked as Hawk began to dig sand out from under the chain where it disappeared underground.

"It's headed back toward where Zack was trapped. The rockslide must have shifted enough sand to uncover it," he said, lifting sections of the giant chain as reverently as if it were made of spun glass and not iron.

Sara didn't need Elliot to tell her, as he was explaining to the boys, why Hawk was being so careful. A hundred and seventy years of being buried in the sand and seawater would have eaten away at the iron links until they were truly not much stronger than spun glass. If the chain snapped, or disintegrated in his hands, they might never locate the treasure at the other end.

"Hurry, Hawk!" Zack cried, the words echoing once before being swallowed up by the wet, porous walls of the cave. "I want to see the treasure!"

"Shut up, wienie," Ben hissed. He picked his small cousin up and set him on a boulder, where he could see but wouldn't be in the way. "Stay put."

Slowly, carefully, squatting in water up to his haunches, Hawk worked to free the chain. Sara took the lantern so that Elliot could help. It was heavy and she had to use both hands to hold it high enough to shed light on their work. Slowly the water continued to drain out of the cave.

Hawk kept working at freeing the chain. He moved forward little by little, each uncovered link taking him closer and closer to the rockfall that had blocked Sara and Zackary's earlier escape. If the chain continued on under the rocks, they'd never get it out. Sara could hear the bubble and sigh of the hole where seawater had rushed in to threaten her and Zack when he was trapped. It sounded now like the cave itself was taunting them with a breathy, mocking laugh. It had guarded Mary Hawk's treasure well for almost two centuries. It wasn't going to give it up easily.

Hawk stopped pulling on the chain and started to dig again. There was only a few inches of water left on the cave floor, but it still made excavation difficult. He and Elliot kept at it, going deeper with each shovelful. Hawk cursed under his breath when the sand kept washing back into the hole, almost as fast as they pitched it out.

Sara glanced at her watch. Nearly half an hour had passed. She'd long ago set the lantern down on a rock. It was much too heavy to hold for any length of time.

"What's there?" Zack asked for at least the tenth time. He wrapped his arms around his scabbed knees. "I can't see. What's there?"

"Nothing yet, son," Elliot answered, just as Hawk's shovel struck metal and wood.

"Got it."

"What is it, Aunt Sara?"

"A box. Or sea chest of some kind."

Hawk kept working with the shovel, slowly, carefully uncovering the chest. Ben leaned over Sara's shoulder to stare down into the water-and-sand-filled hole. Zack demanded to be helped down from his rock perch so that he could see for himself.

"Quiet," Ben ordered.

"Carson, give me a hand. The iron in this box is in worse shape than the chain." Both men were kneeling by the hole now. Sara couldn't see a thing. Then they turned, holding between them a small iron box.

"It's so little," Zack said, standing on his perch. "I thought it would be bigger. A whole big chest, filled with gold chains and jewels and pieces of eight."

"It is kind of small," Ben agreed, trying not to sound disappointed by the size of their prize.

"It's a dispatch box or something similar," Elliot explained. "It was probably one of the strongest containers on the ship. See how the edges and corners are bound in brass. Seawater doesn't affect brass the way it does iron. That's probably what's held it together so well all these years."

"Open it, Hawk," Zack begged.

"Perhaps we should take it outside the cave," Sara ventured. "I mean, it would be safer. There might be another aftershock." All four males in the cave looked at her with varying degrees of impatience. They had found a buried treasure, every man's fantasy, and she wanted them to go outside to open it up. She took one more look at the box herself, the brass fittings gleaming faintly against the dark, rusted iron, and the last of her Fort Wayne mother-and-teacher sensibilities spiraled up toward the ceiling, to be forgotten. She grinned. "Forget I even said that. What's inside?"

Hawk took the blade of the shovel and gently broke the heavy, old-fashioned lock on the chain. It fell away in pieces, as did the rotted iron of the chest, crumpling into flakes beneath his hands. Inside was a box, or the shape of a box, wrapped round and round in layers of decaying leather.

"Yuck," Ben said, wrinkling his nose.

"Oiled hides," Elliot explained, leaning closer. "Hawk's ancestor must have done everything she could to try to protect it from the seawater. That means Father Benedicto's journal must be inside."

Sara reached out, touched his arm lightly with her hand. The muscles were corded like wire beneath her fingers. "We don't know. And the water damage..."

"I know, sis." But his eyes were every bit as bright with excitement as Zack's.

Hawk had almost finished unwrapping their prize. The outer layers of leather were as rotten as the iron of the chest. The inner layer, however, still held together. Hawk unfolded it and Sara gasped as the treasure it held was revealed.

"Gold!" Zack shrieked, jumping up and down again. *Gold,* his echo called back.

Sara sucked in her breath. Ben let out a long, low whistle that was more eloquent than words. A small gold box inlaid with jewels and chased with a pattern of corroded and darkened silver lay on the wet sand.

"It is gold." Sara drew her gaze from the dazzling oblong of sun-bright metal, as Hawk lifted it carefully from the still-intact brass shell of the ruined chest. He looked up, his dark eyes reflecting the glow of the lantern, his face expressionless, his manner as controlled as always, except for the quick jump of a muscle along the line of his jaw. His eyes met hers. Met and held for one long, silent moment.

"It's gold, all right. Mary Hawk's gold."

"Yes." Sara tore her eyes away from his and looked at the small golden coffer once more. "You found it. Just as you said you would."

"And with forty-eight hours left on my deadline." She lifted her eyes to his face once more. His voice, his expression hadn't changed, but Sara was certain he was teasing her. How she knew, she couldn't say, and she didn't want to think too closely about it. He was right. There were only forty-eight hours left of her visit to Tyiskita. Far too little time to settle anything that might remain between them.

"Open it," she whispered, dropping to the wet sand, heedless of the small, sharp stones beneath her knees. "Open it."

"It's locked," Hawk said, his voice low. "I'll have to break it."

Elliot nodded. So did Sara. It seemed a shame to ruin the small, ornate lock, but they had no choice. A key was nowhere in evidence. Hawk took a knife from the

pocket of his pants, an ordinary Swiss army knife, not
the lethal-looking weapon Sara had so often seen
strapped to his waist. He inserted the tip of the blade
behind the lock. With a single twist it parted company
from the chest and dropped onto the sand. Elliot picked
it up, admiring the workmanship. Hawk took the tip of
the knife and gently worked it into the seam between the
lid and the base of the jeweled box. Sara knew nothing
of Spanish antiques, but it seemed to her, by the size
and shape of the casket and the blurred outline of the
intricate chasing on the top, that the chest had always
been destined to hold ornaments of great beauty and
value.

"What's inside?" Zack scrambled down off his perch
to join the others grouped around the small golden box.

"This is it," Hawk said and opened the lid. The lantern's hard, yellow glow heightened the distinction between light and dark, throwing half Hawk's face into
bold relief, leaving the other half in shadow—a hard,
handsome, dangerous face; an adventurer's face; a man
eminently suited to the job at hand.

"What is it? What's inside?"

"More leather," Elliot answered, making room beside him for the excited little boy. "Not too much water damage." In the strange, harsh light from the
Coleman, he looked no less hard and dangerous than
Hawk. The boys, as well, looked unlike themselves,
mesmerized by the gold and by the magic of the moment. Sara wondered if she had that same intent look
on her face, that same absorbed half smile on her lips,
and concluded that she probably did.

Hawk laid back the oiled leather, very carefully, very
slowly. No one said a word, no one breathed. Underneath was a layer of gold Spanish coins and several un-

set stones, emeralds and rubies, looking less valuable than they truly were because of the old-fashioned, un-faceted cuts. Coiled among them was a finely wrought gold chain, holding a small, intricately carved crucifix.

"My Lord," Sara said, awed by its delicate beauty. "Hawk, it's magnificent."

"Is that all?" Elliot asked, his voice rising enough to cause a faint echo in the cavern. He was disappointed and showed it. "Is there nothing more?"

"There's more," Hawk said, lifting the piece of leather, jewels and all, from the casket. Swiveling on the balls of his feet, he handed the treasure trove to Sara. "Hold this," he said with a grin. A real grin, wide and uncensored, that revealed strong white teeth and carried all the way to his eyes.

She could think of nothing to say. He'd done it. *They* had done it—found Mary Hawk's treasure. Sara realized suddenly that despite all they'd been through, all the adventures they'd shared, she had no idea what this enigmatic man intended to do with the treasure now that he had it in his hands.

"Take it, Sara," Hawk repeated as she continued to stare at him. "There's more." She blinked and held out her hands.

"More?"

"Yes, there's more."

"Let me see, Hawk." Elliot dropped the gold lock he'd been holding on top of the pile of treasure in Sara's hands. He didn't give the jewels or the beautifully worked necklace a second glance, but pounced on the casket, peering inside. "There *is* something else." His voice was triumphant. He picked up the jewel chest, tipped it over and held his own particular, very personal treasure in his hand. Even before he unwrapped the leather covering that had helped protect it for so many years. Sara knew it was Father Benedicto's journal.

"Congratulations, El," she said, dropping the money and jewels back into the little casket, which Hawk held out to her. Elliot had let it fall to the sandy floor, as though he'd forgotten it even existed. "I know how much this means to you."

"And you, Hawk," she couldn't help saying, "what are you going to do with the treasure now that it's yours?"

Hawk looked down at the casket in his hands. It was small, fitting easily into his palm. Still, the workmanship was exquisite, the crucifix necklace alone, Sara guessed, worth many thousands of dollars. Its value to a museum would be beyond price. But Joseph C. Hawk was not a man to deal in intangibles. He looked first at the gold and jewels he held, then at Elliot, absorbed in examining for damage the small leather-bound volume he'd unwrapped from its hide covering. He said nothing for a long moment, just watched his friend.

As though sensing their interest, Elliot looked up, his face transfigured with happiness. "God, sis. It's a miracle. The journal's intact."

"It looks like a mess to me, Dad." Zack's voice had sobered. As young as he was, he was aware how much of a blow it would be to Elliot if the journal was completely destroyed by all it had been through.

"It'll take an expert to restore it, son. There's been some damage but, all in all, it's remarkably well preserved. I guess we have Hawk's ancestor to thank for that. Maybe there was something special in the way they treated the hides they wrapped it in. Or maybe it was luck. Or a miracle. Who knows? A friend I went to

college with is a crack preservationist. I'll get in touch
with her as soon as I can get through on the radio. This
is priceless. Priceless. And right now I can't read a single, solitary word.'' He laughed, and it was a sound
composed of an equal mixture of exhilaration and
frustration. "Not a single word." He bent his head once
more to study his prize.

"What am I going to do with my treasure?" Hawk
repeated Sara's question. His eyes, shuttered, as always, searched her face. For just a moment she thought
she saw a gleam of light, of satisfaction and triumph,
spark in their ebony depths, but it was gone as quickly
as it had come. "We all have our dreams, Sara. Hard as
that may be for you to believe."

Zack leaned forward to stir the doubloons with his
fingers, paying no attention to Hawk and Sara, or to
Elliot's absorption with Father Benedicto's journal. Ben
reached out to touch the fine gold chain of the necklace. If he was listening to what they had to say, Sara
didn't notice. She felt caught, snared like a small ani-
mal by the intensity of Hawk's gaze.

"What is your dream, Hawk?" she asked very softly.
"You've never told me."

He looked down at the treasure, then lifted his head.
For a heartbeat she held her breath, certain their eyes
would meet once more and he would reveal to her
something of import. And then he was surging to his
feet in one swift, lethal movement that brought Sara
upright as well. The gold and jewels, forgotten, tumbled onto the muddy sand at his feet.

Hawk's momentum carried him several yards closer
to the entrance of the cave before Sara could even turn
her head. His hand went instinctively to his belt. But the
knife he so often carried wasn't there.

"Forget it, Hawk." Bright sunlight silhouetted the figures of two men against the cave opening. Their voices were American, familiar. So was their stance. Sara's blood ran cold. The man who spoke was carrying a gun—and it was pointed directly at Hawk's chest. "Looks like the earthquake did most of the hard work for us, Wheeler," he said. "And the Gilligan's Island crew, here, did the rest."

"Matt? Terry?" Ben came up beside Sara. She put out her arm to keep him from moving past her. "What are you doing here? I thought you flew to San José yesterday."

"We're back. We didn't want to miss out on your little discovery."

"It's Luke's friends from the treasure-hunting boat," Zack said, sounding confused. "What do they want?" From the corner of her eye Sara saw him absentmindedly stuff his pockets with the doubloons and emeralds he had picked up off the sand.

"He's got a gun," Ben said in a disbelieving voice.

"Gun?" The word caught Elliot's attention, as well as Zack's.

"What the hell?" Sara's brother stepped in front of her, still holding Father Benedicto's journal. "What's going on here?"

"You can't have our treasure," Zack insisted, standing next to his father, legs planted wide apart, his expression mutinous. "We found it. It's ours."

"I ain't here for your doubloons, kid," the taller of the two—Matt—said dismissively. They looked and sounded like the clean-cut, all-American college kids Luke had introduced her to just days ago. If she closed her eyes, she could imagine they still were—except for the gun Matt carried in his hand.

Hawk said nothing. He merely waited and watched.

"Then what is it you do want?" Elliot asked, his voice harder, more menacing than she'd ever heard it before.

"C'mon, Carson. You know damn well what we're here for."

"The journal." His partner spoke for the first time. "The priest's journal you spent all that time researching in the Spanish archives. The people who hired us want it bad. Especially now that the damn earthquake has stirred up the bottom of the bay so bad the *Mary Deere*'s scattered from here to Cocos Island." His next words struck terror in Sara's heart. "And they're paying us enough that Matt and me are willing to do just about anything to get our hands on it."

CHAPTER SIXTEEN

"WAINRIGHT," Elliot said, making no move to hand over the small, water-damaged diary he considered more valuable than the gold and jewels still scattered at their feet. "Wainright Pharmaceuticals. Or at least someone who works for them is behind this, right?"

"Do you think we're dumb enough to tell you who hired us?"

"Shut up, Terry," Benson ordered his partner. "Hand over the book, Doc—and can the chitchat."

"No."

Benson shifted the gun until it was pointed directly at Zack. "I said, hand over the book."

Zack whimpered in fear, for the first time realizing the extent of the danger.

"Stop it, all of you." Sara stepped forward to pull Zack into her arms, angered beyond discretion by the deliberate terrorization of her nephew. "Leave the children out of this."

Damn the woman, Hawk thought. *She's gutsy as hell, but someone is going to have to teach her when to keep her mouth shut.* Benson backed up a step or two, bringing the barrel of the gun level with Sara's breast, reacting automatically to her sudden movement. Hawk revised his estimate of his adversaries, raising it a notch or two. For a split second before Sara had grabbed Zack, Benson had been off his guard, but no longer. At that distance, Hawk could have taken him without much trouble, and the odds were that his partner wasn't armed or he would have shown his gun by now. But Sara's initiative had ruined his chances; Benson was now too far away. He was going to have to bide his time and hope for another slipup on the young thug's part.

"Keep still, Mrs. Riley," Benson warned, his gun still aimed at her, but his eyes on Hawk. "Just tell your brother to hand over the journal and we'll be outta here."

"You know," Elliot said, looking down at the small, leather-bound volume in his hands, "I was going to offer the journal to Wainright when I finished my research."

"That may take years. The men who hired us don't want to wait that long."

"You stupid creeps," Zack yelled from the sanctuary of Sara's arms. "What do you want with that dumb old book, anyway?"

"It's probably worth more than all the gold you've got stuffed in your pockets, kid," Benson replied.

"Really, Aunt Sara?" He looked up at her in wonder. "The book my dad's been lookin' for is worth more than the gold?"

Sara nodded. "If there's information in the book about just one plant that your dad can find here in Costa Rica, one that might help to cure cancer or AIDS, it would be worth hundreds of millions of dollars to companies like Wainright Pharmaceuticals."

"Right on the money, Mrs. Riley," Benson said. "To hell with your little pile of doubloons. And to hell with those guys sifting through a billion tons of sand down there in the bay."

"I don't know, Matt. That stuff the kid's got is worth plenty." Wheeler looked longingly at the golden casket and its contents.

"Shut up. We've got a job to do. Don't forget it, or you just might find yourself staying behind with our little group of treasure hunters when the boat gets here."

Hawk had no doubt that the two young hit men meant to kill them all before they left the cave. He wondered if whoever was backing them at Wainright had counted on killing a woman and two kids as part of the deal. He doubted it. Most of the corporate types who authorized these clandestine little operations never did know or care how they were carried out.

"Surely you realize you won't get very far," Sara said. The color had drained from her face at Wheeler's last remark, but she stood her ground. Maybe it was because they looked so damn much like schoolkids that she thought she could talk them out of what they intended to do, Hawk decided. Or maybe, just maybe, she was playing for time to give him a chance to make a move. "The authorities will be looking for you before you get back to San José."

"Who said we were going to San José? Maybe we're heading south to Colombia or Peru."

"Can it, Terry."

Wheeler glared at his partner but shut his mouth.

"I'm telling you for the last time, Carson—hand over the journal or, so help me, I'll shoot you right here in front of your sister and your kid."

"Elliot, give him the book," Sara whispered. Suppressed fear was noticeable in her voice, but Hawk didn't make the mistake of turning his head to see how she was holding up.

"Listen to her, Carson, and we'll make this whole thing quick and painless. The kids first. It'll be over just like that."

"You can't be serious!" Sara no longer sounded scared. She sounded furious.

"He's serious as hell, Sara," Hawk said, speaking for the first time.

"Deadly serious." As Hawk hoped, the younger man focused his attention on him. Now, if Sara would only take the boys and run, head into the shadows that led to the passageway back up the hill, they'd be safe. Hawk intended the attack to be swift and lethal. It was their only chance.

"You can't get away with murdering five people, even here," Sara said, her voice strong again, although her face was ashen in the diffused light of the cave.

"It won't be murder. Just an unfortunate accident."

Wheeler pulled a stick of dynamite from under his shirt. "We saved this from your place the other night," he said with a grin. "I'd rather have had the plastique, but we couldn't find the damn stuff. But it doesn't matter. The earthquake solved our problem just fine. It's a great cover for an *accident*." He stressed the word slightly. "Too bad the next aftershock is going to bring this whole damn cave down on your heads. What a shame, huh?"

"Mom?" Ben's voice cracked with fear. Zack buried his face at Sara's waist.

"You bastards," Elliot growled. "Get out of here now and we'll forget this ever happened."

"No can do, Professor. Give me the book." Benson pointed the gun at Ben, frozen where he stood.

Hawk tensed. If Benson made a move for it, he'd take him.

"Now, Professor!" The young man pulled back the hammer.

"No!" The word exploded from Sara's mouth as she launched herself at Benson. He was armed, dangerous and outweighed her by seventy pounds, but he had threatened to kill her child. Hawk knew the combination of adrenaline and fear that drove her forward, fingers curled to scratch and claw. For the space of one pulse beat he stood rooted to the ground, then he moved, too, surging forward just as Benson lifted his arm to brush Sara aside as if she were a fly, sending her careening into Wheeler, who landed on his backside.

"Get him, Dad!" Hawk heard Zack scream as Elliot lunged at Wheeler and both men went down in a tangle of arms and legs on the sand. Then all he had time for was the deadly one-on-one battle with the still-armed Benson, who came at him low and fast. The young man was strong and well trained, the fighting close and dirty. For Hawk the only objective was the gun. He swept Benson's legs at knee level, bringing him down. He straddled him, keeping him pinned to the cave floor. The world had narrowed to their deadly combat. He neither saw nor heard what went on around him. Repeatedly he slammed his adversary's arm against the sharp coral rock on the cave floor, trying to dislodge the gun. On the third blow the weapon went skittering away across the sand.

Hawk had leaned back, fist upraised to deal Benson the finishing blow, when he heard Sara call out a warning. He turned slightly, enough to see Elliot facedown in the sand and Wheeler coming at him feet first. Lights exploded inside his skull as the blow hit home, and blood poured into his eye, blinding him. Instinctively he parried a strike from Benson's left arm, but he couldn't keep his balance, and the younger man squirmed out from under him, intent, Hawk knew, on reaching his gun.

He rolled to avoid the kicks Wheeler continued to rain down on him. He deflected one with his arm, sending splinters of pain streaking from shoulder to fingertips. He couldn't roll out from under the next blow to his ribs quite fast enough. Fiery pain exploded in his chest, draining the breath from his lungs. Groggily he came to his feet, wiping blood from his eyes, just as Sara once more propelled herself into the fray. She rushed at Wheeler's back and shoved him as hard as she could, knocking him enough off balance that it took only one lethal chop with the side of Hawk's hand against his neck to bring him down. But it was too late. Benson once more had the gun.

Sara was on her knees in the sand, breathing heavily. Hawk spared her one quick glance. Her hands were scraped and raw and blood trickled from a cut on her lip. His hands balled into fists, but he remained standing where he was. Lights and sound rushed around in dizzying company inside his head. He could barely see out of his left eye, but he had the satisfaction of noting that Benson was in even worse shape. The young man swayed on his feet, but the gun in his hand was rock-steady. They were right back at square one and his options were even more limited than before.

"You son of a bitch," Benson hissed, wiping blood from his mouth. "I ought to shoot you where you stand."

Sara lifted her head, her eyes going to the darkest spot on the far wall where the passageway led up the hill.

"Sorry to tell you the bad news, Mrs. Riley. Wheeler and I checked. The earthquake closed the passage about halfway up the hill. When we bring this wall down, you'll be here a hell of a lot longer than Father Benedicto's journal."

"What about your friend?" Hawk asked, jerking his head toward the fallen Wheeler, stalling for time. To Benson's right, Elliot was picking himself up off the cave floor. He, too, swayed unsteadily on his feet. Benson's eyes flickered that way, dismissed the botanist as a source of danger and returned to Hawk.

"He stays here with you. All I want now is the journal. And the dynamite." He motioned to Sara with the gun. "Pick it up."

"Get it yourself." She lifted her head defiantly.

"I said move."

"Enough!" Elliot roared, cocking his arm and sending a rock the size of a softball hurtling at Benson's head. Instinctively the young man lifted his arm to ward off the missile, and the heavy rock struck him full force on the elbow just as he pulled the trigger. The bullet buried itself harmlessly in the sand. The shot echoed loudly from wall to wall and up the passageway. Zack covered his ears with his hands. Benson screamed and dropped the gun from sudden nerveless fingers. Hawk was on him in a heartbeat, dealing one quick blow to the side of the neck that put him out for the count.

"Dad! You did it. What an arm! What an arm!" He catapulted himself against his father's chest. "You did it. You saved our lives. Even Hawk's."

"Are you all right, son?" Elliot asked, wrapping his arms around the child, as Hawk pulled Benson forward and stripped the man's shirt down to his waist, using it to tie his hands behind his back.

Ben had come up with the gun. He stood holding it trained on Wheeler, now coming groggily awake. Wheeler looked into the wavering barrel of the gun with terror in his eyes. "Don't—don't shoot," he stammered.

"Don't make a move, scumbag," Ben growled, his voice cracking in the middle of the sentence. He looked at Sara and grinned. "I've always wanted to say that."

"Be careful," Sara warned. "Give the gun to your Uncle El."

"Aw, Mom, do I have to?"

"Yes."

"Help me tie him up, Ben," Hawk commanded. Nearly getting herself killed twice in five minutes hadn't changed Sara a bit. She still wanted to be in charge. "Like this." He gave the knot around Benson's wrists one last tug. The younger man grunted in pain and Hawk took no small pleasure in the sound before he moved toward his partner.

Ben's eyes gleamed behind his glasses. He handed the gun to his uncle, who'd retrieved his precious journal from the floor of the cave. "This is radical."

"Aunt Sara, are you all right?" Zack asked, reaching up to touch the corner of her mouth with one small, grimy finger. "You've got blood on your chin."

"I'm okay, honey," she said, sweeping him into her arms. "I just bit my tongue." She was lying, Hawk knew. Wheeler had hit her, damned hard. There was already the hint of a purpling bruise on her cheek. Hawk's fingers itched to pound the man into the ground, but he didn't let his anger show. There was still too much to be done. And to tell the truth, he hurt too badly to get the job done properly. He was getting too old for this kind of work.

"Let's get out of here," Zack said, cuddling close to his aunt. "I don't like this place anymore."

"Good idea," Hawk said, giving an approving nod to Ben, as he quickly searched both men for hidden weapons and then shoved Benson, who was conscious again, toward the opening of the cave. "Let's get outside. We'll deal with these two bozos back in the village."

"I'd like to know who set this whole thing up," Elliot said, waving the gun at Wheeler to get him moving. "It must have been someone pretty highly placed at Wainwright."

"Don't tell him anything," Benson ordered.

"Save it," Hawk growled, giving Benson a shove that nearly sent him sprawling. "If your partner here's got enough brains to save himself, let him. The Costa Ricans have the best jails in Central America, but that's not saying a whole hell of a lot," he added ominously.

"Matt?"

"I said keep quiet."

"Head 'em out, Elliot," Hawk said, disgusted. He figured a week or so in a Costa Rican jail would loosen Wheeler's tongue, if not his partner's. "Sara?" He turned to find her and Zack kneeling in the sand, putting the scattered emeralds, rubies and doubloons back in the golden casket. "Let's get out of here."

"Just a moment." She looked up at him, her green eyes enormous in her pale face. She tried to smile, but the cut on her lip made it more of a grimace instead. The sight of her pain made him ache again with the need to annihilate the man who had dared to hurt her.

"We can't leave Mary Hawk's treasure behind," she was saying. "Not after what we went through to get it."

"Then grab it and let's get going. Wheeler's right about one thing—all it would take to bring this place down on our heads is one good, strong aftershock." He limped forward, wincing as each footfall sent a white-hot shaft of pain up through his battered ribs to ricochet off his skull. He wiped the back of his hand across his forehead. It came away covered with blood.

"Hawk!" She came to her feet so quickly the doubloons in her lap were strewn in the sand once more. "You're hurt. Let me see." She lifted her hand to brush back his hair. "Oh God," she whispered, turning paler still. "You're still bleeding."

"C'mon, Sara," he said bracingly. "You can faint outside."

"I'm not going to faint," she insisted, but she didn't sound too sure of herself.

"Good. I'm sure as hell in no shape to carry you out of here again. C'mon, Zack. Grab the loot and let's get a move on."

"Yes, sir," Zack said. His eyes were still bright with fear and overexcitement, but the color was returning to his face. "I've got all of it—all the emeralds and the gold and the necklace. Everything."

"Good job."

Zack carried the golden casket carefully in both hands, leading the way out of the cave. The sun outside was so bright it took a moment for Hawk's eyes to adjust to the light. Sunshine poured down on his aching head like liquid fire. Each step sent a jolt of agony along his bruised ribs. All he wanted was to get to his own bed and collapse, but there was still too damned much to do.

"Good Lord," Sara said. "Half the village is here."

Hawk narrowed his eyes against the light. "Son of a bitch." She was right. Half the village was there, including the mayor, the constable and the snake doctor. Two men, armed with aging hunting rifles, were already guarding Wheeler and Benson, although Elliot still held Benson's gun at the ready.

"Well, my friend Hawk, I see our rescue party is too late to help. What have we here?" Ian Carter-Stone asked, usurping the mayor's place by dint of speaking more loudly and in English. "De treasure dat you been seekin'?"

"I think that's obvious," Hawk replied.

"And dese two gringos tried to take it from you 'fore you could turn it over to de authorities as is proper, eh mon?"

"Right again," Hawk said through his teeth. Carter-Stone had him backed into a corner and they both knew it.

"De punishment for stealin' antiquities is very strict," the snake doctor said, with a grin so huge it threatened to split his face in two.

"I know."

"It is even more strict if you are caught tryin' to take dem out of de country."

"I think if you search those two, you'll find some of the treasure on them," Hawk suggested. It was too late now to keep the knowledge of Mary Hawk's treasure from the authorities, but he could still see that Benson and Wheeler got exactly what they deserved.

Ian Carter-Stone barked out a command in Spanish and the two men with rifles began going through the young men's pockets. They came up with half a dozen doubloons and four small emeralds.

"You bastard, Hawk," Benson yelled. "You set us up. He planted this stuff on us, I swear."

"Dat's not for me to say, mon," the snake doctor said, still grinning. "Tell yo' story to de *guarda*. Take dem away."

"I don't suppose we could just forget this whole thing and send those two packing back to the States," Hawk said equitably.

"Not on yo' life, mon. Justice must be served."

"Yeah. That's what I figured you'd say."

"Wit dem gone, you can sleep safe at night, now."

"No more yellow tails in my Jeep, you mean?"

"Right on, mon." Ian Carter-Stone laughed hugely. "No more snakes."

Hawk let the reference pass. They both knew Benson and Wheeler hadn't planted the fer-de-lance in his Jeep. He glanced at Elliot. Father Benedicto's journal was still in the botanist's pocket, but no one seemed to notice. Wheeler and Benson had too much to worry about to call any more attention to themselves.

"Well, mon," the snake doctor said, stepping forward to open the lid on the small jewel box and peer inside. "De doctor, him found what he wanted." He cocked his thumb toward Elliot's pocket but said nothing else as the mayor came forward to take the treasure into custody in the name of the government of Costa Rica. "You too, eh? But you ain't goin' to win." He smiled again. "Dey gonna be down on you like rats on cheese, mon. Dey gonna take dis all—every bit of it— and lock it away. You ain't never gonna see it again. You ain't never gonna plant yo' trees. And de hotels are gonna come, after all. Just de way I said dey would, mon. And dere ain't gonna be a damn ting you can do about it."

CHAPTER SEVENTEEN

"HOLD STILL," Sara said. "Let me clean that cut above your eye before it gets infected." She settled her hip on the wide arm of the heavy, Adirondack-style chair on Hawk's veranda. The only light came from a kerosene lamp on the table beside her and the moon streaming through the screened windows.

Hawk circled her wrist with his fingers and pulled her hand, holding the damp cloth away from his face. "I'm fine. I don't need taking care of." He watched her from hooded eyes. "You ought to be looking after yourself." He touched the cut on her lip with the tip of his finger.

Sara flinched, not from any pain, but from the jolt of electricity his touch communicated along her nerve endings. She hoped he hadn't noticed the slight, involuntary reaction, but she was wrong.

"Why are you really here?" he asked quietly.

She wasn't ready to answer that question directly. "Someone needed to check up on you," she replied, as though talking to one of the boys. She hoped her officious tone would help hide her anxiety over the beating he'd taken in the cave as well as the uncertainty she felt at entering his home uninvited.

After the excitement and alarms of the morning, the afternoon had been anticlimactic. Thankfully, there were no more aftershocks from the earthquake. Just before nightfall, a plane had flown in from San José with a doctor and medical supplies on board for the villagers, as well as an official from the National Museum, one Señor Gonzales, and Inspector Molinas. Sara knew without asking that they had the snake doctor to thank for notifying the authorities of their discovery so quickly.

The two men had taken possession of the jeweled casket and its contents from the mayor. For the government and people of Costa Rica, or so they'd said. They'd given Hawk a detailed inventory, signed, sealed and very official-looking. And probably not worth the paper it was printed on. Then they'd taken Mary Hawk's treasure away, everything but Father Benedicto's journal. The small leather book seemed to interest no one but Elliot and the two would-be assassins, who were in no condition to argue their claim.

Later, Sara had watched the small plane fly off into the sunset, taking all Hawk's hopes and dreams with it, filling her with a sense of frustration and loss as well. Her unease sent her up the path to his house in the pitch darkness of a jungle night. All she could think about was Hawk, alone and hurting, and stripped of the treasure he'd worked so long and hard to find.

She put her thoughts into words, looking down at her wrist, encircled by his hard, scarred hand. "This afternoon Elliot told me about your plans for the rain forest, for Tyiskita. Why didn't you tell me that's what you intended to do with the treasure if you found it?"

He took a drink from the glass of whiskey he held in his left hand before answering her question. His movements were stiff and hesitant, with little of his usual warrior's grace. For that reason, if no other, Sara knew he was in more pain than he would admit to feeling.

"Would you have believed me if I'd told you I wanted to buy Allied Fruit's land—and just let it grow back into forest?"

"I . . ." She looked into his dark, shuttered eyes. "I don't know." She couldn't lie to him. "At first I wouldn't have believed you at all. It seems so quixotic a gesture for Major J. C. Hawk. But now..." She found she couldn't look at him any longer without letting her true feelings for him show. "Now I'm sorry as hell I was so damned narrow-minded." She lifted her hand again to clean the abrasion above his left eye. She shuddered to think what might have happened to Hawk's face if Wheeler had been wearing boots instead of running shoes.

"It is a quixotic gesture," he said, and for the first time since she'd met him, Sara heard fatigue and defeat in his voice. "It's going to take the rest of my lifetime to even begin to bring a small part of the rain forest back. To tell the truth, I don't even know if it can be done. Time isn't the only thing it'll take. It'll take a lot of hard work and expert land management. You don't just wave a magic wand and restore hundreds of species of plants and animals. I've got to start clearing out some of the scrub, reestablishing the canopy trees. That takes men and machines and a hell of a lot of money. And I don't have it." He stopped talking, looked out over the ocean, calm and shining in the moonlight. "Maybe Carter-Stone's right. Maybe the hotels will be better for Tyiskita in the long run."

The pain and uncertainty in his voice were almost her undoing. Hawk vulnerable, unsure? The emotions that the glimpse of a softer side of him invoked within her were more powerful than she could deal with at the moment. She returned to the attack. "I think Wheeler's kicking you in the head scrambled your brain," she said, leaning back to survey her handiwork. She didn't feel as off balance when they were arguing. She could hold her own with him in a verbal free-for-all. It was when they behaved as man and woman that she didn't know how to respond. "How could turning this place into another Cancún be good for anybody?"

"It would bring money and jobs."

"You can't have hotels and swimming pools and parking lots in the same place as monkeys and jaguars and toucans. People can surf in Hawaii. Here they should come to see nature and be part of it." He couldn't give up this easily, no matter how tired and disappointed he was over losing Mary Hawk's gold. This wasn't the Hawk she knew—and loved. And, oh God, she did love him, but didn't have the slightest idea what to do about it.

"That's a pretty militant stance."

"It's the right one. I'd fight Ian Carter-Stone on this till my dying day if I were you."

Hawk chuckled. And Sara thought, as she had before, that she'd do just about anything to hear him do it again. He leaned his head against the back of the chair and looked up at her. She still couldn't read the expression in his eyes. The barriers he erected around his feelings were so ingrained, she suspected he would never completely let them down. "You never give up, do you, Sara? You don't always know what side you're fighting on, but you never give up."

"No," she said, smiling, too. "And I always lead with my heart."

She looked down at his arm, resting alongside her thigh. His knuckles were scraped and bloodied. She saw the faint silvery tracings of older scars and felt the hard strength of tendon and muscle against her leg. She remembered the quick and ruthless way he'd subdued Wheeler and Benson, and the terrible, concentrated patience with which he'd waited for his chance to take them on, knowing full well the odds against him.

"And your heart tells you that I should fight for my vision of Tyiskita's future?" He turned his hand to trace the outer edge of her palm with his thumb.

"You always fight for your dreams. Even if they're not wise ones. And Tyiskita's future is worth fighting for. I'm sorry I ever doubted you."

He closed his eyes and was silent a long moment. When he spoke again, it was to change the subject. "What are your dreams, Sara?" His thumb still caressed her skin, sending shock waves dancing along her nerve endings.

"To have my children grow up to be happy, healthy adults. To be happy and healthy, myself." She stopped talking and looked at his face, half-hidden in shadows, firm and handsome as burnished bronze. At first she had seen him as a pirate, a mercenary with no thought of anyone's benefit but his own. She had been wrong, of course, terribly wrong. He was a soldier, a professional warrior like the knights of old, with his own personal code of ethics and honor and a fierce determination to save this one small corner of paradise. "And to find someone to share my life with, to grow old with. To fall in love with," she whispered, risking her heart.

Hawk opened his eyes. His hand closed over hers, holding her at his side, although she made no attempt to leave. "Could you fall in love with me, Sara Riley?"

"Yes." He had faced death to save her and her family. The courage it took for her to be the first to speak what was in her heart was at least equal to his. "God help me. It wouldn't be hard at all."

He drained the whiskey in his glass, then stood up, pulling her with him. "Then God help us both, Sara Riley. I don't think I'm falling in love with you. I know damn well I am."

"Hawk..." Sara couldn't dismiss all her misgivings so easily, even though she wanted to with all her heart. She'd told herself over and over that Wade's leaving her was not her fault, that she was still a desirable and desiring woman. But to put herself to the test, to risk everything fragile and feminine inside her, was too big a step to take again all at once. "This isn't wise."

He bracketed her chin with his thumb and forefinger, silencing her. "No more discussions, Sara Riley. No more arguments. I'm tired of fighting you. I'm tired of fighting, period. I've spent half my life in wars. Big wars. Little wars. Wars the rest of the world knows nothing about. I've had a bellyful of war. Now I want peace and quiet—and you."

"Are you asking me to stay with you?"

"Only for tonight." He lowered his head, kissing her into silence, gently, because of the cut on her lips, but thoroughly, very thoroughly, so that she knew exactly what he wanted. He didn't think he'd ever get enough of her. Surely not enough of her in one short night, but gut instinct told him not to ask for more, not yet, not before she agreed to do for him what needed to be done. "That's all I'm asking for right now. Just to have you with me tonight."

"That's all I can promise you," Sara whispered, kissing him back.

Her tongue met his, tasted him, explored his mouth as eagerly as he did hers. She didn't hold back. Her

back arched. She pressed herself close. She moved
slowly, provocatively, in an age-old dance of womanly
power and grace. He felt himself stir and harden. He
pulled her hips closer so that there was nothing between them but layers of cloth. He undid two or three
of the tiny buttons of her blouse. It was some kind of
pale peach color that glowed as softly and as warmly as
her skin in the moonlight. He nuzzled the shaded valley between her breasts and she threaded her fingers
through his hair to hold him there. He lifted his head to
kiss her again. He slid his hand beneath her skirt, caressed the silky skin of her thigh, slipped his fingers
underneath the elastic of her panties.

Sara moaned against his mouth; her breath feath-
ered his lips. Her fingers clutched at the material of his
shirt, holding tight, as he felt waves of sensation rocket
through her body. She lifted her leg, curled it around his
thigh, inviting him with sweet wantonness to touch her
more intimately still.

Hawk felt the pressing roar of need and desire fill his
head. He had only to drop to his knees, pull Sara down
with him, and he could make her his, here and now, on
the floor, beneath the stars. But he didn't want that. He
didn't want a quick, furious coupling, although his
body clamored with need. He wanted their loving to be
slow and glorious. He wanted to see her hair spread out
on the pillow, wanted to trace the rosy circle of her nipples, the soft roundness of her belly, mold his hand to
the contours of the dark secret place between her legs.

Before she could protest, he swept her into his arms,
ignoring the pain in his battered ribs, as well as Sara's
murmured insistence that he let her walk on her own
two feet.

"No, Sara. I'm not giving you a chance to get away tonight." He pushed open the screen door and carried her inside. The main room of the house still smelled faintly of smoke from the explosion and fire. Wood carvings of birds and animals from a score of different lands, souvenirs of his travels, still lay on the floor where the earthquake had tumbled them. Pictures were askew on the rough-timbered walls. The kitchen was a disaster and the bathroom was barely operable, but none of that mattered now.

All that mattered was the woman in his arms and the things he wanted to do to her, for her, with her.

"Love me, Sara," he said, surprised at the roughness of his own voice in his ears. He'd never asked a woman to make love to him before. But then, he'd never wanted—needed—a woman as much as he did Sara Riley. "Let me love you."

She smiled and reached up to unbutton his shirt. He did the same to her blouse. Her fingers were clumsy. She shook her head as he finished with her blouse and pushed it aside to glory in the soft fullness of her breasts. Her skin glowed with the luster of ivory in the pale moonlight shining through the screen behind his bed.

"Help me," she whispered. "Hurry."

He did as she wanted, pulling the shirt from his pants and tossing it aside. Her hands went to the zipper of his slacks. She pulled them down over his hips, then undid the buttons at the waistband of her skirt, which dropped into a pool of pale light at her feet. In a heartbeat they were both naked and he pulled her down atop him on the unmade bed.

She came to him willingly, eagerly, her breasts pressed against his chest, her legs tangled with his as he probed the softness between her legs. There was nothing coy or girlish about her actions. Now that she had decided to give herself to him, there would be no holding back. She was a woman who obviously enjoyed making love and relished the return of intimacy. If there were still faint shadows of doubt in her night-darkened eyes, he didn't notice; he was too caught up in the pleasure of at last having her all to himself.

Sara lifted herself above him. Her breasts, just brushing the hair of his chest, set off explosions of longing deep inside him. He pulled her higher so that he could take one nipple into his mouth while he pushed boldly against her with the tip of his shaft. Sara gasped with mingled pleasure and surprise. She moved restlessly above him, but he held back, not wanting to hurt or frighten her.

What did she want from him? Expect from him? Questions he wasn't used to asking of himself when he made love to a woman nibbled at the edges of his brain.

"Sara? Are you ready for me?"

"Yes." She moved her hand between them, curling her fingers tightly around him. Her eyes widened in amazement at the size of him, but then she smiled and caressed him more intimately still. Hawk groaned. Sara did too. "Oh, yes. I'm ready."

He pushed more strongly against her. She was hot and damp with wanting him. She opened her legs, impaling herself on him. Her eyes were open. Her gaze held his. He surged forward, unable to wait any longer to make her completely his. She pulled her lower lip between her teeth, throwing her head back to take each thrust as she settled into his rhythm. Hawk moved beneath her, caught up in the heat and velvety softness of her, needing more, needing to possess her so completely she could never wipe the memory of their love-making from her mind.

"Hawk!" He opened his eyes. She was staring down at him, pleasure and anticipation mirrored in her clear green gaze. She gasped as he entered her once more and he knew she was very close to her release.

"Slow down, Sara. Wait for me." He didn't want her to find fulfillment alone. He slowed his movement within her, wrapped her in his arms and rolled on top of her, intending to hold himself still until she slowed her reckless, headlong race to satisfaction. But, as always, Sara surprised him.

"No," she said, moving boldly against him. "I don't want to wait. I want all of you. Now. Please, Hawk. Now."

He found his rhythm once more and she matched him thrust for thrust. Her fingernails dug into his shoulders. She wrapped her legs around his waist and held him tightly inside her. Her breathing was ragged. She moaned softly, then cried out more loudly as her body jerked out of control. She buried her face in his shoulder as her climax sent waves of pleasure shuddering through her, communicating themselves to him in tiny intense shockwaves that pushed him quickly into finding his own shattering release and the warm dark oblivion that followed. He welcomed it. Sleep was an aftermath of lovemaking he'd never indulged in. For most of his adult life, sex, like everything else, had never been allowed to dull his warrior's edge.

Moments—or perhaps it was hours—later, Sara moved slightly beneath him, and he realized his full weight was pinning her to the bed. He shifted his position, but still didn't let his body slide away from hers. She reached up and pushed his hair back from his forehead. Her fingers were warm against his skin, her movements languorous and heavy with the satisfaction of a woman well loved.

"Thank you," she said very softly. "That was very, very nice."

He allowed a smile to curve his lips. "Is that all? Just very, very nice? I could have sworn the earth moved again."

"Well," she said, tracing a finger over his breastbone, "I didn't want to be the first one to say it. It wasn't just very, very nice, it was incredible. I've never experienced anything quite like loving you, J. C. Hawk."

He wanted to tell her he loved her more deeply than he'd thought he was capable of doing, but he wasn't yet free to reveal his feelings, so he said nothing at all.

Some of the happiness faded from her moonlit eyes. She was beginning to start thinking again, instead of just letting herself feel. Hawk wasn't ready for that, or for the questions that would inevitably follow. When Sara's razor-sharp brain was engaged, she came up with entirely too many hard-hitting questions. Questions he didn't have answers for right now. He knew even better than she did that she wasn't ready to face the changes a commitment to him would bring in her life. It chilled him to the bone to think that she might never be ready to make such changes or such a commitment. She would have to come to him of her own free will. He couldn't force her to make the choice, as much as he wanted to try. For the next few hours, he was no more ready than she to face the uncertain future.

For now all he wanted was to hold her and to love her, as if this night was the only one they would ever share. He felt himself begin to harden again at the very thought of making love to her once more. Sara's eyes widened, then closed in sweet surrender as he began to move within her. She lay quietly for a moment, then began to move with him, her arms and legs entangling him in the silken bonds of passion and need.

He held her close, moving with her as the spiraling whirlwind of mutual desire built between them yet again. "Love me, Hawk," she said softly, her breath warm in his ear. "Just for tonight. Love me."

"I will," he said, before the tempest of release broke over her, catching him unaware, pulling him with her into the maelstrom. "I do."

This one night was all he could promise her, because tomorrow morning, at first light, he intended to send her away.

CHAPTER EIGHTEEN

SARA AWOKE SLOWLY, her thoughts confused, an unsettling mixture of repletion and anxiety. She wiggled her toes and winced at the slight soreness between her legs. She couldn't recall in all her years of marriage to Wade, even when they'd been young and infatuated with each other, ever making love with the intensity and abandon of last night. She felt her face grow hot remembering the sounds she'd made, the way she'd begged for more, the incredible satisfaction and power she'd felt, as Hawk climaxed within her again and again. She'd fallen asleep in his arms. And, as usual, her dreams had been of him.

Sara frowned and her sleepy lassitude faded away. Her dreams had not been pleasant ones. They'd been filled with longing and loss. And she understood why. Even though Hawk had lain beside her in the night, had loved her as she'd never expected to be loved in her entire life, she knew that it was only an interlude, already a memory. Because as much as she loved him, J. C. Hawk was not, and never would be, a part of her life.

Hawk was standing in the center of the room, studying something lying on the table before him. He hadn't seemed to notice that she was awake. Sara took a moment to survey his home. It was still too dark to make out many details of its design and decor, but it appeared to be clean and simply furnished, the living place of a man who had never cared much for physical comfort and material extravagance. There were paintings on the wall, their details obscured by early-morning shadows, and carvings of birds and animals and people everywhere, which she'd noted the night before. And there were shelves and shelves of books in glass-fronted cases to keep out the damp. Sara longed to read the titles, to learn more about him from the books he surrounded himself with.

"Your clothes are on the chair by the bed," he said without turning around.

"Thank you." She could have sworn she hadn't made a sound, but he had heard her anyway. She reached for her blouse. He was bare-chested, wearing only a pair of slacks, and didn't seem to notice the early-morning damp and chill. But she wasn't feeling strong enough or sure enough of herself to face him in the nude. "What time is it? I—I didn't mean to fall asleep and spend the night."

He turned around. "Didn't you?"

"No." She pushed her fingers through her hair, aware that it was sleep-tousled and so was she. "I...I've never spent the night with any man since my divorce. It would be very upsetting to Ben and...and Zack if they found I'd stayed with you."

"Why, Sara? Because you don't want them to know you have a sex life?"

"It's not that." But it was, in a way. She wasn't ready to share her feelings for Hawk with anyone yet, not even her children.

"Isn't it?" One eyebrow lifted slightly.

"I'm not a prude. If...if I have a committed relationship with a man, I'll tell them about it. I won't go sneaking around behind their backs."

"Like their father did?"

"Yes." She lifted her chin defiantly.

"Then is it because you regret what happened last night?"

"No." She looked down at her bare feet and wondered what had become of her sandals, the last pair of shoes she had with her. The shoes she'd have to wear home to cold and snowy Fort Wayne.

"You're lying, Sara."

"Yes, I am," she said, her heart thumping hard in her chest. "But not because of what you just said. Last night was wonderful, incredible, but it was something that can't happen again."

"Why not?"

"Because you don't belong in my world," Sara said honestly, although the effort it cost her to speak without tears was tremendous. "And I don't belong in yours. It's that simple."

"How do you know you don't belong in my world?" The skin above his left eye looked raw and abraded. There was a dark purple bruise on his rib cage. Sara had traced the scars on his body during the night as they made love again and again. He was a man who had put his life on the line many times and never stopped to count the costs. Yesterday he'd faced injury and death again, this time for her sake. But it didn't make any difference in the end. She owed him her gratitude, she'd given him her love. But she couldn't stay with him, and there was nothing she could do to change that.

"The same way you know you don't belong in mine," she said simply. She saw her sandals peeking out from under the bed and slipped them on her feet before looking at him again.

"I can't change your mind?"

"No." She spoke too loudly and her voice cracked. She swallowed hard to dislodge the lump of tears in her throat.

He was silent for a moment. "Then I have something I want you to do for me."

"What?" She hadn't expected protestations of undying love, but she had expected him to fight a little harder to keep her with him.

"Take these back to the States." He held out his hand. Lying on his palm were five emeralds.

A tiny spurt of excitement made her heartbeat race. "They're from Mary Hawk's treasure, aren't they? You hid them before Inspector Molinas got here, didn't you?"

"No," he said and smiled, a real smile, the one that she seldom saw and craved like a drug. "I didn't have a chance, except for the two or three I planted on Wheeler. Carter-Stone and the mayor took custody of the casket out on the beach, remember? These are the stones that Zack picked up off the sand."

"Yes," Sara said, walking forward slowly, as though drawn by their cool, green fire. "I do vaguely remember him picking them up." Even in the hazy dawn light, they glowed with a life of their own. "But why did he give them to you?"

"He was afraid to tell Molinas he still had them. He and Ben came up here looking for me just before dark last night. He wanted me to smuggle them into the States and sell them to the mob or some Saudi oil sheikh. He thought I could use the money to help get the rest of the treasure back from the government."

"Oh, Zack!" Sara laughed because if she didn't, she thought she might cry. "He's so imaginative."

"He's also dead right, Sara."

She looked up quickly, her eyes drawn to the power of his. "What do you mean?"

"I want you to smuggle these emeralds back into the States for me."

"I can't," she said automatically, speaking the words before the thought was fully formed in her brain. "I can't." Was this why he hadn't tried to talk her into staying with him? Was this why he'd told her he loved her, made love to her over and over again—merely to bind her to him, to make it impossible to say no when he asked her to take the emeralds out of the country?

"Sara, don't get midwestern or self-righteous on me now. I—I need your help."

"You want me to commit a crime for you?" She swept her hand toward the bed. "Is that what this whole night was about?" Oh God, he wouldn't do that, would he? He wasn't like Wade, was he? Telling the truth when it suited him. *Loving her* when it suited him. *Betraying her* when it suited him.

"No," he said, his voice low and controlled as always, although Sara jumped as if he'd roared the denial to the stars. "You've got it all wrong."

Why was he telling her this now, when it was too late? If he'd trusted her, he wouldn't have thought it was necessary to seduce her first. "Have I? Why do you need me? You said yourself last night that Wainright won't be a problem anymore. It'll be cheaper and easier for them to deal with Elliot for the journal than to try another stunt like they pulled with Wheeler and Benson." Last night she'd accepted what he'd said because she'd wanted to believe that her brother would be safe, that Hawk would be safe here in his remote and beautiful corner of the world. Now he was telling her there was someone interested enough in the treasure to make him believe she should risk her freedom to smuggle his emeralds back into the States? What kind of a fool did he think she was? She thought once more of the night they'd just spent together. A compliant and willing fool, obviously.

What did she really know about this man, anyway? She'd met him for the first time less than two weeks ago. She'd loved him for only a few days. *Fools rush in where angels fear to tread.* It was a cliché, but that didn't make it any less the truth. At the moment she was the biggest fool in the world and she was going to have to pay the price.

"Yes, damn it, I did tell you Wainright wasn't a threat." His hand balled into a fist around the emeralds. "They weren't the only ones interested in the treasure. From the moment Molinas and his friend from the museum stepped out of that plane, I've been a marked man. Molinas will be back. Yesterday he was dazzled by the casket and what it held, but by tomorrow or the next day, he'll start putting two and two together and begin to wonder if there wasn't something more. Something extra. Anyone that comes in or goes out of Tyiskita will be suspect. Anyone but you."

"No customs inspector is going to look twice at a middle-aged high school art teacher and two kids—is that what you mean?"

"Yes."

"I see." Pain squeezed her heart and made the blood rush in her ears. She didn't hear the note of pleading in his voice, wouldn't have believed it if she had. She had brought this misery on herself. She'd gotten caught up in her own fantasy, imagined *she* was Mary Hawk, a pirate's mistress, his equal and his love. That was where she'd made her fatal mistake—she'd started to believe her own dreams. And now she'd have to pay the price for that fantasy in years and years of loneliness and regret.

"No, you don't see. But I don't have time to explain it any better. I can't wait years for the government to straighten this all out. Even then, I'll be lucky to see a tenth of what we found in the cave. And a tenth is not enough. I need the money now. For Tyiskita. For the rain forest."

"I'll do it," she said, the expression in her green eyes as cold as the fire in the gems he held in his fist. "Give them to me." She held out her hands. "Tell me how to get them into the States without getting caught. Tell me who to get in touch with when I get home. Get me a plane out of here as soon as possible and I'll get the hell out of your life."

"YOU'RE GOING BACK to the States this morning?" Elliot asked from the bedroom doorway, as Sara packed the boys' belongings. Her hands were trembling, a reaction to her devastating final encounter with Hawk that she couldn't hide.

"That's what I said." She turned to the boys, still lying in their bunks. "You guys get in the shower and get dressed. The plane from Golfito will be here in less than an hour. If you don't hurry, you won't have time for breakfast."

"But Mom, we're not supposed to go home until tomorrow," Ben said. "I promised Luke I'd help work on the snake doctor's house in the village today. It got messed up worse than the others."

"I'm sorry, Ben. I know this change of plans spoils the last day of your vacation, but it can't be helped. Hawk asked us to leave."

"What?" Elliot grabbed the top of the doorjamb with both hands and leaned into he room as if to hear her better. "Hawk asked you to leave? Why?"

She looked up from her packing. "Because the plane's making a special trip in today with supplies. The pilot doesn't want to fly back empty." It wasn't a bad lie for the spur of the moment.

"Bummer," Zack said.

"Go take a shower, honey. The plane really should be here in less than an hour."

"Okay," he said, rolling out of bed and shuffling off to the bathroom. "But I don't want to go."

As soon as his son was out of earshot, Elliot jumped her. "You're not telling the truth, sis."

"What's the matter, mom?" Sara looked at Ben, sitting cross-legged on his bunk. "I'm not a baby like Zack. I know something's wrong."

Ben was right. He wasn't a child, he was almost a young man; she could trust him with the truth. "Hawk asked me to smuggle Zack's emeralds into the States."

"Well, I'll be damned," Elliot said.

She turned angrily on her brother. "Is that all you can say? Why don't you march up there and punch him in the nose for even asking me to do something like that?" she demanded.

"He'd flatten me with one blow," Elliot said reasonably.

"You're no help." Sara was perilously close to tears. "Where's a knight in shining armor when you need one?"

"I'll be your knight, Mom," Ben said earnestly. "I'll smuggle the emeralds."

"Oh, Ben honey, thanks for offering." Sara smiled and leaned over Zack's duffel to give her son a peck on the cheek. "But don't be ridiculous. It's against the law."

"I know that. But sometimes you have to do something wrong to make something right." He shrugged.

"I know what you mean," Sara said, biting her lip.

"Mom, I've read about what happens when people find a treasure and the government tries to get it all. It takes years to get your money. And sometimes the lawyers cost so much they get most of it anyway. It isn't fair. Hawk asked you to help. We've got to do it."

"But smuggling is wrong," Sara said.

"So is what they're doing to Hawk." Ben folded his arms across his chest, looking stubborn. "Tell him you'll do it, Mom."

Sara sat down on the bunk, her knees suddenly too weak to hold her. "I already did."

"It'll be okay, Mom." He got off his bunk and patted her awkwardly on the shoulder. "It'll be okay, I'll help. I'll go right now and make sure Zack washes all the parts that don't show."

"Thanks, honey."

"He's going to be one hell of a fine young man," Elliot said when Ben had left them alone.

"If we don't all end up in jail. Oh, El, I don't believe I'm doing this."

"What? Smuggling emeralds or leaving Tyiskita?"

Her head shot up. "Smuggling emeralds, of course. Why—why should I be upset about leaving Tyiskita?"

"Maybe because you spent the night with Hawk."

Sara groaned. "How do you know that?"

"I couldn't sleep. I was out on the veranda when you went up the path. I was there for three hours and you never came back."

"It was a mistake."

"Was it?"

"Yes." Her voice rose in pitch.

"Why?"

"Elliot, stop it. You sound like a psychiatrist and I don't need analyzing. I know perfectly well what's wrong with me. I made the mistake of falling for a man I can't have. And who used me for his own ends. This whole two weeks has been a fantasy. Unreal. And a huge mistake."

"Don't say that, sis." Elliot cocked his head, listening to the boys arguing back and forth over whether or not Zack should wash his hair. He smiled. "Your coming here has given me back the chance to know my son. He isn't ready to stay here with me yet, but we're making real progress and it's all because of you."

"I'm glad you feel that way." It wasn't a very gracious or supportive statement, but it was all she could manage at the moment.

"I'm thinking of coming home this summer," he said. "When the rainy season gets going real good, it slows me down a lot. I'll be able to spend time with Zack on his own turf. Really cement our relationship. Maybe even get him to come back here with me part of the year, at least."

"That's wonderful, El. Maybe Zack *should* be with you," she said, letting her inner turmoil burst forth in words. "I don't seem to be doing a very good job raising him or Ben lately."

"What do you mean by that?" Elliot came into the room, shoved Ben's duffel out of the way and sat down on the low narrow bunk.

"My son just offered to turn smuggler. I'm sure Zack would be more than willing to become his accomplice. I'm raising a pair of unprincipled gangsters."

"Sara, lighten up. I'm not trying to tell you this isn't a serious situation. It is. But don't come down too hard on the boys. This whole vacation has been a fairy tale for them. Don't spoil it by trying to make a morality play out of it."

"It's not a fairy tale, it's life," she said in desperation. "It's the difference between right and wrong." Tears pressed hotly against her eyelids, but she refused to let them fall.

"Are you angry because Hawk asked you to smuggle the emeralds into the States? Most women would be."

"No. I'm angry because he thought he had to get me into bed before he could ask me to do it." Unbidden, a picture of Hawk holding the emeralds in his big scarred hand came into her mind, followed by the equally unwelcome recollection of those same hands on her breasts and thighs and the pleasure they had given her. She pushed the memory ruthlessly aside.

"Do you really think that's what he meant to do? Because if it is, I'll go up there and try to avenge your honor by letting him knock my block off, if it'll make you feel better."

"It won't make me feel better."

"Good." He rubbed his hand over his jaw. "I prefer not to have to eat with my jaw wired shut for six weeks.... Consider this while you're at it. Could it be that you swept him off his feet last night and he didn't have a chance to ask you before you got him into bed?"

She laughed. She had to, or she might break apart into tiny shards of misery and dissolve at his feet in a flood of tears. "Don't be silly. Hawk swept off his feet? Give me a break."

"Don't underestimate yourself, sis," Elliot said with a smile. "You're a pretty sexy broad."

She didn't dignify the statement with a response for a moment. "My heart's been pretty unreliable the last couple of years," she said finally. "Let's just say I've figured out the difference between fantasy and reality and leave it go at that. I don't want to talk about Hawk anymore, okay?" She pulled the zipper on Zack's duffel closed with a jerk.

Elliot was quiet for almost a minute while she dealt with Ben's tote. When he spoke, his voice was low and serious. "I won't argue with you anymore about Hawk. But I need your help, too. I have to get Father Benedicto's journal out of the country just like Hawk does the emeralds. Will you help me, sis?"

"I figured this was coming," she said wearily. "Why not? I might as well be hanged for a sheep as a lamb."

HE'D NEVER BUNGLED a job so badly in his life. Hawk stood at the edge of his veranda watching the plane carrying Sara and the boys take off into the blue sky, its noisy ascent ignored by the frigate birds circling gracefully far above it. Everything he'd said and done since he'd woken up that morning had been wrong, including not making love to Sara one last time. She had been pliant and willing and more desirable than any women he'd ever known, but something had held him back. He still wasn't certain what it was.

Maybe it was because when he'd opened his eyes to find Sara's head on his pillow and had felt the true strength of his need for her hit him like a blow between the shoulders, he'd panicked. Maybe it was the kick to the head he'd taken yesterday that slowed his thinking and made him say all the wrong things at just the right moment. Maybe it was because he wanted and needed her in his life and didn't know what to say or do to make her want to stay. But mostly it was because facing that longing and that need was the hardest thing he'd ever done in his life. And in the end, it didn't matter where he'd screwed up; the damage was done.

Sara had taken the emeralds, just as he'd wanted her to do. But she wouldn't be coming back. He'd saved Tyiskita. He'd have enough money to fight the bureaucrats and lawyers for his share of Mary Hawk's treasure, but he'd have to do it alone. He'd let himself weave pie-in-the-sky dreams of the future with Sara beside him, instead of keeping his eye firmly on the objective at hand. In the old days, that lack of focus and concentration would have cost him his life. This time, it had cost him his soul.

"WE DID IT, Mom," Ben whispered, leaning back in the middle seat as the plane took off from Miami, heading north into the lingering cold and snow of late March in Indiana. "We did it."

"We did it," she said, whispering as well, so that they didn't waken Zack, asleep in his seat, his baseball glove in his lap.

"Where are they? You can tell me now," Ben insisted.

"They're in Zack's glove. Uncle El and I stuffed them inside the lining this morning while you guys were in the shower."

"Radical," Ben said, smiling his approval. "No one even gave that baseball glove a second glance." He settled himself more comfortably in his seat. "This smuggling business is a lot easier than I thought. They never looked at Zack's baseball glove, and they never even looked in your purse to find Father Benedicto's journal.''

"Who'd a thunk it?" Sara replied, with a smile that was so hard to form it took a direct effort of will.

"But I don't think I want to do it again," Ben added. "It's too nerve-wracking. Did you know Costa Rica has a prison on an island? In shark-infested waters? I looked it up."

"I don't think any of us is cut out for a life of crime."

"I'm not. I'll pass the next time you need an accessory."

"I'll remember that." Sara leaned her head against the back of the seat. She was so tired she could hardly keep her eyes open, but her thoughts wouldn't let her rest. What was Hawk doing now? It would be dark already at Tyiskita. Was he reading a book, or looking out at the night sky? Or wondering what had become of her and her children and the bits and pieces of Mary Hawk's treasure that they carried with them?

She didn't know and she told herself she shouldn't care. But she did. Because she'd suddenly recalled Elliot's last words to her before the plane took off from Tyiskita. At the time, she had been so completely focused on what was going on between her brother and his son that she'd missed the underlying meaning in his words. Only now, when it was much too late to do anything about it did she understand what he'd been trying to tell her.

"Goodbye, Ben," he had said, holding out his hand to his nephew.

"See ya, Uncle El."

He'd turned to his son. "I'll see you in Fort Wayne before school starts again in the fall, okay?" He'd stood there uncertainly, then held out his hand.

Instead of shaking hands, Zack threw himself into his father's arms. "You mean it? You won't forget to come?"

Elliot dropped to one knee and wrapped his arms around the little boy, holding him tight. "I won't forget to come. I promise." He looked at Sara over the top of Zack's head and Sara knew she hadn't failed in her mission to help reunite her brother and his son.

"I'll show you everything there—where I play baseball and football and the zoo and the coliseum." Zack hugged his father back for all he was worth. "And I'll tell Grandma and Grandpa Carson that you were a hero and saved us all from the bad guys. They'll like that."

Elliot laughed; he couldn't seem to help himself. "Great, you do that."

"I will, Dad. I'll see you soon."

"Soon." There was a catch in his voice and for a moment longer he'd held the little boy tightly against his chest. "Be good, Zack."

"I'll try," Zack had said, torn between honesty and a desire to please his dad.

"Good enough. Mind Aunt Sara now."

"Don't worry about that." Zack's response had been fervent.

Elliot laughed and gave him a man-to-man punch on the shoulder. "I know what you mean. She's my big sister, remember." He stood and gave Sara an embarrassed peck on the cheek. "So long, sis. And thanks. Thanks for everything."

"Hurry home, El," she said, wrapping her arms around him in a hug. He gave her a quick hard hug in return, one that conveyed far more emotion than his words.

"I'll be there." It was a promise and a pledge. "And I know I can trust you with the journal the same way Hawk has trusted you with securing the future of Tyis-kita."

CHAPTER NINETEEN

"GREAT PARTY, Sara," Wade said, bestowing a look of mingled pity and curiosity on her from across the table on which Megan's high school memorabilia, band trophies and senior pictures were displayed. "Megan's having a blast, but you look pretty bad."

"Thanks, Wade," Sara said, wishing she could contradict his remark. But she did look bad. Eleven weeks of mostly sleepless nights tended to do that to a person.

"Wade, that wasn't very tactful," the new Mrs. Riley admonished her husband. "Sorry, Sara."

"That's all right."

"It really is a very nice party." Felicity made a second attempt at polite conversation, and Sara forced herself to respond in kind, although carrying on a conversation with the younger woman in front of most of her friends and relatives was the last thing she wanted to do.

For a moment Sara wished her divorce hadn't been so damned civilized. Maybe if she'd had the chance to rant and rave and vent her anger at Wade and Felicity, work out her frustrations and confront her own feelings of inadequacy and rage in a couple of screaming matches and good hard crying jags, she wouldn't have made such a damned mess of her affair with one J. C. Hawk. But she hadn't done any of those things. The entire proceeding had been very discreet, very friendly and wholly unsatisfactory. The trouble was, deep down she knew her inability to make a commitment to Hawk couldn't be blamed on Wade and Felicity or the trauma of dissolving a marriage that had lasted fifteen years— as much as she'd like to do just that.

She was just plain scared of making such a momentous change in her life. Even for the love of a lifetime. And that was what it would have been, she was absolutely certain—the love of a lifetime. It was her own fault and no one else's that she now faced the prospect of spending the rest of her life by herself.

Wade and Felicity moved off toward the punch bowl to greet other friends and accept congratulations on Megan's graduation and on the great party they'd helped pay for.

Megan herself had long since deserted the festivities to cruise the neighborhood with the boys and a couple of friends in her father and stepmother's graduation present, a new car. Sara couldn't believe her eyes when Wade had presented the teenager with the keys immediately after the ceremony at the high school.

"Where's Meggie?" her mother asked, coming up to the table to thumb through the picture album she'd helped Sara put together.

"Out cruising in her new car," Sara said in a low voice, smiling sweetly at Megan's band director as he passed them on his way to the buffet table. "She'll be back by nine."

"A brand-new car." Marvelle Carson was not pleased by the extravagant present, either. "I thought you two had agreed he would give her a CD player."

"We did," Sara replied, smiling at no one in particular this time. "The car was supposed to come later. A

used car that she could take to college in the fall and
that she's supposed to help pay for out of her summer
wages at the pool.''

"That man's a fool. I can't imagine what's come over
him since you were divorced. Guilt, I suppose, at not
being around for the kids. At least that's what Oprah
would say." Marvelle replaced the picture album exactly where she'd found it.

"Mother, don't start on me again."

"I'm not. But I can't believe he had the nerve to bring
that woman here with him this afternoon." She gave
Felicity the once-over from beneath dark eyebrows that
arched in exactly the same sweeping curve as Sara's.
Marvelle Carson was sixty-eight years old, ramrod thin
and formidable. But beneath her acerbic exterior beat
a heart of gold. She was fiercely loyal to her husband,
her children and her many friends, and woe betide the
unlucky soul who caused pain to any of them.

"It's over and done with, Mother," Sara said wearily. "I'll just look like an ogre if I make him take it
back. Megan's still going to have to help make pay-
ments on it. And she can't keep it with her at college
until the second semester—I made him promise me
that."

"Whatever happened to the good old days when college freshmen weren't allowed to have cars on cam-
pus?"

"They went the way of the dinosaur and flattops and
sock hops," Sara reminded her. "Excuse me, Mom. I
have to check with the maître d' and see if there're
enough cold cuts to last until the band's finished playing." She had to admit that having Megan's party at the
country club—Wade and Felicity's idea—was a big

help. The staff was excellent and everything was running more smoothly than Sara could have hoped.

Marvelle snorted. "Playing? Is that what you call that noise? I just pray one of them blows a fuse before they start back up again." Even though Wade had made good his promise not to have the band start playing until later in the evening, so that his mother and Sara's parents wouldn't suffer the overly loud and enthusiastic performance of *Wrecking Crew*, the three elders were still in attendance. And were complaining. Marvelle had wasted no time in letting her ex-son-in-law and his new wife know how she felt about the quality of the entertainment.

"Hello, Marvelle," Wade said cautiously as he approached the table again, this time without Felicity at his side. "I want to talk to Sara. Alone, if you don't mind."

"I have to check with the staff about the food," Sara said.

"It can wait a few minutes, can't it?"

"I guess so."

"Sara?" Marvelle asked, raising her eyebrows in a look that said just as clearly as words that she wasn't going anywhere unless her daughter told her to, point-blank.

"It's all right, Mom. Maybe you could check on the food for me."

"Okay. And I'll check on Ben and Zack as well. I haven't seen them around for a while."

"Megan's giving them a ride around the block in her new car. They'll all be back in about five minutes. Megan doesn't want to miss the second set." He glanced at his watch. "The *Wrecking Crew*'ll be back on stage in fifteen minutes."

"Then I'd better get my talking over with in a hurry," Marvelle complained, turning away. "You can't hear yourself think, let alone carry on an intelligent conversation, with that racket going on."

"Your mother hasn't changed a bit," Wade remarked as he watched her walk away.

"No, thank goodness. What do you want to talk about, Wade?" Sara asked warily. She was really very tired. In the weeks since she'd returned from Costa Rica, there had been so much to do—the end of the school year, Megan's graduation plans, spring sports and school projects for Ben and Zack. The days had been busy and fulfilled, but her nights had been long and wakeful, and she was beginning to feel the strain.

"There's got to be someplace more private we can talk." He motioned toward the French doors leading out onto the terrace.

"If you want to explain why you bought the car without asking me if I approved, isn't it a little late?"

"It isn't about the car. I'm sorry I did that without consulting you. Felicity's already cleaned my clock over that one. But what's done is done and hell, Megan really got a kick out of it, didn't she?"

"What eighteen-year-old wouldn't get a kick out of a brand-new red sports car?"

Wade frowned as he held the heavy glass door open for her. The irony in her words had gotten through to him. "She's a good kid," he insisted. "She'll use her head. Both our kids are good kids. And Zack, too. You should be proud of them."

"I am proud of them."

"I want to ask you something else," he said, changing the subject. "It's about Zack's education fund. I got a cashier's check from this Hawkslair for the entire fifty thousand. Plus interest.''

"You did? I'm glad Hawk kept his word." The end of her odyssey with Mary Hawk's emeralds had been as prosaic as you could hope. The day after she returned from Costa Rica, she'd called the number Hawk had given her. An older-sounding woman answered, took the information, thanked her kindly and hung up. A week later, a very nice-looking, clean-shaven, elderly man rang her doorbell, wished her good afternoon and handed her a letter from Hawk. She'd only seen Hawk's handwriting once or twice, but she had no doubt the bold sweeping signature was his. She'd turned over the emeralds without another word. The old man had inclined his head in thanks, walked down her front steps and driven away. That was the last she'd seen or heard of him or the emeralds.

"Yeah. He did. I guess Elliot's a better judge of character than I ever gave him credit for."

"Yes," she said, smiling just a little. "He is."

Surprisingly, the terrace was deserted. The country club sat on a low rise and the hillside dropped away sharply beyond the terrace wall to a stream at the bottom of a wooded ravine. Through the lacy patchwork of newly leafed trees, Sara could see the fifteenth green, gilded by the fading gold of a lingering June twilight. The hole was a par five dogleg, she recalled, and it always gave Wade fits. Maybe that's why he was scowling as he looked at it now.

"What the hell happened in Costa Rica? Zack keeps giving me this cock-and-bull story about finding that lost treasure you went looking for." He sounded incredulous. "I thought the kid was making it up. He's always had one hell of an imagination. But Ben backed him up. Ben. Our Ben, who hasn't got an imaginative bone in his body."

"Ben's got a great imagination," Sara said, rushing to her son's defense.

"Okay, maybe he has," Wade admitted. "Then all that stuff about poison snakes and witch doctors and skeletons in caves was true?"

"Snake doctor, not witch doctor," Sara corrected him. "And yes, it's true. All of it, even the skeletons. Poor souls. We may never learn who they were."

"My God." He looked at her with new respect. "How much of this have you told your mother?"

"Only bits and pieces. She nearly had a heart attack over the earthquake. She still can't make up her mind whether or not it's safe for her and Dad to plan a visit to Elliot."

"And the part about Wainright sending the fraternity brother hit men to steal the journal and leave you all to die in the cave? That was true, too?" He wasn't smiling any longer.

"Yes. It's true."

"Son of a bitch," he said reverently. "I didn't think Ben would make up a story like that. But it's so..."

"So unbelievable?" Sara prompted.

He nodded. "But it makes sense. Did you know Wainright Pharmaceuticals has deferred its year-end dividend? The stockholders are so up in arms over it that heads are still rolling. All the way to the top. Seems word got out that they lost a hell of a bundle on some fly-by-night investment scam."

"The treasure salvager's ship," Sara explained. "That's where the two young thugs worked. The setup was legitimate, as far as I know, but it cost millions to keep going. Then the earthquake tore up the bottom of the bay. They were close to finding the wreck of the *Mary Deere* before that happened. Afterward, they didn't stand a chance. And of course, what they really wanted was Father Benedicto's journal.''

"Which you smuggled into the States."

Sara nodded. "I simply put it in my purse along with the doubloons we found earlier. No one asked to see it," she said, smiling at the memory. "Smuggling's a lot easier than I thought. We brought back the emeralds Hawk used to repay the loan as well."

Wade looked as if he were going to have a stroke. "You what?" he gasped, then hastily lowered his voice as two other couples walked onto the terrace. "How?"

"In Zack's baseball glove."

"I'll be damned. Do you still have the journal?"

"No. As soon as we got home, I air-expressed it to the restoration expert Elliot's been in contact with."

"And now your adventure's over."

"Yes." She couldn't keep a hint of sadness out of her voice. "It's all over. I'm back to being just plain Sara from Fort Wayne."

"Is that what you want for the rest of your life?"

"No." The insightful question coming from Wade, the least insightful of men, surprised her enough that she'd answered without thinking.

"Then why don't you do something about it?"

"The way you did?"

A red stain darkened his neck and the tips of his ears. "Yes, as a matter of fact."

"I can't, Wade. There are the kids to consider. My job. Mom and Dad."

"Your parents are happy and healthy. They've got a lot of good years left together, with any luck. You don't need to mother-hen them quite yet. Megan's almost

ready to leave home. The boys..." He fell silent, as
though sifting through his thoughts, trying to decide
just what to say and what to keep to himself.

"Good Lord. They told you about Hawk." Sara felt
the color drain from her face and then come flooding
back again. How much had Ben and Zack guessed
about her feelings for him?

"Then it's true." He looked pleased with himself for
obtaining the admission. "There's something going on
between you and this Hawk guy."

"No." Wade was the last person on earth she wanted
to talk to about Hawk.

He grinned at her discomfiture. "I thought so. He
must be something. Ben and Zack act like he's Errol
Flynn, Superman and Arnold Schwarzenegger all rolled
into one. Hell, even I'd like to meet him."

"Just what exactly did they tell you?" Sara demanded, imagining all kinds of things.

"Don't worry. They didn't see or hear anything you
didn't want them to. It's just that they never stop talking about the guy, and what the two of you were always doing together. It's 'Mom and Hawk' this and
'Mom and Hawk' that. I just put two and two together
and asked a couple of relevant questions here and there.
It was easy to figure out the rest. You lead with your
chin, Sara. You always have. You'd no more have a
fling with some macho soldier of fortune with only one
name than you'd fly. You're in love with the guy, aren't
you?"

"No!" The denial was fierce and automatic, a defense mechanism she'd perfected over the last eleven
weeks. "Certainly not."

"You're also the free world's worst liar. You're lying
now."

"All right. I'm lying. But that doesn't change the fact that falling in love with Hawk is just about the biggest mistake I've made in my life."

He laughed. "I guess that finally lets me off the hook."

Sara smiled weakly at his joke. It was all she could manage. "You did us both a favor, walking out of our marriage," she admitted at last. "I would have stayed for the children's sake. Because I was afraid of facing the future alone. For a lot of reasons, all of them the wrong ones. You were right to ask for a divorce."

"Maybe your going back to Costa Rica is the right thing to do as well."

She looked out over the golf course so she didn't have to meet his eyes. There were now more than a few people on the terrace, even though she and Wade remained fairly isolated where they stood. "What could I do in Costa Rica?" she asked in a low voice.

"Marry this Hawk guy."

"Wade, please."

"Okay. Teach, then. I know you think I never look past the bottom line of a balance sheet, but I've got some idea of what's going on in the world. In places like Costa Rica, teachers are worth their weight in gold and emeralds and lost Spanish journals."

"I don't speak Spanish," she pointed out, suddenly wanting very much to be convinced by his argument.

"Hell, Sara. You can learn."

"All right, I'll admit I've thought about it. Teaching, I mean. There's a little school in Tyiskita. The kids don't have diddly compared to what Ben and Zack and Megan have in their classrooms, but they're so eager to learn. I could make a difference there," she said, barely above a whisper.

"You sure as hell could."

"But the children..." The second most important reason she couldn't return to Costa Rica was that it would disrupt her children's lives.

"Megan's going to be off to college in three months. She can stay with Felicity and me between semesters. Ben can't stop talking about that place. He loved it there. And school would be no problem for him. The kid's a genius, or as close as makes no difference. Between you and Elliot, he'll probably be ready for college himself by this time next year." He shook his head, as if wondering how he had fathered such a prodigy, or maybe wondering how he would afford double tuition if his prediction came true. "And Zack would be with his father."

"But leaving their friends, their sports—it would mean taking them away from everything they know and care about. It would deny them so much."

Wade snorted. He shoved his hands into the pockets of his sport coat. "Look past Fort Wayne for once in your life. It's not the center of the universe, for Pete's sake. Forget how we were raised. This is the chance of a lifetime for Ben and Zack." He laid his hand on her arm, the first time he'd touched her since long before he'd moved out of the house. "Give it a try, Sara. Follow your heart."

"What if it doesn't work out?"

"Do you really think you're going to let that happen?" He laughed and pulled her into his arms for a hug. Sara went, not unwillingly, feeling charitable toward him for the first time in years.

"It's not up to me," she said, looking up into the face of the man she'd once loved. As a young, unfinished girl, she realized now. Not as Sara, the woman she was today. There was nothing between them anymore except the shared bond of their children, a tie that could never be completely broken. But that was all.

He stepped back, as though remembering they were no longer entitled to such moments of affection. "Don't give me that meek-and-submissive-little-woman-sitting-by-the-fire-waiting-for-her-man-to-come-home routine. It won't wash. And from what Ben tells me of this Hawk fellow, he's not going to show up on your doorstep, anyway."

"No," she said. "He's as stubborn as a jackass."

"And I'll bet you a year's worth of greens fees that you were the one who walked out on him." He tilted up her chin with his knuckle. "Am I right?"

"Yes. I left him." The uncertainty wouldn't go completely away, although she was beginning to let herself hope, for the first time since she'd walked out of Hawk's house that March morning. Maybe she *could* make it work. And because of Wade, the last person on earth she'd thought she'd ever take advice from again, let alone advice on matters of the heart.

"Then you'll have to go back."

"It's not that simple," she said, panicking again. "Megan. And the boys." What if she went back and Hawk wouldn't even see her?

"Yes, it is. The kids can stay with Felicity and me for as long as it takes. Jeez, Sara." Wade looked exasperated, as if the strain of giving counsel was beginning to tell on him. "He's a man. He won't come to you. You women are always telling us you're stronger and better and smarter than us. Then prove it. Go to him. Put your money where your mouth is."

"What if he doesn't want me back?" She was horrified to hear herself voicing the question, but she couldn't keep the words from leaping off her tongue.

"You'll never know unless you go down there and ask."

CHAPTER TWENTY

HAWK WAS STANDING on his veranda when the plane from Golfito appeared through a break in the clouds and set down for a landing on the beach. He watched it with idle curiosity. He hadn't been expecting it today. There were no guests scheduled to arrive until the end of the week, and the mail had come in on yesterday's flight.

Still, he could make good use of its being here. He had papers that needed to go to his attorney in San José. He'd decided to move fast, using some of the funds he'd received from the smuggled emeralds to set legal proceedings in motion to retrieve the rest of Mary Hawk's treasure trove. So far, the government hadn't seen fit to reply. He hadn't expected anything else. Despite the fact that nothing in Costa Rica moved swiftly, most certainly not the wheels of justice, he'd served notice to the museum officials, Inspector Molinas and the rest, that he didn't intend to stand idly by and do nothing while they sat on the gold.

Hawk headed back inside to get the papers. The plane wouldn't be staying long. The break in the clouds was only temporary. The rainy season was well advanced and all-night downpours were the norm. The pilot wouldn't want to be grounded at Tyiskita, where the landing strip wouldn't dry out enough for him to take off again until well into the morning.

It took him a couple of minutes longer to find them than he had expected. Too many restless nights had gotten him into the habit of carrying his reading material from one place to another around the house, instead of leaving it on his desk where it belonged. Where, until the advent of one Sara Riley from Fort Wayne, Indiana, into his well-ordered life, it would be right this moment. Grabbing the papers from beside a chair in the main room, he stuffed them into an envelope, addressed them to his lawyer and hurried back outside to start the Jeep.

The sound of a motor revving alerted him to the fact that his search had indeed taken too long. He moved to the edge of the veranda just in time to watch the plane taxi down the landing strip and take off into the rain-dark sky.

"Damn!" He rolled the envelope into a cylinder and banged it against his palm. "Now what the hell was that all about?" Planes that landed at Tyiskita usually stayed long enough for him to get down to the beach with mail or with messages to be forwarded to the tourist agency that handled the bookings for the lodge.

Perhaps someone in the village had been taken seriously ill and needed to be flown into hospital in San José. Olivia hadn't mentioned any unusual illnesses in the village at breakfast that morning, as he recalled. That didn't rule out a serious accident, however. Hawk decided to take the Jeep down to the village anyway and see what was going on.

He'd taken about six steps toward the back of the house when he saw movement on the path up from the beach out of the corner of his eye. "Sara." He didn't know if the word was a prayer or a curse when it left his mouth. He waited where he stood and watched her come across the grass toward him.

The clouds had closed in again. It was starting to rain. She hesitated, glanced up at the sky and resolutely kept on walking. He continued to watch her, making no move forward to greet her.

Raindrops glistened in her hair, which was longer than he remembered. Pulled up in back with a big pink comb of some kind, it just brushed the nape of her neck. Curling tendrils framed her face and forehead. Her green eyes were enormous, dark-shadowed, as though she hadn't slept any better than he had during the past three months. The apprehension she was feeling was plain to see in their clear emerald depths, although the smile pasted on her face was meant to look both assured and reassuring.

"Hello, Hawk."

"What are you doing here, Sara?" He spoke too abruptly. His tone was too harsh, but he wasn't in the mood to have his insides kicked out by this woman a second time. He was going to be damned sure why she'd come back to him before he let his heart have any say in the matter again.

She looked as if she'd hoped for a little friendlier greeting, but she didn't let it stop her advance across his yard. "I had to come," she said simply, holding an oversized canvas tote in front of her with both hands. She watched him steadily, and he was awed by the courage it must have taken for her to maintain eye contact, when she was so nervous her knuckles were white on the handle of the duffel and her lower lip was clamped tightly between her teeth.

"Does Elliot know you're here?"

"No."

"Where are your children?"

"With their father."

"How long do you plan to stay?"

"I don't know. I guess that depends on you." It was raining harder now, but neither of them moved.

"Why did you come, Sara?"

"Because I needed to see you again." She took a deep breath. "I needed to talk to you. Was that a mistake?"

"I don't know." His heart was pounding in sledgehammer blows against his chest.

"Does that mean you want me to leave? The plane will be back tomorrow afternoon for the mail. I'll stay with Elliot until then." She turned as if to go.

"No! Don't go."

She looked over her shoulder. A small, satisfied smile curved her mouth for just a heartbeat, then disappeared. "Good," she said. "I didn't intend to. I didn't fly three thousand miles to a foreign country, on my own, just to have you turn me away without saying what I came to say."

He wanted to smile but didn't, not yet. "I would have been surprised if you had walked away without a fight, Sara Riley." He moved closer, towering over her, making her tilt her head to look up at him so he could see the smooth, creamy curve of her throat and the thrust of her breasts against the soft damp cotton of her blouse. "Why are you here?" he repeated, his voice a low, demanding growl.

"I'm here because my ex-husband talked me into coming."

"What the hell?"

She smiled, another tiny, private smile that made him think she was enjoying a joke at his expense. "You heard what I said. My ex-husband told me to come."

"Since when did you start taking advice from the bastard who broke your heart?" he asked roughly, goaded beyond silence by her revelation.

Sara shook her head. "He didn't break my heart, Hawk." He had to lean forward slightly to hear her, she spoke so softly, softer than the raindrops falling all around them. "You did."

"Me?"

"When you sent me away."

"I sent you away because you wanted to go," he said with a growl that held as much pain as anger. "You were leaving anyway, remember? Going back to Fort Wayne. Running away. Back to your own world. Where I couldn't follow you."

"It's where I belong—"

"*I* can't belong there," he said, taking the duffel from her hand, tossing it aside so that there was nothing between them but their pain. "My life has been war and the business of war. I can't be part of a nine-to-five, business-lunch, country-club life, Sara. Maybe I never could have."

"I know that. I would never have asked it of you," she said, lifting her hand as though she might touch his face, then pulling it back. "And I know one of the reasons you choose to live here is because Costa Rica has no war and no business of war. The problem was, I thought I couldn't give that world up myself."

"And now you think you can?" He curled his hands around her upper arms, tightening his grip just enough to keep her from escaping if she decided to bolt. He wanted this settled between them, here and now. He didn't want her running away again.

This time she didn't hold back, but framed his face with her hands. Her skin was warm against his cheek, her fragrance filled his nostrils and made his head spin and his gut tighten with anticipation and need. "Yes. For you. If you'll have me."

"You can stay," he said, his heart hammering away inside his chest, "but only till the day I die."

"Hmm," she said, her smile so brilliant it was as if the sun had come out from behind the clouds just for him. "That should be at least thirty-five or forty years."

"With an option on another ten," he said, beginning to believe. "My family is very long-lived."

"I'm glad to hear that." The smile dimmed slightly. "I come as a package deal, you know," she said, focusing on the top button of his shirt for a moment before raising her eyes to his once more. "Zack, of course. It will be wonderful that he can be with Elliot. And Ben. He loves Tyiskita as much as I do."

"And your daughter and her friends for spring break?"

"And my parents, too," Sara said, tilting her head. "Sorry. We're very close. But I promise they'll only visit once or twice a year. And one thing more..."

"What's that?"

"Puddles. Our dog. We can't leave him behind."

"A dog?" He tried not to laugh. He'd slain dragons for her. Did she think he'd actually balk at a dog? "I think I can live with that."

"Can you?"

"For thirty-five or forty years," he said, allowing himself to smile at last. "With an option on another ten."

"Hawk, do you mean it?"

"Yes," he said, lowering his mouth to hers. "I mean every word of it."

"I love you," she whispered when he allowed her the breath to speak again, a long time later.

"I love you," he repeated. It was really very easy to say.

"Let's go inside," she said after another kiss charged the air around them as though lightning had struck nearby. "I'm soaking wet."

"Afraid you'll melt?" he asked, picking up her duffel and tucking her against his side as they headed for the house.

"I won't melt. But I'm not sure about you." She brushed her hand boldly across the front of his slacks.

"Don't worry," he said. "I won't melt, either." He lowered his head for one more quick kiss. "Not before you want me to." She blushed, just as he hoped she would.

"You might just be surprised how long that will be," she replied, recovering her poise in the blink of an eye. "I'm a very hard woman to satisfy."

"I know. And I wouldn't have it any other way." Life with Sara was never going to be boring, Hawk decided. But the long march of the future without her didn't bear thinking of. There would be arguments and disagreements, he had no doubt, differences they'd make up with lovemaking afterward. They'd work hard and play hard. Go to bed together at night and wake up together in the morning. That alone was worth all the adjustments he'd have to make. Kids and pets and in-laws were a small price to pay for never being lonely again.

"I suppose I should let Elliot know I'm here," Sara said as they stepped onto the porch. The sound of rain on the thatched roof over their heads was much louder than it had been outside. "Don't you agree?"

"Later," he said, working at the buttons of her blouse. It was wet and clung to her skin in ways that did strange things to his insides. "We've got a lot to talk about."

"Yes," Sara said dreamily as he bent his head to kiss the silky rise of her breast above the lacy fabric of her bra. "We need to make some plans for the future. I mean, I'll want to take Spanish lessons from Olivia and help Emily at the school, as soon as I get settled back here for good. And I'll bet I'd be good at figuring out ways to earn money to restore..." Her voice trailed off as he unhooked her bra and let it drop to the floor beside her blouse.

"Shut up, Sara," he said with a growl as he scooped her up in his arms and carried her inside the house. "I know you're going to turn my world upside down, but not today, not now. I don't want to talk business or trees or anything else. I want to talk sex."

"Love," she corrected, looping her arms around his neck, for once not making any kind of protest about being perfectly capable of walking on her own.

"Love," he agreed. "Not business."

"But our future—"

He dropped her onto the mattress hard enough to shut her up for a moment. "Our future can wait until morning. We'll have plenty of time to work it out in detail." Now that she'd made her decision, her commitment to him and to Tyiskita, she would back it with all the energy and loyalty she possessed. Of that he had no doubt at all. "I'm glad you want to learn Spanish and teach the village kids and find ways to make someone else pay for planting trees. But right now I want you to stop talking and kiss me."

"Gladly," she said, suiting action to words. "But there's one more thing I'd like to ask you."

"What?"

"Do you know how to scuba dive?"

"I know how," he said warily. He knew exactly what she was going to say next. No, life with Sara was not going to be dull.

"I figured as much. Will you teach me?"

"Why?"

"The wreck of the *Mary Deere* is still out there in the bay somewhere, you know."

"I know." He rolled over her, covering her body with his. She wrapped her arms around his neck and moved against him.

"Why?" he demanded again, although he didn't give a damn why, as long as she was with him this way, as long as she would always be with him this way.

She smiled. "I just thought you might like to help me do a little more treasure hunting on the side."

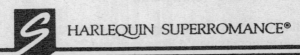

Fifty red-blooded, white-hot, true-blue hunks from every
State in the Union!

Beginning in May, look for MEN MADE IN AMERICA!
Written by some of our most popular authors, these
stories feature fifty of the strongest, sexiest men, each
from a different state in the union!

Two titles available every other month at your favorite
retail outlet.

In September, look for:

DECEPTIONS by Annette Broadrick (California)
STORMWALKER by Dallas Schulze (Colorado)

In November, look for:

STRAIGHT FROM THE HEART by Barbara Delinsky
(Connecticut)
AUTHOR'S CHOICE by Elizabeth August (Delaware)

You won't be able to resist MEN MADE IN AMERICA!

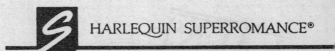

Calloway Corners

In September, Harlequin is proud to bring readers four involving, romantic stories about the Calloway sisters, set in Calloway Corners, Louisiana. Written by four of Harlequin's most popular and award-winning authors, you'll be enchanted by these sisters and the men they love!

MARIAH by Sandra Canfield
JO by Tracy Hughes
TESS by Katherine Burton
EDEN by Penny Richards

As an added bonus, you can enter a sweepstakes contest to win a trip to Calloway Corners, and meet all four authors. Watch for details in all Calloway Corners books in September.

CAL93

Relive the romance...
Harlequin®is proud to bring you

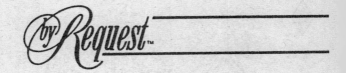

A new collection of three complete novels every month. By the most requested authors, featuring the most requested themes.

Available in October:

DREAMSCAPE

They're falling under a spell!
But is it love—or magic?

Three complete novels in one special collection:

GHOST OF A CHANCE by Jayne Ann Krentz
BEWITCHING HOUR by Anne Stuart
REMEMBER ME by Bobby Hutchinson

Available wherever Harlequin books are sold.

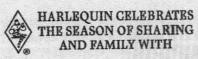

Where do you find hot Texas nights, smooth Texas charm and dangerously sexy cowboys?

THE THUNDER ROLLS
Fireworks—Texas style!

Ken Slattery, foreman at the Double C, is a shy man who knows what he wants. And he wants Nora. But Nora Jones has eyes for only one man in her life—her eight-year-old son. Besides, her ex-husband, Gordon, has threatened to come between her and any man who tries to stake a claim on her. The more strongly Ken and Nora are drawn together, the more violently Gordon reacts—and Gordon is frighteningly unpredictable!

CRYSTAL CREEK reverberates with the exciting rhythm of Texas. Each story features the rugged individuals who live and love in the Lone Star State. And each one ends with the same invitation...

Y'ALL COME BACK...REAL SOON

Don't miss THE THUNDER ROLLS by Bethany Campbell.
Available in October wherever Harlequin books are sold.